A Fortnight of Fury

David Culberson

CALUMET EDITIONS

Minneapolis

**CALUMET
EDITIONS**

Minneapolis

SECOND EDITION DECEMBER 2022

A Fortnight of Fury. Copyright © 2019 by David Culberson.
All rights reserved.

This is a work of fiction. All of the characters, names, incidents, organizations, and dialogue are either the products of the author's imagination or are used fictitiously.

10 9 8 7 6 5 4 3 2

ISBN: 978-1-960250-09-4

Cover and book design by Gary Lindberg

To all those who helped make my young, informative years in the Caribbean very special. Many are gone but are forever alive in the pages of these books.

Acknowledgements

Thanks to Calumet Editions and my many friends who take time to read drafts that they know will change many, many times before being deemed acceptable.

Also by David Culberson

Alterio's Motive

Back Time on Love City

A Fortnight
of Fury

David Culberson

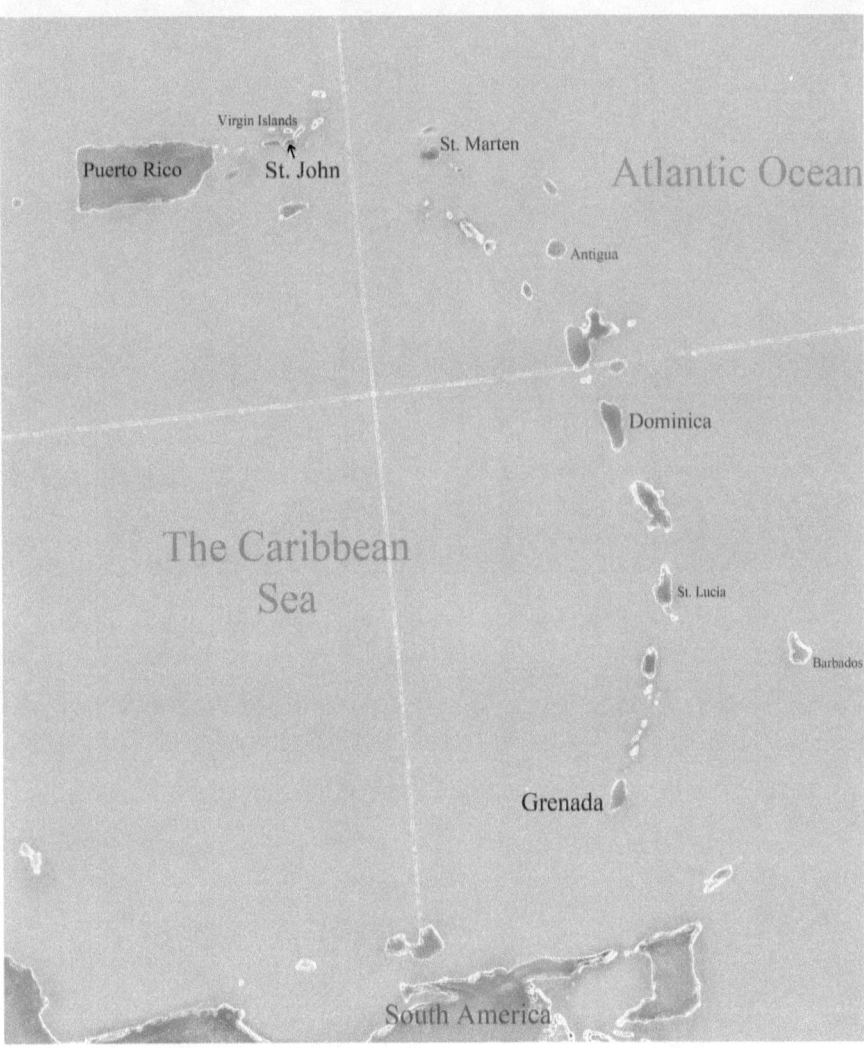

Virgin Islands

Puerto Rico

St. John

St. Marten

Atlantic Ocean

Antigua

Dominica

The Caribbean
Sea

St. Lucia

Barbados

Grenada

South America

Pearls Airport

Grenville

GRENADA

Grand Mal Bay

Fort Rupert
St.Georges •
Prison

Grand Anse Bay

Calivigny

Point Salines Airstrip

True Blue Campus

Prickly Bay

Preface

October 1983

The world witnessed an escalation of the Cold War as the Soviet Union grasped for financial straws in the wake of Ronald Reagan's anti-communist rhetoric and defense spending. Fidel Castro, after failing to gain a foothold for his unique revolution on the African continent, sought one closer to home and was knocking on the doors of Grenada and Dominica. On October 23rd, a suicide bomber rammed his vehicle into a US Marine barracks in Beirut and killed, besides himself and a passenger, two hundred forty-one marines. Reagan was loaded for bear. America needed a win. Reagan pounced. His target was an idyllic island in the Windward Chain of the lower Caribbean whose primary export, besides tourism, was nutmeg. Maurice Bishop, Grenada's prime minister and a Marxist who wanted better medical care and education for the people of his island, was not interested in becoming a regional military power. He had recently been placed in jail by an extreme faction of his political party that wanted a stronger military presence on the island, but not before bringing in six hundred Cuban construction workers to build a nine-thousand-foot runway that, according to the US, could possibly land Soviet military aircraft. The runway and Bishop's closeness to Castro were two ingredients that stoked the fires of an invasion by the United States. Then Bishop was executed, which brought the world's attention to Grenada and the safety of foreigners on the island. The final ingredient needed to justify Reagan's invasion was a medical

1

school on the island where eight hundred American students hoped to receive degrees.

Operation Urgent Fury, the invasion of Grenada, began on October 25th, 1983. Bombs dropped against a backdrop of lush mountain jungles and sugary sand beaches bleached by the Caribbean sun. In the villages, chickens strutted around brightly painted wooden shacks with metal roofs. Roosters crowed. Goats huddled under trees and in makeshift bus stops, trying to avoid humans. Locals that were not part of the People's Revolutionary Army went about their daily routines. Children played soccer and cricket. Women opened shutters and swept porches; some carried baskets of fruit on their heads to local markets. Many men, on their way to clear brush, rode bicycles with machetes strapped to their backs. A few locals set up coolers and folding tables along roadsides so they could sell a jonny cake and an ice-cold bottle of beer for less than a dollar. All wore thin clothes and broad smiles.

As mighty as it was, the military invasion could not obscure the backdrop. As acrid smoke from exploded ordnance filled the air, roosters still crowed. The rat-tat-tat of automatic firearms enveloped the island, and the goats still huddled. Locals lined the roadsides to cheer the US forces as they flooded the country. The beaches remained pristine, beckoning tourists... who didn't show up. Soldiers died. Calypso music played through cheap speakers set up at road intersections or near the cricket fields. Helicopters crashed while the intense Caribbean sun shone through the smoky haze of gunfire. Chickens led their chicks through the marauding armies, just another nuisance in the chicken's quest to avoid the mongooses—who have an insatiable craving for baby chickens.

And the war went on.

The world saw none of this. Journalists weren't allowed on the island during the first few days of the invasion. But a handful of locals from a neighboring island, on a totally different mission, unwittingly landed on Grenada on the eve of Operation Urgent Fury. What they witnessed was surreal—a harsh brushstroke of battle painted across the colorful, whimsical canvas that was the Caribbean.

It was as though Disney had gone to war.

Chapter 1

DAY 1: OCTOBER 14

A full moon shone on Pillsbury Sound, its mirrored image warped by the rough seas between St. John and St. Thomas, transforming into clearer detail on the calmer water in the bay. Boiled Bob sat under a palm tree on an overturned fiberglass fishing boat that he knew had been in the same spot for as long as he'd been on the island. He watched the moon's reflection slide up the beach on lapping waves, disappearing each time the water retreated back into the sea, its shiny remnant sucked into the sand. A wave crawled over his sandaled feet, and Bob moved higher up on the boat's hull, scraping the back of his thigh on a new patch of fiberglass that had not yet been sanded. He rubbed his skin checking for blood and sneered at the unkempt boat.

"Fucking locals," he mumbled. "How in hell does anything get done on this shithole?"

Boiled Bob looked into the bay and then glanced at the surrounding hills. It was midnight, and the island had shut down, but the light from the moon bothered him. He and his minions had work to do. Anybody could step out onto their deck in the middle of the night and be alarmed by unusual activity in the moonlit bay. This was the first of two bays he planned to visit this night, and he needed all the time he could get, particularly given the bumbling misfits at his command.

He shook his head in disgust at the thought of the crew he'd assembled over the past three years. They were loyal but provided him with multiple frustrations. He simply couldn't understand why those attracted to his brilliant political and social theories were such… idiots. He sighed and thought of the revolutionary writings introduced to him during his six-month foray into college life. He read Marx, Proudhon and Lenin. He even picked up on Bakunin and Emma Goldman. He didn't understand their philosophies, but he could repeat many of their writings, which impressed his minions but sometimes got him kicked out of local bars by patrons who tired of Boiled Bob's incoherent diatribes.

A dog barked nearby, and Boiled Bob looked up the hill to see if anybody had come out of one of the scattering of homes across the street. He didn't see anybody but started to wonder what was taking his crew so long—a crew with an uncanny ability to bungle the simplest task. Bob shook his head. One of the first things he'd realized after he landed on the island was that it was as if somebody had grabbed the world and shook it, and all of the loose ends and broken pieces had fallen to the Caribbean. Boiled Bob befriended as many of these broken souls and goofballs as would listen to him. Many seemed to think he was a natural leader, a role Bob readily accepted, and he took those he could control under his wing—for as long as they believed his bullshit. After a couple of years and multiple changes in the group's membership, they'd worn out their welcome on the island that tolerated just about anything—except a loud group of misfits led by Boiled Bob. Locals sometimes shouted them down and demanded that Boiled Bob and his cult leave the island. Bob felt mildly responsible for his small group of broken pieces and had begun to think that a move to a different island would improve his stake in life, or at least allow him to start over someplace where he and his followers were unknown.

Tonight was the night he'd chosen to make the move. He hadn't really chosen it. He had coerced his crew into the conclusion that this was the opportune night to take action—a conclusion not based on research of the moon's phases or which night would be darkest in order to conceal their plan. The decision was made a week earlier after psilocybin mushrooms, plucked from cow dung on Tortola's Sage Mountain, were added to the group's pasta dinner. Around a campfire an hour after dinner, a passage from Carlos Castaneda's *The Teachings of Don Juan* was read to them over and over by Boiled Bob—until the sun came up. His warped interpretation of the passage was that they would leave the island together in one week. Deep into their hallucinogenic condition, the group enthusiastically agreed with their *too cool* leader.

Another shiny wave lapped at his feet, and Boiled Bob stared into the bay and then to St. Thomas, four miles in the distance, where house lights clung to the symmetrical volcanic slopes, making the island look like a squat, lit up Christmas tree. The noise of an approaching vehicle turned his attention landward. He stood and ran his hand through his scruffy, black hair and then placed his thumb and fingers on either side of his beard and absentmindedly stroked downward. A small, beat-up Toyota pickup truck came to a stop along the concrete seawall. His crew bailed from the truck and stepped off the seawall onto the beach. Boiled Bob started toward his crew, passing another overturned dinghy closer to the seawall and tied to a palm tree. He looked back at the dinghy he'd been sitting on and decided it was too small for his crew. He'd take the one closer to the wall. He heard a thump under the dinghy just as a mosquito bit his neck. He slapped at the mosquito and paused. His crew, two men and three women, all thin and wearing shorts, tank tops and sandals, stopped a few feet from him. One of the women giggled, causing Bob to glare at his crew. All seemed enthusiastic and ready to start their new lives as modern-day pirates. Once they had settled he smiled at the women, all of whom he'd slept with. They smiled back. The two taller women, Mary and Pam, both had dark complexions and long auburn hair and could have passed as sisters. Neither currently shared his bed. Tricia, the short woman with long, dark curls and the nice ass, did.

Boiled Bob stepped close to Tricia, patted her butt, stood back and said, "It's the *Happy Hobo*." He pointed to a seventy-one-foot wooden yawl, built in the 1930s by John Alden, anchored in the bay fifty yards from shore and said, "That's the one we'll take."

The crew looked out to the boat, which they all knew well. There were a dozen other boats in the bay, but this was the prize. It had sailed in many regattas and had been featured on the cover of more than one

US boating magazine. Most importantly, it belonged to the father of Captain Jay's girlfriend. Boiled Bob had nothing against the father, but he hated his daughter—just a little less than he hated Captain Jay.

The tallest of the men, thin and topped off with a mop of red hair, blew out a breath and said, "You sure, Boiled... I mean, Boss? I know the owner of that boat. He's got lots of friends."

Boiled Bob glared up at Long Bill's six-foot-seven frame. He despised the name *Boiled Bob*.

"Of course he's got a lot of friends, idiot," he snorted. He then added, "Why aren't you called Tall Bill? I mean Long Bill is a stupid name. It's like you were named while lying down. What the fuck's with that, LB? Who named your tall, skinny ass anyway?"

"I don't know. It just happened," Long Bill said with a shrug, nervously rubbing the bump on the bridge of his big, crooked nose. "But are you sure about this boat? Some of his friends are kinda mean."

"Yeah, I'm sure," Boiled Bob said, nodding at Long Bill's nose. "You shouldn't have let that asshole Captain Jay do that to you. You're bigger than him by five inches or more."

"It wasn't Captain Jay who broke my nose. It was that stutterer, Tommy Lowell. But he cheated. He smiled, and I thought that meant he was done with the fight. Then he hit me again. Hurt like hell."

"Well, you've got a good seven inches on him. You should have kicked his ass."

"I don't think anybody has ever been able to kick Tommy's ass, Boss. Besides, I kinda like him."

Boiled Bob stared at Long Bill for a long time and finally said, "You in love with Captain Jay too?"

"No, Boss, he's a prick. He's got a nice girlfriend though."

Boiled Bob looked out to the bay and thought about his own experiences with Captain Jay, the worst at a rental house Boiled Bob maintained. A friend of Captain Jay had rented the home for a week so that he and his family could dive with him. The asshole captain happened to have walked in on Boiled Bob while he was having his way with his friend's beautiful daughter. It didn't matter to Boiled Bob that she was thirteen. Captain Jay pounced, and Boiled Bob had spent

6

a month in the St. Thomas hospital. He absentmindedly rubbed his ribs. It still hurt to sneeze or cough.

Boiled Bob shook his head, looked around at the rest of his crew and said, "We're taking this boat because we can. Fuck the owner and his friends. They think they're so tough. I'm smarter than them, and taking this boat will prove it. It'll make them look like the meathead idiots they are."

Boiled Bob looked at each crew member. All but Long Bill nodded with enthusiasm. Long Bill looked confused.

Boiled Bob smiled and said, "Okay. Let's get this done." He then pointed to the overturned fishing boat next to them and said, "Grab some oars from some of these dinghies pulled up on the beach, and grab the gear from the truck. Then paddle this boat out to the *Happy Hobo*."

Boiled Bob walked to the truck and took out a canvas bag. He pulled out hand augers and said, "I want you three to drill holes in the bottoms of every boat tied up along this beach. After you've paddled this one out to the *Happy Hobo*, sink it."

Long Bill, Pam and Mary grabbed the drills and walked toward the dozen or so dinghies spread out up the beach. Tricia walked down the beach in search of oars. Boiled Bob untied the overturned fishing boat from the palm tree. He and the other male crew member, Maynard, uprighted the boat. A crab that had found refuge in the boat's shadow skittered between their feet and into the shadows of the seawall.

Jumping back, Maynard yelled, "What the hell is that?"

A small, unshaven West Indian man wearing a dirty T-shirt and who smelled of stale beer sat up, wiped sand from his face and shouted, "Hey! What you doing wit my house? Leave me alone." He wiped more sand and sweat from his face, squinted at the three men and said, "I know you."

"Calm down, Willie," Boiled Bob said, holding up his palm.

Maynard pulled out the large knife he kept in his baggy shorts.

Boiled Bob stepped toward the short, wiry Frenchie and said, "No, Maynard."

Maynard hesitated. He lowered the knife and ran his left hand through his wavy blond hair.

Boiled Bob had several advantages over his crew. One was his intelligence. Another was that he was a good fighter, or so he'd convinced his followers. They'd never seen him fight and, in reality, Boiled Bob had been on the losing end of every fight he'd been in, including a thrashing at the hands of Captain Jay. He'd learned a couple of martial arts moves in his youth, knew fighting jargon from movies and told his crew of numerous fights he'd won over the years, many times putting his opponents in the hospital. It was all bullshit, but Boiled Bob knew that what he lacked in experience he could make up with brazenness. He could bluff his way out of anything— most of the time.

"But he saw us," Maynard said, waving the large knife. "He'll run to town and tell anybody who's awake that we stole the *Happy Hobo*. Besides, I'm tired of seeing this homeless asshole stinking up the bars."

Long Bill, who'd drilled holes in the dinghy Boiled Bob had been sitting on, saw what was going on and stepped back to the boat Boiled Bob and Maynard had just uprighted. Maynard continued to wave his knife.

Boiled Bob pushed Maynard and said, "No." He then looked at Long Bill and said, "Drag that lighter dinghy you just put holes in over here."

Maynard sneered at Boiled Bob and walked away, sliding his knife back into his baggy shorts. Boiled Bob shook his head, wondering how Maynard had never cut his prick off taking that damned knife in and out of his shorts.

Long Bill dragged the smaller dinghy next to Willie's while Boiled Bob dragged the dinghy Willie slept under to the edge of the surf. Then he and Long Bill turned the smaller dinghy over on top of the piece of cardboard Willie used as a mattress.

Boiled Bob lifted one side of the dinghy and said, "Okay, Willie. This is your new house. See? It's lighter and easier for you to get in and out."

Willie, still wiping sand from his face and looking in the direction Maynard had walked, said, "That mon is bad. He always been treaten*in* me wit dat stupid knife. Somebody needs to keel that mon."

8

Boiled Bob looked at Maynard, who said, "Like I said, I don't like this homeless piece of shit coming in and smelling up the bar when I'm trying to enjoy a few beers."

Bob set the dinghy back onto the sand, walked to the truck where their provisions were and came back with a fifth of rum. He lifted one side of the dinghy, placed the bottle under it and said to Willie, "Take it. It's a housewarming gift for your new dinghy."

Willie hesitantly crawled under the dinghy, and Boiled Bob let the side he'd held up settle onto the sand. He heard the metal cap turn on the glass rum bottle followed by several loud gulps. He then heard a muffled voice say, "Der holes in dis boat. I can see de moon."

Boiled Bob heard another gulp from the rum bottle and then silence.

"He won't remember a thing," Bob said.

A few minutes later the three women returned with the drills, two oars and a paddle.

"LB, you crewed on the *Happy Hobo* a while back, didn't you?" Boiled Bob asked.

"A couple of times, Boss."

"You'll be the first mate."

Boiled Bob reminded the crew that Long Bill would captain the *Happy Hobo* in his absence and turned to walk in the opposite direction.

"Where you going, Boss?" Long Bill asked.

Boiled Bob turned back toward the crew and said, "Going to do some more damage while you get the boat ready."

Maynard snorted and said, "I'm the most experienced captain here. Don't you think I should take charge?"

"No. LB knows the boat better," Boiled Bob said.

After a brief stare down, Maynard shrugged and stepped into the only functional dinghy left on the beach. The rest of the crew followed. Boiled Bob walked away, glad he could still intimidate Maynard—at least for now.

Boiled Bob walked down the beach to the ferry dock and a row of grey inflatable dinghies tied close to shore. They all were in good shape and had small, three-horsepower motors clamped to their wooden sterns. He knew which dinghy belonged to the *Happy Hobo* and hopped in, starting the three-horsepower motor with a pull of the rope, and steered toward its mother ship. Halfway to the *Happy Hobo*, he turned around and headed back to the dock, where he untied the remaining inflatable dinghies and tied them behind his.

On the ride to the *Happy Hobo*, Boiled Bob thought about two things. One was to figure out how to get rid of Maynard, who had become unmanageable. The other was the name given to him shortly after arriving to St. John, having been reminded of it earlier by Long Bill. It was a name given by the locals, who had a propensity for making up names for newcomers with abnormal behaviors, which was just about everybody who stayed on the island for more than a week. Boiled Bob arrived on the island as Bob—Bob Blight from Miami. He'd heard the whispers as he passed locals who thought of him as a burned-out druggie. Shortly after, he'd started to hear *Boiled* in front of *Bob*. Bob bristled at the description. His hair and beard were scruffy, and his wardrobe was a little ragged, but *burn out... boiled?* He did a lot of drugs, but only mind-expanding hallucinogenic drugs like LSD and magic mushrooms from Tortola. The drugs were an important part of his evolution as a philosopher of social revolution—and as a sex magnet. Young women were often attracted to him, at least compliant, when given enough liquor and quaaludes. That's how he'd landed all of the women who'd followed him in the past three years. Most had gone away, stealing off with sailors in the night or returning to the US. It didn't matter to Boiled Bob either way. He'd tired of them and was glad to see them go. He still had Pam and Mary and Tricia, proving that he wasn't *boiled*—he was brilliant.

"Fucking locals," he mumbled and motored to the *Happy Hobo*.

"What are we going to do with those?" Long Bill asked when Boiled Bob arrived at the *Happy Hobo* with the dinghies.

"We'll take them with us. It'll slow down any chase, and we'll sell them for a lot of money down island."

"Should I set sail?" Long Bill asked as he and the crew prepared the boat to leave the bay.

"Not yet. Secure the dinghies, and motor to the resort."

Boiled Bob looked around at the few boats in the harbor and said, "Do it as quietly as possible so we don't wake up anybody on those liveaboards."

They headed north with six dinghies behind the ketch. Two dinghies upended after crashing into each other at the crest of a large wave just outside the bay.

"LB, what the hell are you doing? You've just ruined two good motors," Boiled Bob said, looking behind them.

"I tied them up and thought I left plenty of room between them, but these seas are getting pretty big," Long Bill replied.

The rest of the crew, except Maynard, watched the exchange, shrugged and went about their business of stowing their gear and readying the lines and sails for the sail down island. Maynard stood with a smirk and stared at Boiled Bob for a minute before turning to help the crew.

The resort was located two bays to the north, and the *Happy Hobo* and its new crew were there in less than twenty minutes. Several sailboats and a couple of dive boats were at anchor in the quiet bay. The sailboats were for day-charters. Nobody lived on them. Boiled Bob ignored the sailboats and stared at the dive boats. They belonged to Captain Jay, who Boiled Bob knew was off-island. If there was time, he'd sink them on his way out of the bay.

Long Bill leaned toward Boiled Bob and asked, "What's the plan?"

Boiled Bob stared at the shoreline, looking for anybody who might notice the stolen yawl. "You, me and Tricia will take one of the dinghies to the dock. The rest will stay on the boat. Maynard will drive the boat. Don't anchor. Motor near the mouth of the bay, and keep the lights off," Boiled Bob said loud enough for the crew to hear. He saw questioning looks from a couple of his crew and added, "We don't want any of the nighttime employees to see it, especially those useless security guards. Both are sailors and will recognize the boat and know something's up."

Maynard reached to the handle of his knife and said, "I want to go with you."

Boiled Bob didn't want Maynard near the security guards, who were armed only with two-way radios.

"You're staying on the boat, Maynard." He gauged Maynard's reaction and then added, "With me and LB gone you're the only one who can handle the boat in these seas. You'll be more useful manning the helm until we come back."

Maynard puffed out his chest and stepped into the cockpit.

Boiled Bob went below, opened his bag and grabbed two handguns. Returning to the deck he passed one to Long Bill and put the other in his front pocket. Neither gun was loaded. They stepped down into a dinghy, headed to the dock and tied up close to shore next to a half dozen other inflatable dinghies. Boiled Bob climbed onto the dock and looked back into the bay. The *Happy Hobo* was a couple of hundred yards from shore and partially screened by the anchored boats. Satisfied, he led Long Bill and Tricia past the dock and into the open lobby, which was empty of guests and employees. He told Tricia to keep watch and then led Long Bill up a flight of stairs. Once on the second floor, Boiled Bob took the handgun from his pocket and motioned Long Bill to do the same but saw that Long Bill had already taken his gun out.

Boiled Bob knew the layout well, having worked in the night auditor's office for a couple of months during his first year on the island. He'd taken an accounting class during his short stint in college and learned little, but his general knowledge of the discipline's principles and his ability to bullshit landed him a part-time job with the resort during the off season when employees were hard to find. He was fired after being accused of using Friday night deposits to buy and sell drugs on the weekend for a profit and then return the cash he'd taken on Sunday nights, before Monday's deposit into the local bank. Boiled Bob had denied the charge, but management persisted in their accusation, and for days Boiled Bob stewed. He ended up carrying a large revenue posting machine down the steps on a dolly and dumping it off the end of the resort's dock into the bay. That was the end of his short career as an assistant to the night auditor.

Revenge on the resort wasn't the reason for his visit to the comptroller's office. The night auditor happened to be Captain Jay's girlfriend, Lisa. She'd humiliated him in front of people when he hit on her in a bar a couple of years earlier. After she'd called his behavior "obnoxious," she grabbed his crotch, frowned, turned to her friends and said, "I think his penis is missing."

Boiled Bob could hear the pecking of adding machines around the corner—too much noise for a single employee to make. This complicated things. He paused, and before he and Long Bill could turn the corner to the office, Tricia bounded up the stairway. At the top she whispered, "Two security guards are hiding in the bushes between the lobby and the bar. They saw us come in."

Boiled Bob let out a sigh and said, "Shit."

"Why aren't they coming after us?" Long Bill asked.

Bob glanced down at the handgun Long Bill held and said, "Because, dipshit, they saw your gun. You should've kept it hidden like I told you to do."

He told Tricia to return to the lobby and stay out of sight and motioned Long Bill to follow him. He watched Tricia head back down the stairway and admired her tight butt.

Giggles from the accounting office brought Boiled Bob back to real time. He and Long Bill entered the office and found three women busily adding receipts and shoving cash into zippered bank bags. They didn't look up until Boiled Bob cocked his revolver and pointed it at them.

Bob ran his eyes up and down Lisa's tall, athletic body and stayed on her long, brown hair for a moment. She was beautiful—and, as far as he was concerned, a royal bitch. Boiled Bob could never understand why she was so popular around the island.

"Hi, Lisa. Miss me?" Boiled Bob asked. He nodded to her co-workers and asked, "Why all the help? Is this place making that much money? It's off-season. Can't be that busy."

She stood, looked at her co-workers and, with a nod, indicated for them to stay calm.

"We're busy," Lisa said and then smirked. "Oh, yeah, I miss you like I miss a venereal disease. What do you want, asshole?"

Boiled Bob waved the revolver and moved forward a step. "Still a ballsy, smart-ass bitch, aren't you?" He stepped up to her desk and hit her on the side of her head with the revolver. She wavered, almost toppling over. Blood trickled down past her ear. He'd hit her harder than he'd expected to.

Long Bill backed up and asked, "Boss, you sure you want to do this?"

"Fuck you, LB. You can leave anytime you want."

Long Bill looked toward the stairs and then back to the room. He stayed where he was.

"Good. Now, LB, find a bag and get those two to put all of the cash in it," Boiled Bob said.

Lisa moved toward Boiled Bob. "Take the cash and leave, asshole," she said, holding the side of her head. "You won't get far."

Boiled Bob hesitated and said nothing for a moment. He'd hoped to take any cash there was and rough up Lisa before sailing away. The presence of the guards and witnesses changed things. He'd thought about kidnapping Lisa but had not mentioned it to his crew and was undecided about it—until now. Now he had no choice. He needed her as a hostage now that he'd been seen. And there were her two co-workers. He could kill them or drop them off down island, but he wasn't a killer, and having all three on the boat would be complicated—and there were the guards.

Boiled Bob looked around the room, thinking. He glanced at the door and said to Lisa, "You're coming with us. You're going to be our protection. Too bad your boyfriend can't save you now."

With that, Lisa bolted toward the door. Boiled Bob caught her arm and spun her around, pointed the revolver at her face and said, "Down." He tightened his grip and twisted. She grimaced and went to her knees.

Long Bill held a plastic garbage bag with a fair amount of cash in it. "What do we do now, Boss?"

"Find some rope or tape, and tie those two up and gag them."

Long Bill went through desk drawers and found two rolls of packing tape. He bound the two women to chairs and wrapped tape around their heads, covering their mouths.

Boiled Bob led Lisa down the stairs. At the bottom he called out to Tricia in a heavy whisper, "They still there?"

She backpedaled to the base of the stairs and said, "They're still there. I heard them talking about their radios. I think they're broken."

Bob looked around, knowing there was no other way back to the dinghy. "Okay. We walk out of here and to the dock. LB, keep your weapon out."

They walked out of the lobby and toward the dock. Boiled Bob saw the guards in the bushes. One of them shouted, "The police are on their way."

"Bullshit!" Boiled Bob shouted. "Those clowns couldn't find their way out of Cruz Bay. You pricks come after us, and she's dead." He held his gun above his head, making sure they saw it and then grabbed Lisa. One guard backed off and ran in the opposite direction.

"Let's go," Bob said to the group.

Lisa hesitated, and Boiled Bob wrenched her wrist up behind her back hard enough to make her cry out. They reached the dinghy dock, and Long Bill folded his tall frame into the rubber dinghy they'd come in. He pulled the chord to start the motor. Nothing. Boiled Bob nervously looked back toward the lobby. The police might be on their way if the guard who ran had found a phone, which didn't worry him much. The police didn't have a boat, and the coast guard boats were in St Thomas or Puerto Rico. With Captain Jay off-island they couldn't call him, but a guard could call some of the island heroes—the part-time mercenary bastards who were always in his way, like Tommy Lowell and that big son-of-a bitch, Charlie Kline. They worried him. They were close to the *Happy Hobo*'s owner and, if currently on the island, might, no, *would* come after him, especially if Lisa was his hostage. He thought about leaving Lisa on the dock but dismissed that as soon as he realized that, sooner or later, he might need her as a hostage to negotiate his safety if they caught up with him. If Long Bill didn't get the dinghy started he'd need her sooner rather than later.

"Come on, LB. Get the damn thing started," Boiled Bob said, looking out into the moonlit bay. He couldn't see the *Happy Hobo*, which was good. Maynard had hidden it behind the anchored boats in the bay. The seas had worsened. He saw large swells break onto the rocks on either side of the bay, sending white, frothing spray over and around them.

Long Bill tried a dozen more times to start the motor.

"Check the gas tank," Boiled Bob said, nervously waving the revolver and looking toward the lobby.

"Damn, Boss. It's empty, or close to it."

"Jesus, LB. How can you be such a dipshit?"

Boiled Bob raged and waved the revolver aimlessly. Long Bill stared back wide-eyed and slunk as low as he could. He was still a big target.

All eyes were on the revolver, which only Bob knew wasn't loaded. Everybody ducked or twisted sideways each time it pointed in their direction. It finally settled on Lisa, who managed to say, "Steal one of these dinghies, asshole." She nodded to the group of inflatable dinghies tied next to theirs.

Boiled Bob wanted to shoot her. Her suggestion was genius. Why didn't he think of it?

"LB, get into one of those dinghies, and check the gas," Boiled Bob said and looked to the lobby again.

"Good news, Boss. This one's full," Long Bill said and started the motor with one pull.

"Get in," Boiled Bob said to the two women.

Tricia hurried into the dinghy. Lisa had to be shoved. Boiled Bob followed, still waving his gun around. Long Bill took them out into the bay toward the *Happy Hobo*. The swells had found their way into the bay, rocking the boats at anchor with each passing wave and making for a rough dinghy ride.

Boiled Bob spotted the *Happy Hobo* motoring in circles at the bay's entrance and ordered Long Bill to head out into the swells and come back to the sailboat with following seas. He reasoned it would be easier to land the dinghy and safely off-load in the dangerous seas going with the swells, rather than into them, though he wasn't sure. Either way would be bad.

Long Bill swung the dinghy close to the rocks on the south side of the bay in order to run parallel with the swells before turning northeast to run with them. Boiled Bob looked over at Lisa and saw her unclasp her bracelet. He wondered why. At the closest point to the rocks, just as Boiled Bob decided to grab Lisa, she jumped, taking with her the plastic bag of cash that Long Bill had tossed into the bottom of the dinghy. Boiled Bob was able to grab the bag, which tore, sending most of the cash into the rough sea and some into the dinghy. He paid no attention to the cash. He saw the heavy seas smash Lisa into the rocks and the backwash bring her back toward the dinghy, face down. In seconds the water covered her.

"Shit!" Boiled Bob shouted. "Get us over there. We need her— alive."

Long Bill drove the dinghy to where they had last seen Lisa. They were dangerously close to the rocks. Boiled Bob reached into the water and luckily grabbed an arm just as a large wave hit the dinghy. Long Bill gunned the motor and turned the handle as far as he could to the left, swinging the dinghy to the right and out into the bay, away from the rocks. Boiled Bob lost his grip on the arm and stared back to the churning sea near the rocks.

"Shit!" he shouted again. "Get us back there."

"But, Boss!" Long Bill shouted and turned the bow of the dinghy into the next giant swell. Water crashed over the boat and drenched everybody in it.

Boiled Bob glared at Long Bill, water dripping off his face. "Get us back there. We need her with us."

Chapter 2

DAY 2: OCTOBER 15

Arlan O'Brien slipped on his flip-flops and stepped onto the sunlit deck of a massive, plastered, concrete house that overlooked the north shore of St. John and the Sir Francis Drake Channel, the mile-wide channel that separated the US Virgin Islands from the British Virgin Islands, or the BVI. He glanced to the east and saw whitecaps breaking over Johnson's Reef. The seas had settled only a little since the front that passed the night before when, in the bright moonlight, he could see the large breakers on the reef from the same deck.

Arlan looked at his giant titanium watch, the only watch he'd ever worn. It was given to him by Captain Jay, Arlan's mentor and the person responsible for all things dangerous and mischievous he'd experienced since arriving on the island a few years earlier. Arlan smiled as he remembered being handed the watch on Captain Jay's dive boat while on his second dive ever—a wonderful nightmare of a dive in very deep water filled with sharks, blood and thrashing fish on the ends of spears. Just before going into the water, Captain Jay had handed Arlan a speargun and a mesh bag, pointed to Arlan's new watch and told him he had to be back under the boat in forty minutes. The dive had been a recreational spearfishing expedition that consisted of a group of seasoned local divers, many of whom owned their own dive operations. They gathered every month or so to go on a "play dive." These were aggressive dives, normally in deep, current driven and shark infested water where few recreational divers had any business diving, particularly tourists who had been certified in pools and gravel pits. This was the seasoned diver's escape from the monotony of the daily grind of dealing with tourists who showed up with matching wetsuits and underwater knives strapped around their shins. Only Captain Jay had known Arlan was a rookie diver who had never been certified—in a pool or anywhere else. As soon as Arlan entered the water he'd realized he'd be on his own. The last words he'd heard before going underwater were, "Don't worry, Rookie, it's as easy as screwin'." A few minutes later, once comfortable in the deep water, Arlan had experienced an underwater adventure that divers who'd been diving for decades rarely saw. Forty-five minutes later and back on the boat, Arlan was happy to be among the living.

Arlan walked back through the house, out the entrance and into the driveway. He left the doors open, the way they'd been for most of the life of the house. There was no reason to close and batten down doors on the island unless a hurricane was close. Burglaries were unheard of. Iguanas and smaller lizards, fruit rats, hummingbirds and an occasional goat could be found passing through or becoming part-time roommates in most island homes, but that was a minor tradeoff for the ability to live in a wonderfully open environment.

The house was owned by friends who had convinced Arlan to come for a short visit a few years earlier. He missed his return flight and had never left, eventually finding other places to stay on the island. When the owners of this home traveled or were back at their US home they often asked Arlan to house sit, which he was happy to do. The home's architecture was stunning, and the views were even more so.

Arlan squinted in the bright Caribbean sunlight. The immediate pain behind his eyes reminded him that he'd stayed up far too late. He placed the sunglasses that hung from his neck onto the bridge of his nose, grabbed the handlebars of his Kawasaki 175CC dirt bike, lifted his right leg over the seat and settled in. Once comfortable, he raised the kickstand with his left foot, then used his right leg to kick the starter arm, at the same time twisting the throttle with his right hand.

Ring-a-ding-a-ding-ding-ding.

The two-stroke engine came to life, and Arlan fishtailed out of the long gravel drive and onto Centerline Road, one of three main roads on the island. He had five minutes to make the ferry which, contrary to most island things, was always punctual.

Why did I agree to meet the early boat? he thought as he glanced at his watch again.

Tommy Lowell, Arlan's construction supervisor for the project he was developing, had called the night before to remind Arlan that he had a meeting with the building inspector at the ferry dock at eight in the morning.

It wasn't really a meeting. Arlan had volunteered to pay for Blake's daughter's dress she needed to compete in a local beauty pageant coming up in a week. Arlan liked Blake and his family and knew they didn't have a lot of money. He had to meet the boat and hand Blake an envelope with one hundred and eighty-three dollars in it, the cost of a bright-red dress on display in a shop on St. Thomas. Arlan could have had his secretary or Tommy deliver the money but preferred to keep the transaction quiet, lest anybody thought it a bribe. Arlan frowned at the thought that such a fine young lady had been thrust into the competition. She was a sweet person but was a hundred pounds overweight and had her father's rough facial features. She had no chance to win a competition based on looks.

After three hairpin turns Arlan entered the stretch on Centerline Road that was flat and straight, if only for a half mile. It was the only place on the volcanic island that a standard transmission vehicle could see fourth gear. It was also bordered on both sides by the Iva Moses property—full of pigs, cows and a host of unfinished concrete block buildings that were the beginning of Iva's dream of the first shopping mall ever on St. John. He had a lot of land and endless energy but didn't have bank financing or a business model that would have told him that his dream may have been a couple of decades or more ahead of its time.

It was the pigs that interested Arlan as he increased power and nudged the shifter under his foot into the highest gear. About twenty pigs were huddled on either side of the road. The pigs on the left had already crossed the road and were waiting on their friends to cross so they could be on their way to the nearby landfill and the daily food scraps and other high-quality waste that tourism produces. The six pigs on the right side of the road had yet to cross.

Arlan had increased his speed and was screaming through the flat terrain. He'd be on the other side of the straightaway in seconds and would have to downshift. He glanced at his watch and turned the throttle a little more.

Ring-a-ding-a-ding-ding-ding.

He was a hundred feet from the pigs.

"Don't cross," he said out loud.

All but three crossed. Arlan lightly put his right foot on the brake pedal, and his hands opened to clutch the front brake handle if needed. He paused. The pigs made it across the road. He looked at the three pigs that stayed on the right side of the road and repeated, "Don't cross."

Ten feet away, a sixty-pound pig decided to cross.

"Motherfu..."

Arlan had no time to slow. Swerving would have made him drop the bike and skid down the road. Wearing shorts and no helmet, the slide would hurt and cause him to miss the boat. He chose to take his chances and remained upright. *It was a small pig*, he reasoned. He braced for the collision and wondered what the impact of a dirt bike against a pig would look like to a bystander. The thought made him smile, but only for a moment.

The impact catapulted him forward, his crotch landing hard on the gas tank. His hands found the clutch and throttle cables that were connected to the handlebars. He grabbed tight and was able to control the steering while his feet dragged the ground... Flintstone-style. Everything stayed that way until the bike came to a stop in the grass a few feet off the road.

Arlan looked down at his position on the bike, flabbergasted that he was still upright. He then looked back at the collision site and saw that the pig was alive—kind of. It was on its right side, and its left front leg kicked wildly in the air. It had made it to the other side of the road and, thanks to Arlan's bike, would soon be on the other side of life. He couldn't do anything to help the dying pig short of smashing its head with a rock, which would be messy and, if anybody saw him, he would be accused of pig murder. Arlan winced as he swung his leg over the seat and stood on the side of the bike. His balls would be sore for a while.

He glanced at his watch. "Damn, two minutes."

He wished he'd driven the Jeep, but he had left it at the office the day before, opting to ride home on his little motorcycle.

Arlan made a quick check of the bike and found nothing broken. The topsides of his toes were scraped raw from dragging on the asphalt. He kick-started the engine and gently sat back on the seat. The engine sputtered for a moment and then came to life. He settled into the seat, winced and continued to the end of the straightaway and down the steep, winding road to Cruz Bay. He'd call Iva later in the day and tell him about the pig and remind him once again to fence his animals in or risk seeing them become roadkill, or find a few wrecked motorcycles, or worse, along the road that bifurcated his property.

Arlan sped past the police station and waved at the uniformed Jimmy Dalmida, who laughed and motioned for Arlan to slow down, which he didn't. As he approached the small park across from the ferry dock Arlan could see the crew untying the lines of the ferry. All of the parking spots near the dock were filled with taxis or surrey buses. Trucks with metal benches welded in rows on the frame behind the driver's cab were covered with a canvas top to keep tourists dry. The taxi drivers who owned the trucks had dropped off their passengers at the ferry and were waiting for a different ferry full of passengers that would arrive from St. Thomas about twenty minutes after the hour. He waved and said "Okay" to several locals milling in the park and illegally parked the bike next to the small wooden kiosk used to sell ferry boat tickets.

"Hey mister, dat is no park*in* place. Dat's me kiosk," a very large, uniformed West Indian lady shouted from the park. She hadn't recognized Arlan, who had his back to her. When he turned, the big lady said, "Mr. Arlan, me son, whachu doin mak*in* my life so hard?"

"Sorry, Miss Elsie. I'll be right back. You can take the bike for a spin if you want," Arlan answered.

"Wha? Me on dat motorcycle. Yo whan fo it to be flat as a jonny cake when yo go to come back?" Elsie shouted with a giant smile, making others in the park laugh.

"It's okay. I've got insurance," Arlan said and limped toward the boat, which was now a few feet from the dock. One of the crew had a thick coil of rope draped on his shoulder and was readying to leap from the dock to the boat. Arlan heard Elsie shout behind him, "You can get a ticket on da boat… if you make it der in time."

Arlan limped past a group of boat owners huddled around the second of the two on-duty police officers, Jimmy's brother Alex, who was listening to one of the boat owners explain that his dinghy was missing. Arlan knew all of the owners, who looked as though they had stepped out of a 1969 Woodstock time warp. He knew their boats and most of their dinghies, none of which were tied to the section of the dock close to shore that served as the official dinghy dock. He had no time to ask about the missing dinghies. Instead, he shouted to the crewman who'd finished his leap to the boat, who, upon seeing Arlan, leapt back to the dock and wrapped the heavy line around the nearest cleat while shouting for the captain to back up.

Once the captain brought the ferryboat against the dock, he stepped out of the wheelhouse and shouted, "Arlan, me son, why you always so late?"

Arlan shrugged and said to the captain, "Thanks, Ashley. I just need to give something to Mr. Blake. Can you hold the boat for a minute?"

"You gonna owe me. Maybe some lobsters next time you and Captain Jay go out huntin."

"No problem. How big?"

The captain laughed and stepped back to the controls. Arlan ducked under the metal frame that held up the roof of the main cabin of the old ferryboat, which had been salvaged from the Gulf of Mexico where it transported oil rig workers for years before being retired as a ferryboat in the Caribbean. A few tourists were sprinkled around the cabin on the wood and plastic benches. Their luggage had been piled on the floor in the center of the cabin near the open rail where passengers would disembark. Locals sat together talking and laughing. Inspector Blake sat next to two older West Indian ladies.

"Good day, Miss Gwennie, Mrs. Hall," Arlan said as he approached the group.

Mrs. Hall said, "Mr. Arlan, why you mak*in* the captain turn around. You mak*in* me late fo my weekly shopp*in* trip to da big isl*an*."

"Da big isl*an* tis not gonna go anyplace soon, Mrs. Hall," Arlan said, making everybody on the bench laugh.

Arlan handed an envelope to Mr. Blake, who thanked him and asked Arlan when he'd need another inspection on the construction project.

"I'll let you know." Arlan nodded to all three and said, "Have a good day."

Arlan thanked the captain for holding the boat and returned to his Kawasaki. After a few greetings with locals he sped up the hill to his office at Gallows Point, a run-down building built by Richard, *Duke*, Ellington.

Ellington was a mystery writer who had built seven funky cottages and a bar on the property in the '50s and managed them until Arlan's new partners bought the property. Many people speculated that Herman Wouk's *Don't Stop the Carnival*, written while Wouk lived in the Virgin Islands, was based on Gallows Point. Others were sure that it was based on a little inn near French Town on St. Thomas called Villa Olga. Others thought it might be about a small hotel on Hassle Island. They were all similar, and Wouk may have picked parts of all of them to pen his famous novel.

After an hour or so of phone calls, Arlan left his office to check out the construction progress. Tommy Lowell stood outside the office giving instructions to a masonry crew that had arrived late. Tommy was Arlan's right-hand man, though Arlan often thought it should have been the other way around. Their friendship had come a long way since the awkward start a couple of years earlier. Captain Jay had been dragging the rookie around Cruz Bay and introducing him to many of the island characters. They'd entered one of the three bars on the island early on a Saturday night and sat next to a group of Americans who'd made St. John their home.

The man who sat on a bar stool had looked at him with penetrating blue eyes and asked, "A-are you n-new to the island?" Arlan smiled and shook his head.

"You m-must be th-the rookie C-Captain Jay has t-talked about."

The man was about the same size as Arlan. Arlan had been sure the man was drunk and did everything he could to avoid him, grunting answers to his questions and trying hard not to make eye contact. The more Arlan avoided answering the man's questions, the more intense the man became. After one beer, Captain Jay had saved Arlan by announcing that they'd be moving on. As they left the bar, Arlan found out from Captain Jay that the guy next to him was Tommy Lowell.

"He's drunk," Arlan had said.

Captain Jay had asked, "You didn't piss him off did you?"

"Uh, well, maybe. He kept looking at me like he wanted to punch me."

Captain Jay had said, "He wasn't drunk... he stutters. And he doesn't like it when you don't pay attention to what he has to say. He makes you listen to every word, even if it does take a long time, and you already know how he's gonna finish a sentence. He is kinda old-fashioned and all about chivalry and politeness and all of that shit. Hell, he's even polite when he kicks your ass."

Tommy and Arlan could have passed for brothers. Both were about six feet and rangy, though Tommy was a little more chiseled, and both had dark wavy hair and deep blue eyes. But Tommy, probably because of his stuttering, was a tough and skilled fighter. A state wrestling champ and a Golden Glove boxing champ in a previous life, Tommy didn't like rudeness in people, no matter what size or how many. He especially didn't like people to curse when talking to him. If they did he would ask them to stop. If they did it a second time he would ask them to stop and demand an apology. If they continued, they found themselves on their asses looking up at Tommy wondering what kind of apology would work best.

Tommy was also one of the most knowledgeable contractors on the island, or anywhere, as far as Arlan knew. More importantly, he was liked by everybody, which was difficult on an island full of fiercely independent people with strong egos.

The masonry crew moved on to start their work day. Arlan told Tommy about hitting the pig and limping down the dock.

Tommy laughed and said, "W-we should take the Jeep and d-drive back up there and b-bring the dead pig back. We c-could have a pig roast f-for the workers."

"I'm sure Iva has butchered it by now. He never lets anything wait."

A plumbing contractor arrived and asked Tommy several questions about the job.

Arlan watched the contractor walk away, apparently satisfied with the answers.

Arlan said, "I saw a strange thing on the dock. Alex was talking to several boat owners. Their dinghies were missing."

"I h-heard about that a while ago. But th-that's not all."

Arlan cocked his head, wondering how Tommy knew so much in such a short time. "What else?" he asked.

"The *Ha-Happy Hobo* is m-missing."

"How do you know it's missing? Maybe Stu is out sailing."

"S-stu is off-island."

Arlan shrugged and said, "Oh well, I guess it'll show up sooner or later."

Tommy smiled and said, "P-probably." He then asked, "Is F-frank coming today?"

"He's supposed to be here on the noon ferry. Maybe we should meet him at the dock."

Frank Zapelli was the contractor that Arlan's New Jersey partners forced him to hire as the general contractor for a new project at Gallows Point. Arlan had fought the decision but, as a 20 percent partner, was out-voted. It didn't help that Frank had paid Arlan's partners under-the-table cash for not insisting on a bond that was required in the contract but that Frank couldn't provide because of bad credit.

"Are you g-going to fire him t-today?" Tommy asked as they waited for Frank.

"I don't want to fire him. But what choice do I have? He low-balled the project to get the job. My partners accepted the bid, and here we are. He's broke and wants me to look the other way and allow him to receive construction draws from the bank for work he hasn't completed. He's offered me cash to turn my head. I could use the money, but I can't do that."

Tommy was quiet for a few minutes and then said, "You're r-right, but I'm used to seeing p-people take th-the money."

"Would you?"

"N-no way."

"Right," Arlan replied and smiled.

"D-do you think he kn-knows he's going to be fired?"

"He might suspect it."

"M-maybe he'll be a n-no show—again."

They both laughed at that.

Frank was a likable man. His New *Yawk* accent and quick smile were disarming. It didn't hurt that he looked like the pope. The reason he'd last missed an important meeting was as funny as Frank was charming. Frank lived on Puerto Rico, kept an office on St. Thomas and commuted three or four days a week to St. John to check on his construction supervisor. A month earlier, Frank was a no-show for a meeting at the project site. He'd eventually entered Arlan's office, sat in a chair, wiped sweat from his bald head with a handkerchief and apologized. A commuter flight from San Juan to St. Thomas had crash landed just feet off a beach of a resort on Puerto Rico's northeast coast shortly after takeoff early that morning. Frank was a passenger. Nobody had been hurt, and the passengers and crew waded to the beach resort where they were kept comfortable while waiting for authorities to show up. Frank didn't wait. He'd walked, sopping wet, through the lobby of the resort and out to the parking lot where he handed a taxi driver a wet fifty-dollar bill and asked to be driven back to his San Juan apartment. Frank changed into dry clothes and took the next flight to St. Thomas, then taxied across the island and took the ferry to St. John. Arlan had heard radio reports throughout the day about the downed plane with one passenger missing and the subsequent coast guard search for the missing passenger. Arlan smiled as Frank told his story. When Frank had finished and apologized again for being so late, Arlan handed him the office phone and told him he should call the coast guard so they could call off the search. Frank had looked shocked while Arlan told him of the radio reports and that he was the missing passenger. Frank made the call.

A little after noon Arlan walked out to the parking lot to meet Tommy. They'd decided to pick Frank up at the ferry dock. Tommy shouted at a worker to slow down as he drove his truck out of the parking lot. The worker slowed and smiled back at Tommy. They were about to step into the vehicle when Sherry, a friend who worked at Caneel Bay full-time and helped Arlan with his accounting part-time, drove her Mini Moke into the parking lot and stopped within inches of them. The little British-made vehicle had wheels with independent suspension and could easily climb the island's steep, rocky roads. It was more a Flintstone-type dune buggy than car, and there weren't many left on the island. Larger and faster vehicles like Jeeps and Land Rovers were more in favor, particularly since more roads were being paved, making what used to be inaccessible parts of the island accessible.

"Wh-why don't you let me take th-the floor b-boards out of this car so you can drive it with y-your feet?" Tommy asked Sherry with a laugh.

"Tommy, you don't understand a piece of art when you see it," Sherry said as she sat in the driver's seat, her ass inches off the ground. "This is a collector's item."

"Yeah. A j-junk collector."

Sherry smiled and asked, "Have either of you heard from Captain Jay?"

"No. He's due back in any day. I know they left Florida about eight days ago and planned to stop in the Turks and Caicos and the Dominican Republic. If they spent time at the Hooker Bar in Puerto Plata they might be laid up for a few days," Arlan said with a smile.

"Y-you're no f-fan of Captain Jay," Tommy said to Sherry and then smiled and asked, "You n-need to kick his ass or something?"

Sherry didn't answer Tommy's question. Instead, she said, "Willie's been wandering around town mumbling that Maynard pulled his knife on him last night and that Boiled Bob gave him a new dinghy to sleep under. He's also saying that he heard Boiled Bob and his crew start the engine on the *Happy Hobo* and leave the bay."

"H-he heard them? He d-didn't see them?"

"He was under the dinghy, evidently," Sherry said.

"What's that have to do with Jay?" Arlan asked.

Glancing toward the ground, Sherry said, "Lisa's disappeared."

Neither Arlan nor Tommy said anything. It wasn't unusual for people who lived on the islands to "disappear" now and then and show up a few days or weeks later. Sherry then explained what she knew of the robbery at the resort the night before.

"Are you sure it was Boiled Bob?" Arlan asked.

Sherry said, "He and his crew were definitely the ones who robbed the resort and kidnapped Lisa. Peter was one of the security guards and watched it from a bush outside the lobby."

"He hid in the bushes?" Arlan asked with a smile.

"I guess they were armed," Sherry said.

"Wh-what about Lisa?"

"Nobody's seen or heard from her?"

"No. But the *Happy Hobo*'s dinghy was tied up to the resort dock, and another one was stolen but no one saw where it went," Sherry said.

"Maybe we can take Willie seriously, for once," Arlan said.

"S-so it looks like Boiled Bob and his mis-f-fits have taken the *H-Happy Hobo* too."

"Sounds like it was a pretty busy night for Boiled Bob and his troop of whackos," Arlan said. He looked at Sherry and asked, "Is anybody searching for the boat?"

"The police came out to the resort this morning, but I don't think they've put two and two together and haven't tied the *Happy Hobo* with Lisa's disappearance yet."

"W-we have," Tommy said. "I'll c-call Forrest. H-he'll be able to get a p-plane."

After a few moments of silence, Arlan looked into the bay and then to the east toward Puerto Rico and the direction from which Captain Jay would be returning. He took a deep breath and said, "So. Somebody took Captain Jay's girlfriend. He's going to be very pissed off."

Tommy looked at Sherry, who shrugged nervously. All three knew there would be island-wide, maybe region-wide, repercussions as soon as Captain Jay landed and learned about Lisa.

* * *

Boiled Bob sat in the galley of the *Happy Hobo* with his face resting on his knuckles and his elbows planted on either side of a white porcelain coffee cup that sat on a glossy wooden table, made glossier by the early morning sunlight that shone through the portholes. The *Happy Hobo* was tucked into a bay on the south side of Peter Island, where they'd been forced to anchor before sunrise, just a couple of hours from where they had started.

Boiled Bob had planned to sail east during the night and then take a more direct southerly route to their destination, which would require fifty hours of open water navigation. Soon after departing Caneel Bay he'd discovered that the provisions they'd gathered the week before the heist sat in their beat-up truck parked next to the Cruz Bay beach. His crew had loaded a few small personal bags into the dinghy but had neglected to bring the boxes of provisions. Boiled Bob was livid. After questioning everybody, it became clear that the crew had been too excited about the heist and had forgotten to follow orders. The *Happy Hobo* had little fresh water onboard, no food and no rum. He knew they couldn't make the passage without provisions, and they couldn't sail through the popular BVI islands during daylight—not without disguising the boat. He'd decided they'd need to stop for provisions and then wiggle their way through the Leeward Islands, ducking into as many hidden bays as necessary before heading south. Their getaway would be slower and riskier than he'd planned.

Boiled Bob knew that Peter Island would be the best place to buy supplies. There were no homes and only one resort on the island. They could hide out on the island's south side and dinghy around the island to the resort and buy provisions. Once provisioned, they'd make the direct passage south.

Boiled Bob stood, put the coffee cup in the sink and climbed to the deck. He and Long Bill took one of the dinghies through rough seas around the west side of the island to a bay from where they could hike to the island's only resort. After pulling the dinghy onto the beach they hiked through low-lying island scrub until they reached the resort, which was shut down for hurricane season. They peeked through the palm trees and saw a skeleton maintenance crew working on the landscape and a security guard sleeping on a lounge chair in the shade of a palm tree near the beach. They walked through the lobby and found its only store closed and locked. The bar and restaurant were also locked up tight. Skirting the beach, they walked to the back of the resort and found an unlocked warehouse where they found no food or water but passed a storeroom with tools, paint and other supplies.

"Look at all those supplies, Boss," Long Bill said.

"Fuck that. We need food and water."

Dejected, Boiled Bob led Long Bill back toward the dinghy.

Long Bill ran into a four-foot-wide century plant on the edge of the trail. One of the barbs at the tip of one of the long agave leaves stabbed his thigh and stuck.

"Ouch. Damn that hurt. I didn't even see that damn century plant. It was hidden behind that sea grape," Long Bill said as he wiped the blood from his leg and pointed back at the jumbled beach vegetation.

That's when Boiled Bob had an epiphany.

"Come on," Boiled Bob said. "We're going back to the storeroom."

After three short hikes from the warehouse to the beach, Boiled Bob and Long Bill lumbered their overloaded dinghy back to the *Happy Hobo*.

Chapter 3

DAY 3: OCTOBER 16

The news about Lisa sufficiently distracted Arlan enough to lose interest in firing Frank until he knew what the next few days would bring. He and Tommy might be too busy dealing with Captain Jay and the Black Ops to handle organizing a new crew to take over construction. When they'd met later in the morning Arlan had told Frank he was on thin ice and either needed to bring the construction progress up to the value of the draw requests he'd made or he wasn't going to get paid. Frank argued but eventually smiled and promised Arlan that he'd make more progress. Arlan accepted Frank's plea but knew it was a promise he couldn't make. Arlan would need to deal with that problem later.

In the afternoon Tommy spotted Captain Jay's three-boat flotilla from the top of one of the roofs of the new buildings at Gallows Point. He was showing a construction crew how to cut nineteen-gauge, corrugated galvanized metal roofing by loading a Skilsaw blade backwards and more or less melting it with friction. Modern electric metal snips hadn't made it to the island yet, and this archaic method was mind-jarring work, exacerbated by the Caribbean sun. After a few minutes the person holding the Skilsaw would experience severe headaches. Even from a distance Arlan and nearby workers winced at the metal-on-metal screeching.

Tommy shut the Skilsaw off, shouted to anybody who could hear that Captain Jay had arrived and pointed to the east to Pillsbury Sound. About a mile out were three, forty-foot-plus fiberglass boats running at full speed toward the bay, their wakes washing over the buoy that marked a shallow reef on the north side of Stevens Cay, a half-acre island between St. John and St. Thomas. Arlan squinted from ground level toward the cay and saw the unusual sight of three similar dive boats in formation. It could only be Captain Jay.

Arlan took the Jeep down to the dock to meet Captain Jay so he could be the first to give him the news about Lisa, though he didn't know much more than she'd been kidnapped by Boiled Bob and was likely on the *Happy Hobo*, wherever it might be. It would be better that Arlan told Jay before he heard it from somebody on the dock, who would inevitably tell a version of the story that had circulated through the island's rumor mill, embellished or changed each time it was regurgitated.

By the time Captain Jay returned, most island residents had heard of the thefts, the robbery and the kidnapping. Most shrugged off the thefts and robbery with a smile, assuming that things would end well, and the events would be something to laugh about for the foreseeable future. Only those closest to Lisa or her father gave the news of her kidnapping serious consideration. Unfortunately for Boiled Bob, this group included some of the island's most dangerous characters—a half dozen ex-mercenaries and retired paramilitary from all over the world who happened to have moved to St. John in search of a more tranquil environment. Tranquility, though, didn't fit well into a warrior's personality, and it didn't take long for them to find each other and form a loose covert group that would occasionally hire out for clandestine operations, mostly hostage rescue missions around the Caribbean and Central America. They had plenty of physical talent but lacked literary creativity, calling themselves the Black Ops, and their informal headquarters was the missing *Happy Hobo*. Stu, the owner of the boat and father-in-law of a South African mercenary who'd married his oldest daughter, was too old to be an active member of the group but was happy to let them use the *Happy Hobo* as their headquarters when needed. They sometimes used the sailboat as cover to get to and from their destinations. Few on the island knew the Black Ops existed. Most paid no attention or assumed it was just another rumor.

The Black Ops had its heyday the decade before Arlan moved to the island, but the aging group still carried out operations not too far from home. Charlie Kline, a CIA operative who had started the first dive shop on the island as a front for his real life, was the founder of the Black Ops. Charlie would frequently disappear for months at a time with no word that he was going or that he'd return. When asked about his absence, the large, quiet man would respond with a smile and a gruff, "As the wind blows."

Arlan had no doubt that all or some Black Ops members would take action to find Boiled Bob and punish him appropriately—unless Captain Jay got there first. Captain Jay's level of punishment would go far beyond appropriate.

Arlan parked near the ferryboat ticket kiosk. Two ferryboats were tied to the dock. One was empty. The other was loading tourists and locals and would leave at the top of the hour for a twenty-minute run to Red Hook, on the east end of St. Thomas, where it would load passengers and return to St. John at the top of the next hour, passing its sister ship that would be on the same route at the same times, but in reverse.

Arlan walked onto the dock and looked toward the entrance of the bay. He saw that Captain Jay's flotilla had reached the buoy that marked the entrance to the bay where most boats pulled their engines back to just beyond idle so they could politely navigate the bay and the many liveaboard boats. Two of the boats slowed and proceeded at a crawl. One didn't. Arlan smiled as he recognized who captained the still speeding boat. Six feet two with short blond hair and Hollywood good looks, Captain Jay wore red Speedo bikini swim trunks, aviator sunglasses and a giant grin. He was probably wearing flip flops but Arlan couldn't see his feet. The boat sped toward the dock, pushing its large wake into the anchored boats behind it. Passengers on the ferry took notice, as did most people on the dock and in the park across from the dock. Knowing what was coming, Arlan smiled. Nobody else did. Arlan saw the chiseled black shape of Gizmo, Captain Jay's right-hand man from the island of Jost Van Dyke, step onto the bow with a coiled rope in his hand as Captain Jay's boat headed toward the dock at ramming speed. The captain of the ferry looked over and saw Arlan, who was still smiling, then looked back to the speeding boat and began to laugh.

"Dat be Captain Jay and his new boat?" the captain shouted down from the wheelhouse.

Arlan nodded.

"I guess der will be a show for da passengers today," the captain said.

"You know Captain Jay, Ashley."

"Tis fo true," the captain said as he surveyed the dock and the gathering crowd of onlookers.

Several people on the liveaboard boats had come onto their decks looking for somebody to yell at. Those who recognized Captain Jay smiled and checked their dinghy lines as their boats bounced in Captain Jay's wake. The few who didn't know Captain Jay shook their fists at the boat and shouted obscenities.

Arlan heard a tourist on the top deck of the ferry shriek, "He's going to hit the dock. Oh, my God."

Captain Jay's shoulders heaved up and down as he laughed. Gizmo saw Arlan and smiled as he balanced on the bow. Gizmo was a superb athlete, which was critical for what he was expected to do next. Captain Jay brought his new fiberglass, twin-diesel-engine boat alongside the opposite side of the dock where the ferryboats were tied, still moving forward at a very fast pace. Thirty feet from where the end of the dock met the beach Captain Jay threw both diesel engines into reverse, immediately stopping the boat and churning up a mass of seawater and bubbles. Gizmo kept his balance during the maneuver and, with a pause in the boat's forward momentum, jumped to the dock with the coiled bow line, wrapped it once around the large steel cleat and held tight while Captain Jay shifted the throttles to neutral. The boat settled in its bubbly wake inches from the dock, and Gizmo finished tying off the bow.

Everybody on the dock and ferry stared in fascination. Arlan had already placed himself near where he thought the stern would end up. Captain Jay shut the engines down, walked to the stern with a large grin and tossed the stern line to Arlan. Arlan tied it off, securing the boat to the dock. Captain Jay, whose chiseled body sported a dozen or so scars from knives and bullets, stepped onto the dock with a big Elvis-like grin and gave Arlan a crushing hug.

"Hey, Rookie. You should've come along. We had a great time. What do you think of my new boat?" Captain Jay asked and swept his palm toward his newest asset.

Arlan smiled and said, "I'm glad the transmission works. Otherwise you'd be picking sand out of your teeth."

"Sheeit, Rookie. You still don't know nothin'. How many times you been with me when we've done the same thing? We ever crash?" Captain Jay asked and waved to Ashley, who had stepped out of the ferryboat wheelhouse.

Ashley shook his head and, with a big smile, said, "You still one crazy white boy, me son."

"I'm not white, Ashley. I'm beige."

Ashley laughed, returned to the wheelhouse and blasted the horn, signaling the ferry was ready to depart. For the next couple of minutes, as the ferry motored out of the bay, tourists and locals on the boat craned their necks to look back at the man with short, blond hair, wearing sunglasses and a red Speedo.

The two other boats from the flotilla slowly made their way to the dock, and their crews tied them in the space left empty by the departed ferry. The captains and crews were longtime residents of the island, and a dozen or more locals welcomed them with high fives, backslaps and handshakes. Arlan, not wanting any of them to ask about Lisa, herded Captain Jay away from the crowd.

"Why don't you show me your new boat?"

"Jesus, Rookie. I just got here. Come on. Let's get a beer," Jay said and turned back toward shore. After a few steps he looked back to the boat and said, "Gizmo, we need to leave before the next ferry gets here. We'll take my boat to Caneel after I catch up with the rookie."

As they walked down the dock Arlan deflected conversations with friends who had approached Captain Jay and said, "Let's go to my office. I've got beer there. My Jeep is across from the clinic."

36

"No time. Let's have a beer at Mooie's," Captain Jay said, basking in the adulation from locals and smiles from the few tourists who had witnessed his approach to the dock.

Two young ladies wearing backpacks, tank tops and short cutoff jeans passed Arlan and Jay as they walked to the bar.

"Hey, sugar puddin'," Captain Jay said to the taller of the two, lifting his aviator sunglasses and resting them on top of his head. "You two needin' a ride to the campground?"

The girls giggled, and the taller one said, "We missed the taxi and were told we'd have to wait for the next ferry to arrive and can catch the taxi to Cinnamon Bay with the next batch of tourists."

"Well, darlins, this is your lucky day. I can take you in my boat," Captain Jay said and pointed to the dark-blue boat on the port side of the dock. "That's Gizmo standin' next to the boat. He won't bite and will help you with your backpacks. I'll be along in a few minutes."

The shorter of the two women smiled, looked at her friend and said, "I don't know…"

Arlan stepped over and bought two Heinekens from a vendor in the park a few feet away. He looked back at Captain Jay and shook his head at the familiar scene as Captain Jay charmed the two ladies that stood with him at the end of the dock. They smiled and giggled and were smitten with the rogue southerner who looked and sounded like a blond Elvis. Arlan could never understand how easy it was for Captain Jay to be… Captain Jay.

Arlan interrupted the trio and shoved a cold bottle into Jay's hand.

"Come on. We need to talk," Arlan said and stepped off the dock onto the beach.

"Keep your panties on, sugarplums. I'll be right back," Jay said and followed Arlan.

Both girls laughed and stayed where they were.

"Damn, Rookie. Not many tourists around durin' hurricane season. Wonder what those two beauties are doin' here."

"Probably here on a research project," Arlan said.

Captain Jay cocked his head and started to say something, but, once out of earshot from anybody near the beach, Arlan turned and told Captain Jay about the *Happy Hobo*, Boiled Bob and Lisa.

Jay chugged half the beer and said, "You sure?"

"I'm not sure of anything except Lisa's gone. The police know nothing more than what the security guards could tell them, and the coast guard can only look for the boat as long as it's in US waters. With the BVI a mile from here, they finished their search in a day. We've called friends in the BVI to be on the lookout for the boat. The BVI police have been notified." Arlan paused and said, "Nobody's seen anything."

"That motherfuckin' Boiled Bob. I should've killed him a long time ago when I had the chance."

"You beat him senseless, if I remember right," Arlan said.

"Should've killed him," Jay said and stomped back to his boat, ignoring the two young women as he passed them.

Arlan followed and shrugged as he passed the two women, who seemed more than a bit slighted. "Sorry. You'll need to wait for the next taxi to the campground," Arlan told them and walked to catch up with Captain Jay. As an afterthought, he looked back and with a smile said, "He's been a bit unstable since the accident."

The two ladies shared confused looks and backed away toward the park.

Arlan caught up to Captain Jay as he jumped into his new boat and started the engines. Gizmo untied the lines and held them while Captain Jay rummaged through a bag below the center console. He pulled a T-shirt out and told Gizmo to shove off.

"Rookie, you need to get packed. We're gonna go after that little weenie son-of-a-bitch."

"Don't you think we should wait until we get a little more information?" Arlan asked.

"From who? He's goin' down island. That's the only thing that makes any sense. We'll leave in the mornin'. I'll pick you up," Captain Jay shouted as he pushed the throttles forward, turning hard to starboard and motoring out of the bay as fast as he had entered.

Several liveaboard boat owners returned to their decks and shouted at Captain Jay as he sped out of the bay. Arlan wasn't sure, but he thought he saw Captain Jay turn a smile at him as he rounded the point and sped north to the resort.

Arlan walked to his Jeep and drove up the hill to Gallows Point. Captain Jay would stop at nothing to find Boiled Bob. What wasn't clear to Arlan was whether Captain Jay's priority was to find Lisa or to exact revenge on Boiled Bob for taking his girlfriend—if that's what happened. Arlan wasn't sure of anything, other than he was in for another adventure with Captain Jay—likely a dangerous one. Maybe he should tell Captain Jay he wouldn't go along. He shook his head. Two things stood in the way of Arlan telling Captain Jay that he wouldn't help—he had a difficult time turning down an adventure, and he was part of an island culture that demanded residents help each other when called upon. If you didn't, you were either brand new to the island or on your way out, never having fit in.

* * *

After offloading the dinghy, Boiled Bob had meted out instructions to the crew and then instructed Tricia to take one of the dinghies, a bottle of water and a radio to the western tip of the island to watch for any boat that was heading to the south side of the island, which was not the normal navigation route through the BVI. If she spotted a power boat it would likely be a pursuit vessel, and she could at least warn Boiled Bob and the rest of the crew to defend themselves. There would be no chance of outrunning it. She was to return to the boat in the evening only to start her vigil the next morning.

For the better part of two days, while the crew worked on deck, Boiled Bob had spent his time in the stateroom studying the charts he had found on the *Happy Hobo*, mapping out a new course. He'd only occasionally climbed up top to check on the progress of the crew and give orders. He allowed none of his crew below deck except to eat and to use the aft head. Late in the afternoon of the second day anchored off Peter Island, Boiled Bob radioed Tricia, who'd reported that she'd seen no boating activity on the south side of the island. Bob told her to return and then stepped into one of the dinghies to see what the newly disguised *Happy Hobo* looked like from a distance.

Long Bill had untied the line and tossed it into the bow of the dinghy. Boiled Bob made a pass around the *Happy Hobo* and saw that the raised wood cabin in the center of the deck, once varnished mahogany, had been painted white, and the gunwale, which had also been a brilliant natural wood finish was now an ugly green. The crew had found extra sail covers in the fo'c's'le. They were dirty beige, not the usual burgundy covers that made the unique boat stand out while at anchor. They'd wrapped the stainless steel cable rails that ran the length of the deck on both sides and kept people from falling overboard in rough seas with strips of white sheets they'd taken from the bunks below. Up close they looked shabby but from a distance it helped change the character of the boat. Boiled Bob was elated that his crew had done such a good job. The boat had started to take on a new identity—a clunky one.

He stopped a few feet off its stern and shouted, "What the fuck is this?"

The crew stopped what they were doing and looked toward Boiled Bob and then to Long Bill.

"What the fuck is a Pappy Bobo?" Boiled Bob shouted, pointing to a few scraggly, hand-painted lines that had been added to what was left of *Happy Hobo.*

After a long silence Long Bill said, "Boss, you wanted us to get rid of the name. I altered the letters a little."

"I told you to get rid of the name, not change it to one only a moron could come up with."

"Boss, every boat has a name. I thought getting rid of it all together would raise a few eyebrows."

Boiled Bob shook his head and asked again, "What is a Pappy Bobo?"

LB looked down, shuffled his feet and then said, "It's the name of our new boat. I was going to change it to, Bappy Bobo, but I wasn't sure bappy was a real word."

"And Bobo is a real word?"

Long Bill shrugged and smiled.

Boiled Bob gave up and climbed back on the *Happy Hobo*, or the *Pappy Bobo.*

The rest of the evening they discussed their new plan to get down island.

"Now that we have disguised the boat we'll sail to Cooper Island early tomorrow for provisions," he told them.

"But Boss, there's no store on Cooper," Long Bill said.

"Old Man Samuels will sell us provisions from the restaurant he manages."

Maynard said, "How do you know it's open. It's hurricane season. There'll be no tourists."

"Old Man Samuels is always there. He lives there."

"What if he doesn't want to sell us any provisions?" Maynard had persisted, his hand absentmindedly reaching for his knife.

Tricia said, "Maybe we should go back."

Pam and Mary nodded their heads in agreement.

Tricia continued and said, "We screwed up by leaving the provisions in the truck. We've taken too long to get away, and St. John is just right over there." Tricia pointed to the lights of the east end of the island.

Boiled Bob fumed through his wooden smile. He had good reason to question Tricia's loyalties. She seemed brighter than any of the other people who'd fallen under his spell. She'd shown up on the island a year earlier with a story that Boiled Bob knew was bullshit. Everybody had a story. He guessed she was running from a bad marriage or bad parents, or both. What bothered him most was that she seemed to have a stronger moral compass than any other of his misfit crew. *Hell*, he thought, *she's the only one with any morals.* She had one foot in and one foot out of his control. He'd tried to keep an eye on her but couldn't resist her adorable ass and gave her more leeway than he knew he should.

He looked at his crew and realized that, for now, he needed to bolster the morale on the boat. He said, "We're home free. Look at this boat. Nobody's going to recognize it."

"Why are we going down island anyway?" Tricia asked.

"Because we all hate St. John and the idiots that live there," Bob said, looking around at his crew. "We all decided this more than a week ago." He then looked directly at Tricia and said, "It's a little too late to back out now."

Tricia and the other two women exchanged glances.

Boiled Bob couldn't afford a mutiny, and he didn't want to share the real reason for moving down island with anybody other than Maynard, who had given him the idea several weeks earlier.

Maynard had grown up in Frenchtown on St. Thomas but was close to the Rastafarians on the island. His uncle owned an old wooden sloop and would often take Maynard along on his trips down island where he traded in illegal goods and, more recently, smuggled firearms from Grenada to the Dreads on Dominica. Nobody was sure if it was the Rastafarians who lived on Grenada or if it was the Cubans, invited by Maurice Bishop to help build a new airport, that were supplying firearms to the Dreads. The intention was clear, though—the supplier wanted to help the Dreads create their own revolution on Dominica, and the Dreads were highly motivated to overthrow the government of Dominica. Prime Minister Regina Charles was part of the government movement that passed the Dread Act in the mid-70's—a law that allowed imprisonment and worse to anybody on the island who grew dreadlocks. The police shot scores of Dreads, forcing many to escape to mountain hideaways. Many Dreads became violent and used theft, kidnapping and murder to meet their goal of overthrowing the Charles regime.

Boiled Bob looked toward Maynard, who sat with his permanent scowl near the bow of the boat sharpening his knife with a whetstone. Boiled Bob had met Maynard in a St. Thomas bar when he'd first arrived on the islands several years earlier, before he moved to St. John and gathered his group of flunkies. Bob was about to get his ass handed to him by a couple of locals when Maynard stepped in, brandishing his knife. The locals recognized Maynard and backed off. Boiled Bob learned later that Maynard was not saving him as much as he was interested in hurting the two locals with whom he'd had a long history. Boiled Bob and Maynard became loose friends, and a year later, when Boiled Bob found his way to St. John, Maynard, when not sailing down island, joined him and his followers. He often told Boiled Bob about the profitability of running drugs up and down the chain of islands, and Bob joined Maynard on a few trips. Running drugs didn't appeal to him, but the more recent opportunity to make money transporting weapons to Dominica from Grenada did. Not only would he make money, but he'd be contributing to a revolution. Thanks to Maynard's idea he now had a boat, a new vocation and a place to go where he'd be accepted.

A large fish, or something else, splashed a few feet from the boat, which brought Boiled Bob back to this new dilemma—what to tell his crew. He thought for a moment and decided to tell them his plan, but he'd leave out the violent nature of the Dreads and the gunrunning.

He told them that from Cooper they'd make their way to Dominica, where Maynard had introduced him to some local Dreads a few months earlier. There they would join the Dreads in their effort to overthrow the government. He stopped talking and waited for a reaction from the crew. Maynard's eyes brightened. He was eager to get into a fight with anybody. Long Bill seemed confused but didn't question the plan. Tricia looked shaken and glanced down the companionway. She started to say something but kept quiet. The other two women said nothing.

Boiled Bob knew he needed to have a private talk with Tricia. He might take her behind some bushes on the beach and give her what he was sure she wanted. She'd brushed off his advances lately, but he knew she'd come around after he showered her with compliments and gave her a thorough humping. They all did. He smiled at the thought.

"Are you with us Tricia?" Boiled Bob asked.

Tricia paused and then quietly answered, "Yes."

Boiled Bob sighed and said, "Good. This is the new beginning we've wanted. And it'll be perfect for us. Once the Dreads have taken over, we'll be superstars on the island. They'll protect us and our boat from anybody from St. John who'd be stupid enough to come after us. You'll see."

Long Bill and Maynard smiled. The women didn't seem to share their enthusiasm. Boiled Bob would need to keep an eye on them. He stood and said to his crew, "Get some sleep."

He then disappeared down the companionway and closed the hatch after him, leaving the crew to sleep on the deck.

Chapter 4

DAY 4: OCTOBER 17 (Morning)

The forward motion of the boat brought a rare smile to Boiled Bob. The boat listed as a strong gust of wind hit the sails. Long Bill, charged with captaining the newly disguised boat, had fallen off the wind slightly, but not enough that Boiled Bob needed to grab on to the table, fixed to the floor in the galley, to keep his balance. Boiled Bob stood and tight-roped his way to the sink where he poured out the remainder of his coffee and climbed the companionway onto the deck. Looking directly at Maynard, he told the crew that he'd be going onshore alone and that none of them were allowed to go below while he was gone. Maynard shrugged. The other crew members exchanged glances and went back to work.

Under an hour later the *Pappy Bobo* anchored on the northwest side of Cooper Island, and Boiled Bob took one of the dinghies to the wooden dock that served the small resort run by Old Man Samuels. Two small outboard fiberglass boats were tied to the dock on the lee side. He recognized one as belonging to the guesthouse. He wasn't sure who owned the other boat, a typical narrow-beamed, twenty-four-foot fiberglass fishing boat with a fifty-horsepower outboard engine clamped to the stern, and he didn't care. After tying off the dinghy he looked back at the *Pappy Bobo* and thought that the new disguise was sufficient enough at a distance to fool anybody familiar with the boat. Other than the five bunched up dinghies tied to its stern, the *Pappy Bobo* looked like a typical Caribbean sailboat and no longer like the impressive historic sailboat it was a couple of days ago.

Bob trudged barefoot through the sugary sand to the restaurant, the sun hot enough to cause sweat to roll off his brow by the time he reached the covered open deck of the restaurant. A small radio blasted a calypso song that the owner of the resort sang along with. The music was mixed with the sound of clanging utensils and the intermittent spray of running water splashing against a metal sink.

"Inside?" Boiled Bob called out.

"Outside," Ray Samuels answered, inviting Bob to come into the kitchen in the back of the restaurant.

Ray turned and said, "Bob, me son, wha brings you to my little isl*an*?" They shook hands and Ray said, "Tis been a while. Where yo been keep*in* yoself, Bob?"

"You know… just limin' here and there. I see your son on St. John quite a bit."

Ray frowned and said, "Tis hard to keep Tony work*in* here wit me. He likes to dally around wit da ladies too much on your isl*an*."

They both laughed, and Boiled Bob said, "I need some provisions for my new boat," and pointed to the bay at the sailboat with five dinghies tied to its stern.

Ray followed Bob's gaze and said, "Dat boat look familiar… kind of." Then he shrugged, smiled and said, "Hope yo gonna paint dat ugly boat when you get to where yo go*in*."

After looking at the boat a while longer he asked, "Whatchu do*in* wit all dem dinghies?"

"I'm dropping them off for Stewart Black up on Virgin Gorda," Bob lied. "He's helping a friend who's starting a charter business."

"I tought Stewart wanted all a de business fo hisself," Ray said with a laugh.

"Me too. I'm just doing him a favor before I sail my new boat across the Altantic."

"Woah, me son. Dat's a long trip. Yo sure yo up for it?"

"Come on, Ray, you know me. I'm up for anything," Boiled Bob said.

"Okay, okay. I can give you some provisions, and you can pay me now or on your way back tru," Ray said and took off the apron he was wearing. He then cocked his head and said, "Maybe yo not be com*in* back tru. You better pay now."

Boiled Bob shrugged and pulled a wad of cash from the front left pocket of his shorts.

"Whatchu need*in*, me son?" Ray said as he walked into a storage pantry filled with nonperishable food, water and booze.

"I need the normal stuff for a week charter. We'll make Bermuda in a few days and get more supplies there."

Ray looked back at Bob as he walked into the pantry and said, "If you make it dat far. Tis hurricane season, ya know."

Boiled Bob smiled and said, "I checked the weather. No weather systems are on their way from Africa this week."

Boiled Bob gauged Ray's expression and was fairly sure he'd planted his lie well. He thought for a moment and decided that, as much as he'd like to broadcast that he'd successfully stolen the *Happy Hobo*, he couldn't do it yet. The delay caused by his crew had cost him valuable time—time he needed back. He hoped that the red herring about crossing the Atlantic he'd thrown to Ray would find its way back to Captain Jay, or anybody else who might give chase.

Ray went about gathering provisions and said nothing.

Boiled Bob decided he could push his lie a bit further and said, "Did you hear about the boat theft and robbery of Caneel?"

Ray, still in the pantry loading provisions into a cardboard box, shouted, "Wha? Fo tru?"

"Yeah, the *Happy Hobo* was stolen from Cruz Bay, and the thieves pulled into Caneel Bay and robbed the night auditor's office."

Ray brought the heavy box out of the pantry and set it on a table in the kitchen.

"Who be do*in* something so wicked?" Ray asked.

"Nobody knows, but I heard that Lisa, Captain Jay's girlfriend, was kidnapped but jumped out of the dinghy before the thieves got back to the boat. The seas were rough that night. She was thrown against the rocks at the mouth of the bay. She's probably dead."

Ray looked shocked and said, "I know Lisa and her fadder. He brought his boat here many times. Dat is bad, bad news."

"I think it was somebody from St. Thomas. I heard that a boat was seen heading that direction a few minutes after Lisa was taken."

"Der are many bad men on dat island. Hope dey catch dem, and soon. Tis a bad ting," Ray said as he shook his head.

Satisfied, Boiled Bob asked, "How much do I owe you?"

"How about fifty dollar?"

"Sounds good to me," Ray said. He peeled off three twenties and handed them to Ray. "I only have twenties. How about you throw in five bottles of Cane Garden Rum, and we'll agree to sixty?"

"Okay, mon," Ray said, still shaking his head about the news about Lisa.

Boiled Bob thanked Ray, carried the provisions to his dinghy and sped out to the *Pappy Bobo*. He felt good for the first time in days. The *Happy Hobo*'s disguise seemed to be working. He'd secured provisions for at least a week, nobody was hot on his trail and, best of all, he had Lisa in the forward berth—tied up and ready for more abuse.

* * *

The *Pappy Bobo* set sail as soon as the provisions were loaded. Boiled Bob didn't look back. If he had he would have seen Ray standing outside his restaurant with his son, Tony.

"I saw you sneakin round in da bar when I was talkin to Bob. I tought he was yo friend. Why yo be hidden out like dat?"

"I know him, but he's not a friend of mine. He and his crew are jus a bunch of crazy white folk who be doin too many drugs and always talkin bout de revolution," Tony said, pointing to the boat that had just raised anchor and was setting to sail. "Dat is the *Happy Hobo*, and Boiled Bob stole it and kidnapped Captain Jay's girlfriend two nights ago."

Ray squinted toward the boat, whose crew was setting its sails. After a minute he smiled and said, "Tis the *Happy Hobo*. Looks different, dough." Ray then asked, "Yo hear bout wha Bob say bout Lisa?"

"I heard everyting, Pops."

"Yo believe Bob bout her be*in* dead?"

"Don't know. He took her dough. Dat's fo true."

"Why yo didn't tell me bout Boiled Bob and Lisa when yo arrive?" Ray asked his son.

"I'm glad I didn't. Boiled Bob tis an angry mon and might have tried to hurt you if he tought you knew bout Lisa. If dat crazy Maynard is wit him he would have fo true carve yo up wit his knife."

Ray looked at his son and said, "I didn't know dat Bob was such a bad mon. I only saw him when he'd sail tru now and again. He was always behav*in* hisself. I didn't see no problem wit him. Now I know different."

"I need to get to Tortola and to a phone."

"Yo can use da marine radio to call da police."

"I can't Pops. Da police doan have boats—none dat are work*in* anyway. I got to call Captain Jay by phone. I doan know if he is on his boat or has his radio on. Dis is someth*in* fo his ears only."

Tony paused and then said, "Captain gonna be mighty pissed."

Ray looked at the sailboat before it disappeared around the point and said, "Tis a pistarckle."

"Fo tru, Pops. Tis a big cluster fuck."

* * *

Tommy and Arlan stood in the parking lot discussing the project and keeping an eye out for Captain Jay. A small truck filled with sawdust and construction debris stopped next to Tommy on its way to the island landfill. The driver waited for Tommy to look in the truck bed and give him approval to continue out to the main road. Tommy pulled a six-foot-long piece of cypress wood from the bed, smiled and waved the driver on. Construction materials are hard to get on an island. Shipments come from the US and take weeks to get there. What would normally be discarded lumber on a project in the US is saved and reused on the island. Arlan looked over at a stack of good boards that Tommy had taken from trucks that were heading to the landfill earlier. He didn't keep track of how much money Tommy had saved the project so far but guessed it was easily into the thousands.

Tommy threw the board on the grass next to the other boards and said to Arlan, "I-I could build a h-house with all of th-the boards I've saved from th-the dump."

Arlan grinned and said, "Why don't you?"

Tommy cocked his head and frowned.

"I'm serious, Tommy. You've been building that shack on your property for a couple of years. Why don't you use some of the wood you pull out of the trucks to finish it? Consider it a bonus. You've more than earned it."

"Th-that's mighty b-big of you. Thanks."

"Don't worry. You'll earn it even more before this Lisa thing is over."

"Do y-you think C-Captain Jay is c-concerned that m-much about Lisa?"

"No. Somebody took something from him. Not just anybody, but Boiled Bob. It doesn't matter that it was Lisa. It could have been a car, or a chair. Captain Jay wants it back."

"Wh-what is Captain Jay going to do?"

"He's going to go after Boiled Bob. I guess I'm expected to go along. Who knows how long it will take."

"Wh-when are you l-leaving?"

"I don't know. Soon, I think. Is the Black Ops going after the *Happy Hobo*?"

"Charlie's been d-down island on D-dominica or Grenada. I don't kn-know which, but I h-heard from Henry and F-forrest. I think they're going to organize a search, but I don't kn-know the details yet. I th-think they're waiting to hear from Charlie."

"Charlie's heard about Lisa?"

"I th-think so."

"If the Black Ops give chase I hope they find Boiled Bob before Captain Jay does."

"Why's th-that?"

"Captain Jay won't be as forgiving as the Black Ops."

Almost before Arlan finished the sentence, Captain Jay sped into the parking lot and slid his baby-blue Willys Jeep to a stop in the graveled parking lot a couple of feet from Arlan and Tommy.

"Rookie, I just heard from Tony Samuel. He was on Cooper Island helpin' his father, and Boiled Bob sailed in on the *Happy Hobo*," Captain Jay said as he stepped out of the Jeep. He was wearing sunglasses, shorts, a Polo shirt and flip-flops. He didn't wear his normal grin and offered none of his normal good-natured, off-color trash talk. "He says the boat's been painted and has a new name... *Pappy* somethin' or other."

"D-did he see L-lisa?"

"No. Tony says he hid in the bar while Boiled Bob told his father a bunch of bullshit about the boat heist and robbery. Said he thinks it was somebody from St. Thomas and that he heard that Lisa was kidnapped and jumped from the dinghy near the rocks and was probably dead."

"Why would Boiled Bob say anything to Tony's father about that? Doesn't make sense."

"Boiled Bob told Ray that he and his crew were deliverin' a bunch of dinghies to Virgin Gorda and then headin' across the Atlantic to the Mediterranean. He bought some provisions from the restaurant and sailed away."

"That's a long trip," Arlan said.

"It's bullshit, Rookie. He's goin' down island."

"Do you believe Lisa jumped?"

"She certainly has the balls to jump. She's a strong swimmer. You know that. But there's only one way to find out, Rookie. We're goin' divin' off Caneel and the cays in the sound."

"That was a few nights ago. Nobody's seen her or found a body. If what Boiled Bob said is true, her body could be anywhere," Arlan said.

"Maybe. Or just as likely to have drifted into some coral heads or underwater rocks. We'll motor around the closest cays and look on the rocks. If we don't see anythin' we'll dive the cays. If she got caught up someplace it'll be the Durloes."

Or she could've drifted out into the Atlantic, or south into the Caribbean, or been shark food, or still on the boat, Arlan thought.

"What if it's a r-red herring? What if B-boiled Bob could have m-made it all up just to th-throw us off his trail?"

Captain Jay said, "Probably is, but we've got to check out the water before we go down island and kill the son-of-a-bitch."

"We?" Arlan asked.

Captain Jay ignored Arlan and got back into the Jeep. "You're comin' with me, Rookie." He looked at Tommy and said, "You comin'?"

Tommy sighed and said, "I m-might need to go with Forrest. He's g-going to be flying down island tomorrow t-to search from the air. I'm t-taking my parachute."

Arlan smiled. Tommy could land a parachute on a dime. He didn't know how he'd land on the deck of the *Happy Hobo* but knew Tommy had done this type of work before and didn't question him.

Captain Jay said, "Okay. You can dive with us today though."

"I c-can do that."

"We'll leave in an hour. The two of you and I will dive. Gizmo will follow and pick us up when we surface. We've got a lot of territory to cover."

Chapter 5

DAY 4: October 17 (Afternoon)

By early afternoon Captain Jay, Arlan, Tommy and Gizmo had checked most of the island's northwest coastline from the boat and had circumnavigated all of the cays in Pillsbury Sound. They'd found a dinghy that had broken loose from somewhere up on the rocks on the east side of Lovango Cay and decided to grab it and drop it off at the national park headquarters in Cruz Bay later in the day so its owner had a place to reclaim it. Arlan and Gizmo suffered more than a few cuts after snorkeling through the breaking waves and climbing onto the rocks to rescue the dinghy. Other than the dinghy they'd found nothing.

It was time to check underwater, which normally would have given Arlan a surge of excitement, but this was different. They were looking for a body. He and Captain Jay had recovered bodies before, but this was a friend—a friend Arlan didn't want to find shoved by the seas into a rock crevasse or coral head. He suspected that Captain Jay was right; Boiled Bob and his crew of misfits had taken the *Happy Hobo* down island. Jay was also correct in that they had no choice but to search for Lisa's body before giving chase.

Three days had passed since the kidnapping—six changes of current alternating north to south, then south to north, every twelve hours. If not washed up on a beach or rocks, a body could have drifted out of the sound and into the open ocean and could be anywhere. The coast guard, the local DNR and national park rangers had all searched for two days and found nothing. Captain Jay had reasoned that nobody had gone underwater to search and that the body could be hung up on a coral head or an underwater rock formation. He'd checked the tide charts, which showed a northerly current when the kidnapping had taken place. In its path, about a mile north, were three small spits of land that made the Durloe Cays.

"We'll check the Durloes first," Captain Jay said. "The current's goin' slack. I'll have Gizmo drop me off at Ramgoat Cay. Tommy, you take Rata, and you get to swim around Henley Cay, Rookie."

"Why do I get the big one?" Arlan asked. "Henley's twice the size as the other cays."

Captain Jay said, "Because you swim faster than us and breathe a lot less air. Tommy and I would have sucked our tanks dry by the time we got halfway around it."

Arlan shrugged. He knew he could make it around the cay on one tank but hoped he didn't have to stop to recover a body.

The three divers geared up and walked to the stern carrying their flippers, spearguns and a mesh bag. They sat on the stern with their feet on the large, grated dive platform that had been lowered on hinges for easy water access. Arlan put on his flippers, checked his air and then spit into his mask. He rubbed the spit around the glass and dipped the mask into the ocean water that bubbled through the aluminum tubing that made up the grate.

Arlan looked at the speargun he'd placed, unloaded with the spear tip pointed to the sea, on the dive platform and said, "I thought we were looking for Lisa. Tell me again why we're taking our spearguns."

"Jesus, Rookie. We're goin' on a trip, and we'll need provisions."

Arlan shrugged. He felt more comfortable diving with a speargun anyway, just in case a shark or a barracuda got a little too curious and he'd need to push it away.

The cays were grouped close together with the largest, Henley, in the middle and the two smaller cays a couple of hundred yards away on either side. Gizmo drove the boat to Rata Cay where Captain Jay put his regulator in his mouth and slid off the dive platform. As Captain Jay sank feet-first in the crystal-clear water, Arlan could see him rest the butt of the speargun on his stomach and pull the first of three surgical rubber bands that hung from the front of the three-foot gun and clip it into the first of three notches on the top of the back end of the spear, just above the short handle at the shooting end.

Gizmo dropped Arlan off next. He went through the same ritual he'd seen Captain Jay go through a couple of minutes earlier—sink feet-first while placing the butt of his speargun against his stomach and start to pull the three thick, bronze-colored surgical rubber bands back toward his stomach and into a notch on the spear. He knew Tommy would be doing the same thing a couple of minutes later.

The plan was for each to circumnavigate the island, covering as much vertical coral and rocks as possible, checking more closely in deep holes and caves. They went in the water just twenty minutes after the northerly current slackened and knew they had another twenty-five minutes before the current would turn and carry them south. Each was dropped off at the southwest side of the islands and would swim counterclockwise, using slack tide to swim north and east and the southerly current on the opposite side of the cays. Gizmo would eventually pluck them from the water as they drifted back toward Caneel Bay.

Arlan finished loading his speargun and dove to where the coral met the sandy bottom, about sixty feet under the surface. The visibility allowed him to see a hundred feet in all directions. He looked up to scan the shallow coral and then spent time checking the large coral heads near the sand. Some were as large as Volkswagens, with deep holes that housed scores of fish. He spotted a large Nassau grouper that swam into the depths as soon as it saw Arlan. From deep within a hole a few yards farther a dogtooth snapper showed its gnarly head. If he was free-diving he could have fit into the hole and found the retreating snapper. Wearing bulky SCUBA gear and a tank, all he could do was stick his head into the hole, which was met with the open mouth of the snapper's roommate—a five-foot long and very fat moray eel. Arlan pushed himself back from the hole and continued his search.

He rounded the north side of the cay and noticed that the current had turned. He knew that the coral on the west side of the island would turn to rock on the east side. He continued to swim in the deeper water and scan the shallower rocks closer to the island, thankfully seeing no bodies. A movement out over the sand out in the deeper water got his attention. A medium-sized kingfish swam near him and turned away. Arlan raised his speargun and waited. Fast swimming pelagic fish like kingfish were some of the most difficult to shoot, but he knew there'd be more kingfish swimming the same course. He'd be lucky to land one. The fish were in your sights for just a second or two, and spearguns were extraordinarily inaccurate. The thick rubber bands were used to catapult a two-and-a-half-foot spear about eight feet from the speargun where it either hit its target or abruptly stopped when it reached the end of the nylon line that connected it to the gun. Getting that close to a kingfish would be difficult.

Arlan kept his speargun pointed out over the sandy bottom and saw nothing but distant blue haze. A second kingfish whizzed by about twelve feet from him. He'd need to move out over the sand and risk spooking the next one, which was sure to come. His patience paid off. The third and largest fish approached, causing Arlan to hesitate. The kingfish was at least forty pounds, large enough to take him for a ride. Any larger and Arlan might lose the speargun, something Captain Jay and Tommy would never let him forget.

The fish swam by within ten feet of Arlan, who fired and hit the fish about midway down its body. Not a kill shot. *Damn*, he thought. *This will be a problem.* Not only would the fish tug him around for a while, but the low-frequency vibrations caused by the fish's thrashing would attract any predator in the area. Arlan had to hang on to the speargun with both hands and had no chance to pull the fish to him while it was this active. He could only wait for it to tire and watch the periphery for hungry sharks, which didn't take long. Five minutes after he shot the kingfish, he spotted the first shark out in the blue haze. Its long caudal tailfin told him that it was a thresher shark, which was not likely to approach. A few minutes later, just as the kingfish started to lose energy, Arlan saw an eight-foot bull shark, which he knew would approach, and if he couldn't bag the fish soon he'd have to fight for it.

Arlan had managed to haul the fish closer to the submerged rocks near the cay, where he could back up to a rock and bring the speared fish to him while watching the shark. The shark made another, more aggressive run at the fish, making Arlan pull the line attached to the spear to him and causing the fish to thrash again, further exciting the shark. He brought the tired fish close to him and turned his speargun around so he could use its butt to poke the shark, which swam back and forth about twenty feet from him. Arlan knew that if he saw the shark point away from him, drop its pectoral fins and hump its back, it would explode in a one-hundred-eighty-degree turn and attack. Whether it would attack him or the fish, he wasn't sure, but he was prepared for either.

Two seconds later it was over. Two swipes of its tail, and the shark vanished into the blue. A second later Arlan heard the twin screws of Captain Jay's dive boat and looked up to see its hull knife through the medium-sized waves on the surface. Gizmo was on his way to pick up Tommy, he surmised. Lucky for Arlan sharks hate the sound of boat engines. He pulled the near dead fish to him, removed the spear, put the fish into the mesh bag and continued to search the east side of the cay.

The current picked up and sped Arlan through the remainder of his search. Satisfied he didn't see Lisa's body crammed under a rock, he acquiesced to the strengthening force and let it carry him south, beyond the land mass and into the sound, his kingfish in tow. When down to five hundred pounds of air, he surfaced, blew air into the buoyancy compensator and floated with the current.

Gizmo, Captain Jay and Tommy were waiting, Captain Jay and Tommy having finished their search twenty minutes earlier. Gizmo drove the boat past Arlan and backed the dive platform toward him.

"See anythin', Rookie?" Captain Jay shouted from the boat.

Arlan spit his regulator out of his mouth and said, "No."

"Did you get any fish?"

"One," Arlan answered and kicked toward the boat.

"One? That's all? There was activity all over the place. I got a bag full, and Tommy got three big snappers. How could you only get one?" Captain Jay shouted.

Arlan reached the platform and handed the mesh bag to Tommy, who'd stepped onto the dive platform to lift Arlan's gear into the boat.

"J-jesus. This is h-heavy."

Tommy pulled the bag up and tossed it onto the deck. Captain Jay and Gizmo stared at the big kingfish, which weighed more than all the other fish combined.

Gizmo said, "Dat's a big fish."

"You got lucky, Rookie," Captain Jay said and stomped to the helm.

Arlan smiled and gave his tank to Tommy. He then grabbed the edge of the platform and used his flippers to kick up and out of the water, turning halfway around and landing his ass on the dive platform, facing away from the boat.

As Arlan expected, nobody had found a body or parts of a body or clothing that Lisa might have worn the night she was abducted.

"Let's go to the point where she jumped," Captain Jay said.

"The water there is no more than ten feet deep. You can see the coral and the bottom from shore. She'd have been found if she was there," Arlan said.

"We're goin' there anyway," Captain Jay said and took the wheel from Gizmo.

Tommy and Arlan looked at each other and shrugged.

Five minutes later Captain Jay pulled back the throttles and idled fifty feet off shore at the south side of the entry to Caneel Bay—the place Jay speculated where Lisa had jumped from the dinghy.

"H-how do you know this is wh-where she jumped?" Tommy asked.

"How do you know she jumped at all?" Arlan added.

Captain Jay ignored Arlan and said, "Had to be here. The guards said they took off this way, and they couldn't see the *Happy Hobo*. That's because it was out here behind the anchored boats, so it couldn't be seen from shore."

"Wh-when did you become Sh-sherlock Holmes?"

Captain Jay ignored Tommy's comment and said, "Rookie, get your snorkel gear on and look around down there."

"What am I looking for?"

"Anythin' that doesn't look right."

Arlan donned his mask, snorkel and fins and stepped off the dive platform and into the shallow water. He held his breath and glided down to the small coral heads and rocks. He swam around them, checking under anything that had a ledge and was about to surface when he saw a glint of sunlight reflect off something twenty feet away. A few seconds later he kicked up and onto the dive platform with a bracelet in his hand.

Captain Jay inspected the bracelet and said, "She's alive." He turned the boat toward the dock and said, "No more huntin' for Lisa underwater. We're goin' down island."

"How do you know she's alive?" Arlan asked.

"We've looked everywhere for her body and haven't found squat."

Not everywhere, Arlan thought. *She could be drifting toward Puerto Rico or out into the Atlantic.*

Captain Jay held up the bracelet and said, "This is her bracelet. I gave it to her a few months ago. Look. It's not broken. It came off because she took it off."

"Why would she do that?" Arlan asked.

"It's a signal. She sent us a signal that she's alive," Captain Jay said.

Arlan looked to Tommy and shrugged. Tommy did the same. Arlan had no idea why Captain Jay saw the bracelet as a signal that Lisa was still alive. But it was clear that they were heading down island—soon.

* * *

The *Pappy Bobo* sailed under the bright Caribbean sun, knifing into long, shallow swells while on its way to Anguilla or St. Marten, whichever island Boiled Bob could find a quiet bay near the main port of entry so they could sneak in and out of the country without clearing customs. They'd snug up into a small bay from where they could quietly get to shore to try to sell the dinghies and buy more supplies.

Halfway to their destination, while the crew busied themselves on deck, Boiled Bob went below, drawing glances from crew members as he climbed down the companionway. None of the crew members were allowed near Lisa. She was tied and gagged when Bob wasn't in the cabin with her. He'd untie her and allow her to use the head and shower during his visits, taking care to remove anything that could be used as a weapon and standing outside the door with a four-foot gaffing hook each time she emerged from the head.

Boiled Bob opened the cabin door and smiled. Lisa was in a sitting position on the bunk. Her wrists were individually tied to a beam attached to the ceiling of the small cabin. As soon as Boiled Bob reached out to untie one wrist, Lisa used her free hand to remove the gag. Boiled Bob handed her a bottle of water.

"Are you here to see if you can get a hard on, dipshit?" Lisa said and took a long drink from the bottle.

Boiled Bob sneered and reached over to slap her. She recoiled, and Bob backed off and sat on the far end of the bunk. Lisa's face was already bruised from the beatings he'd delivered the day before. Any more bruises and she'd start to look less sexy to him.

"Bitch," Boiled Bob said, looking at her body. Boiled Bob had discarded all of her clothes except her panties as soon as he tied her up.

"Go ahead, pervert. Look all you want. You can't seem to do anything else."

"I've already had you, while you were unconscious."

She stared at him and shook her head.

"Don't remember, do you?"

He waited to see her squirm.

"It must have been good for you," Lisa said. "I wouldn't have felt that little thing of yours even if I'd been conscious."

Boiled Bob couldn't help himself. He reached over and slapped her, then sat back and said, "I should have left you in the water. You'd have been dead in minutes."

"Why did you save me then, asshole?" Lisa asked and rubbed her cheek. She took a drink from the water bottle and added, "Why did you kidnap me in the first place?"

Boiled Bob said, "I needed you as a hostage to get past the guards or anybody else who might have stumbled into the lobby."

"Why keep me? I'll never give in to you or your moronic friends."

Boiled Bob didn't answer.

"You shouldn't have jumped," he said.

"Yeah, right. All I ever wanted to do was to go sailing with you on my father's stolen boat," Lisa said. "And I couldn't wait to be tied to this fucking bunk." She took another drink of water and said, "Why do you think I jumped, asshole?"

Boiled Bob thought about his decision to tell Long Bill to make another pass near the rocks to save Lisa, which could have easily been a disaster. The truth was that he couldn't have Lisa's death on his hands. Kidnapping was one thing. He'd eventually drop her off on one of the islands and disappear. Murder was a totally different thing. Captain Jay or the crazy mercenary friends of her father would haunt him to hell and back if they ever found out he'd caused her death. And they'd find out. There were five witnesses on the boat who'd give him away in a second if confronted by the Black Ops or Captain Jay.

"Why keep me?" Lisa repeated.

Boiled Bob smiled, then gazed at her body and said, "For entertainment."

"You'll be Captain Jay's entertainment when he catches up with you," Lisa said.

Her smart-ass attitude pissed him off. She needed to suffer a little more before he let her go.

Boiled Bob snorted and said, "I'd like to have seen Captain Jay's face when he learned you drowned."

Lisa looked surprised and said, "What are you talking about?"

"I put the word out that you jumped and were smashed into the rocks. Everybody's going to think you're dead."

Lisa stared at him and said, "Jay and my father and who knows who else will come looking for this boat. It'll be easy to find. I wouldn't want to be you when they do."

Boiled Bob shrugged. "No big deal. I've changed the appearance of the *Happy Hobo*. Changed the name too. It's now the *Pappy Bobo*," Bob said with a smile.

Lisa cringed. Boiled Bob smiled.

Lisa's expression then changed. She frowned and said, "What the hell is a Pappy Bobo?"

Boiled Bob looked away. He stood and said, "We're heading down island, and nobody's ever going to find you. Not even your badass boyfriend."

Lisa slumped onto the bunk.

Satisfied, and tired of the banter, Bob said, "I'll untie you and let you wash up. Don't try anything."

Bob lifted the gaffing hook he'd brought with him and had placed on the floor by his feet.

"After you're clean I'll bring food. After you eat I'm going to fuck you—again," he said and opened the cabin door.

"Oh, gee, honey, I can't wait to see that little baby weenie again," Lisa said.

Bob slammed and locked the cabin door with the padlock and hasp he'd found on the boat and installed soon after they'd sailed from Caneel Bay. He looked through a port window in the galley and saw Tricia and Long Bill look at each other with smiles. He saw Maynard out of the starboard porthole looking inside with a smirk.

"Bitch," Boiled Bob said to himself and started to prepare food.

Chapter 6

DAY 5: OCTOBER 18

Captain Jay wanted to start the search for Boiled Bob immediately after their dive and finding Lisa's bracelet. Tommy suggested he wait until the next day so they could talk to the Black Ops members to find out what plans they had made to search for the boat and Lisa. Arlan agreed with Tommy. Captain Jay snorted and walked ahead of them up the path to his Jeep. They rode to the village in silence.

Tommy and Arlan met early the next morning at the ferry dock in separate vehicles to pick up workers and shuttle them to the jobsite. They returned to the project site, parked next to the office, and the workers bailed out to start their work day. A few minutes later Forrest Fishman arrived in an old Jeep with a marine plywood body, the metal having rusted out years earlier.

A member of the Black Ops, Forrest had come to the islands a decade earlier from California, where he'd flown then Governor Reagan around the state. Once, failing to stop the governor's plane at the end of the paved runway during a landing, he opted to use the rudder and spin the aircraft into a three-hundred and sixty degree turn rather than run off the tarmac and into a muddy field. Reagan, nonplussed, unbuckled his seatbelt, smiled at Forrest and said, "That was an interesting landing." Forrest's value to the Black Ops was that he was qualified to fly just about any aircraft and was considered to be an excellent pilot, even when inebriated.

Forrest flashed his Jimmy Carter smile and stepped out of the doorless Jeep.

"Where's Captain Jay?" he asked.

"He'll be here. He's champing at the bit to go after Boiled Bob but agreed to hear what you and the Black Ops have planned," Arlan said.

Just as Arlan finished talking, Captain Jay sped into the parking lot and braked to a stop a few feet from Forrest's Jeep. He smiled, stepped out of his baby-blue Willys Jeep and removed his aviator sunglasses, letting them hang from his neck by a black nylon line.

"What do you got?" Captain Jay asked, without a hello or a smile.

Forrest smiled, used to Captain Jay's abruptness.

"I talked to Charlie last night," Forrest told them. "He asked that I meet with you so we can organize a search and rescue."

Captain Jay said, "The Rookie and I are headin' down island to kill that son-of-a-bitch."

Arlan looked at Tommy and Forrest and shrugged. He was pretty sure there'd be no killing, at least not by him.

Forrest said, "Charlie wants me to warn you that something big is about to happen down there, either on Dominica or Grenada. Probably Grenada. Word is that Maurice Bishop is under house arrest by his military."

"What's that got to do with anythin'?" Captain Jay said.

"Who knows where the *Happy Hobo* is going, but you could be heading into a shit storm, and Charlie asked that you work with us on this."

Captain Jay snickered, clearly not caring about island political upheavals. He didn't care about anybody's politics. He didn't understand them. Captain Jay couldn't hold an intellectual conversation about anything. He never reflected on the past and never planned for the future. Jay was all about doing, about the moment. He had one of two reactions to everything—joy or anger. At the moment, Captain Jay was angry, and there was a job to do—find Boiled Bob. Beyond that he didn't care what anybody else did, as long as he was in charge.

"Wh-what's going d-down there?" Tommy asked Forrest.

"You know that Bishop New Jewel Movement overthrew Gairy a few years ago?"

"Wasn't Gairy the prime minister who believed in UFOs and rigged the Miss World contest in London a few years back?" Arlan asked with a smile.

"He also had secret police called the Mongoose Gang. They terrorized and murdered his political enemies. That's how Bishop took over. The island residents were fed up with Gairy," Forrest said.

"So what's the big deal?" Captain Jay asked.

"Turns out Bishop has been friendly with Castro, and Cuba has sent construction workers to help build a new airport," Forrest said.

"What's any of that got to do with goin' after Boiled Bob?"

"You might want to know what you'll be getting into if the chase goes that far."

"Who cares about a damn airport?" Captain Jay persisted.

"Cuban construction workers sent to offer help in countries friendly to Cuba are always paramilitary—highly trained and heavily armed."

"So, you're saying that Cuba wants to take over Grenada?" Arlan asked.

"Hard to say. Bishop asked the US to help build their new airport, and the US declined. Bishop found funding elsewhere, and Castro sent workers and aid. Bishop says the airport is to keep up with increasing tourism. The US thinks it's to land Cuban and Soviet military planes," Forrest said.

"How do you know so much about all of this political shit?" Captain Jay asked Forrest.

Tommy answered for him. "Ch-Charlie."

Arlan smiled, remembering the first few times he'd seen Charlie around the island. He was barrel-chested and had beady eyes and a military crew cut. An avid diver and snorkeler, his daytime wardrobe was usually a black Speedo swimsuit and a T-shirt. He had the nickname on the island of the White Whale, because his broad back was an imposing feature on the surface of the water when he snorkeled in the bays near the village, which he did almost every day. He maintained a perpetual smile and said little. When he did talk it was always in a quiet, gruff voice, and those he talked to listened intently. Arlan had once witnessed Charlie throw a lightning fast karate chop across a man's throat, sending him stumbling from the restaurant where he'd made the mistake of harassing Charlie and his guests as they sat at a table enjoying their dinner. It was so fast that most people in the open-air restaurant didn't see it happen, and Charlie didn't watch the outcome. He continued to sit and enjoy his dinner and his guests, who must have seen the confrontation but acted as though nothing had happened. Arlan left the restaurant wanting nothing to do with the large man and his penchant for nonchalant violence. But, on a small island, it is hard to not come in contact with everybody who lives on it sooner or later, and over the next few months Arlan and Charlie had talked and sometimes shared a dive on Captain Jay's dive boat. More recently, Charlie had approached Arlan and asked him to set up a business on Grenada so he could track Cuban sponsored military movements to and from the island. Arlan had declined, not sure why he would want to become a spy, especially after questioning Charlie about what would happen to him if he was caught and getting nothing but a beady-eyed smile in return.

"Wh-where is Charlie?"

"Dominica. I think the CIA is worried that whatever is happening on Grenada might spill over onto Dominica through the Dreads," Forrest said.

Arlan said, "I met some Dreads a few months ago while on Dominica. They're a pretty rough group." He then looked at Captain Jay and added, "Charlie should know when and where to find trouble. He's always in the middle of it. Maybe you should work with him."

"That's not gonna happen," Jay said and looked at Arlan, who was still smiling at the memory of meeting Charlie. "What are you smiling about?"

"Nothing. I was just thinking about something."

Captain Jay seemingly had heard enough. "We're wastin' time," he said and stepped into his Jeep, started it up and made a wide u-turn in the parking lot. "We're leavin' in an hour, Rookie," he shouted as he drove out of the lot and sped down the road toward the village.

"Wh-what are you planning?" Tommy asked Forrest after watching Jay leave.

Forrest smiled and said, "Well, I guess it won't include Captain Jay."

He went on to tell Arlan and Tommy that he'd arranged to lease an old twin-engine Aero Commander from a dentist on Tortola. It could seat seven, take off and land on short airstrips and had a range of about a thousand miles. Forrest told them he planned daily runs from Tortola throughout the islands until they spotted the *Happy Hobo*.

"We're leaving tomorrow morning. Henry and Case are coming along as extra eyes," Forrest said and stepped into his plywood Jeep. Before driving away he asked Tommy, "You going with us or are you going with Captain Jay?"

"I c-can do more good from the a-air. I'll bring m-my chute."

After Forrest left, Arlan asked Tommy, "What do you think is the big thing that's going to happen?"

"I think th-the US is going to in-invade Grenada."

"What makes you think that?"

Before Arlan finished the question, they heard a distant rumble that sounded like thunder. They hadn't seen a cloud in two days, and there were none in the sky then.

Tommy smiled and said, "B-because of that..."

They both smiled.

"...and s-something Charlie t-told me b-before he left to go down island."

While waiting for Tommy to explain, Arlan looked toward Puerto Rico. He couldn't see the island, which was eighty miles to the west and hidden by St. Thomas or the much smaller island of Vieques just off the east coast of Puerto Rico. The US owned the western half of Vieques and used it as a bombing range to train US ships and aircraft. The distant rumbling of exploded ordnance could be felt and heard by all St. John residents every time the US military decided to test new bombs, which was about once a month.

"Ch-Charlie told me about a m-mock invasion of Grenada that the US m-military staged on Vieques t-two years ago—two years after Bishop took o-over and started to rub e-elbows with Castro."

Arlan shrugged and said, "It could be just a rumor. Besides, I'm betting that Boiled Bob and his crew run aground someplace a lot farther north of Grenada."

Tommy laughed and said, "I-I wouldn't bet a-against that."

Both looked west as they heard another rumble.

"I guess I better get going," Arlan said. "I know that you'll be flying with Forrest, but you'll be coming back every day. Try to keep Frank's crews in line as much as you can."

"N-no problem."

Arlan walked to his office to retrieve an overnight bag he kept packed for emergencies. He wondered how long this would take and if he'd packed enough clothing. He laughed out loud and said to himself, "How many pairs of shorts and T-shirts could I possibly need?"

After answering a few phone calls, he slung the bag over his shoulder and walked to the parking lot where he straddled his motorcycle, kicked the starter and took off toward the resort where Captain Jay would be waiting.

* * *

After sailing from Cooper with some provisions, Boiled Bob had to decide to make the long passage to Dominica or make a shorter sail to St. Marten. He looked back to the trailing dinghies and sighed. If there was any type of air search initiated by the Black Ops the dinghies would give them away, regardless of the cosmetic disguise they'd applied to the yawl. What boat drags six dinghies behind it? Or even three or four? He needed to get rid of all but one dinghy as quickly as possible and decided that St. Marten would be the next stop.

Just before dawn the *Pappy Bobo* glided into Great Bay on St. Martin's south shore. Lights from the hundreds of businesses and the street lights of Phillipsburg lit up its beach and shone out into the bay, giving Boiled Bob plenty of light to navigate around the dozens of anchored boats and anchor near the center of the bay. An hour after sunup, Boiled Bob and Maynard towed all of the dinghies to a dock in the center of the town where Maynard quickly spread the word at a few stores and restaurants that they had dinghies for sale. He'd told them that he and his crew had purchased five used dinghies from a charter company on St. Thomas and that they were all in great shape. Maynard then joined Boiled Bob on a bench near the dock to wait for a prospective buyer.

An hour later and tired of waiting, Maynard left the bench to look for coffee and croissants. Boiled Bob stayed behind and noticed a small group of local sailors sitting together at a nearby outdoor restaurant. Bob was convinced that they were looking at the *Pappy Bobo* with more than passing interest. He scanned the shoreline in both directions and looked back at the sailors, who continued to look out at the *Pappy Bobo* with more animation in their discussions. Bob thought, *How many Alden yawls sailed the Caribbean. Not many. Maybe the boat's disguise isn't good enough.* He continued to watch. As he sat, he stewed. His paranoia grew. *He'd wasted too much time getting away from St. John. Maybe he shouldn't have taken Lisa. Maybe he should drop her off and make a clean escape before Captain Jay or the Black Ops come for him.*

Maynard interrupted his thoughts when he returned with two cups of coffee and a paper bag with grease seeping through the bottom. Boiled Bob took a cup and ignored the food. He looked to where he'd seen the local sailors. They were gone.

Boiled Bob sat his cup on the bench and said, "Stay here. I'm going for a walk."

Maynard shrugged and bit into his croissant.

Twenty minutes later Boiled Bob returned carrying a heavy cardboard box. He walked past Maynard and onto the dock where he placed the box into one of the dinghies. Maynard followed.

"I'm thinking that our boat needs to look like a fiberglass boat. It's still too conspicuous. Let's take the dinghies and go back to the boat. We'll find a quiet bay on the French side of the island and paint more disguise on the *Pappy Bobo*."

Maynard looked confused.

Boiled Bob said, "We'll be able to find buyers for the dinghies there."

Maynard frowned and stepped into the lead dinghy.

Three hours later the *Pappy Bobo* sailed into a small, isolated bay just west of Grand Case, on the north shore of the island. Boiled Bob broke open the box and handed out paint cans, brushes and masking tape. After giving his crew instructions he told Maynard to go to the village of Grand Case and spend the afternoon spreading the word that they had five dinghies for sale—cheap.

* * *

Arlan drove to the resort, parked in the employee parking lot and walked down the concrete path that led through the resort's lobby and to the dock.

"Arlan, me son, where yo hedd*in* so fast?"

Arlan looked behind him and saw the giant shape of Norman Doway walking behind him. He was a mass of muscle, more genetic than earned. He wore resort maintenance clothes and a big grin.

Arlan smiled and said, "Norman, what's up?"

Norman, a native of Dominica, walked ahead of a group of co-workers. He stepped close to Arlan and whispered, "It's de Bull. Call me de Bull."

Arlan looked back at the other workers and said quietly, "I forgot." He gave Norman a local handshake and said loudly, "De Bull? Everyting irie?"

The workers passed with several "Okays."

Norman smiled and, after his friends passed, said, "Captain Jay tell*in* me yo going to look fo Lisa. Tis fo true?"

"If she's still alive."

Norman shook his head and said, "Dat a bad ting Boiled Bob did."

"Yeah."

"I hope Captain Jay kicks his ass. He's a bad mon."

Norman and Arlan walked together for a while.

"Where yo go*in* to be look*in*?"

"Everywhere."

"Dat's a lot of look*in,* me son." Norman paused and said, "He might be head*in* to my isl*an*."

"Dominica?" Arlan asked.

"Yeah. Saw him der you know."

"Who?" Arlan asked.

"Boiled Bob and his crazy friend who's always carry*in* dat knife."

"Maynard?"

"Yeah, de short mon. When you went wit me to carry dose Bob Marley cassette tapes to my island and I went to deliver some of dem to de Dreads up in de mountains I saw Boiled Bob and Maynard lim*in* wit dem."

Arlan smiled at the memory of the trip they had taken together to Dominica a few months earlier. The Prime Minister of Dominica, Regina Charles, had a problem with Rastas and reggae music. She considered them bad influences and didn't allow reggae music to be sold or played over radio airwaves on the island. Norman had convinced Arlan to carry a bag full of Bob Marley cassettes to the island, arguing that tourist's carry-on bags were never checked. He was right. Arlan successfully carried a bag full of reggae cassette tapes through Dominica customs, and Norman sold them to the locals who craved them. Norman made a little bit of money, and Arlan got a free trip to Dominica, where he had a blast hanging out with Norman and a few locals for a couple of days.

"What was he doing there?" Arlan asked.

"Dunno. Up to no good if you aks me. He must be supply*in* dem wit some drugs or somth*in* else. De Dreads don't like white boys much. If dey hang*in* wit de Dreads, der's a good reason."

"I met the Dreads who came to your village to pick you up with the Marley cassettes. Remember?"

Norman nodded.

Arlan said, "Some of them weren't very friendly."

"Yeah, mon. But I tink deh would have been irie wit you if you had come along. Especially my friend Slim. I grew up wit him. He's become a Dread, but he's peaceful. He doesn't like de radicals Dreads."

Norman stopped at a fork in the path and said, "Tanks again fo tak*in* dose tapes fo me."

"No problem Norman… I mean de Bull."

Norman laughed and said, "Yo and de Captain be careful. Specially if you find Boiled Bob wit the Dreads. I hear dey been gett*in* weapons from Castro so dey can take over de isl*an*."

Arlan paused and thought about how volatile Grenada and Dominica had become. He then smiled, fist-pumped Norman and continued toward the dock.

Is Boiled Bob joining a revolution? Arlan wondered.

A minute later he walked onto the dock and saw that Captain Jay had tied the boat alongside and was ready to go. Arlan tossed his bag onto the deck of the boat and told Captain Jay of his talk with de Bull.

Jay snorted, stepped to the helm and said, "Untie us."

"Where's Gizmo?"

"He's gonna stay here to run the other dive boat."

"I thought you'd want him to come along," Arlan said, hoping for more muscle if they had to confront Boiled Bob and his crew.

"Just because we're goin' to kill Boiled Bob—"

"You mean to find Lisa," Arlan interrupted.

Captain Jay paused and then said, "Right. But I still got a business to run here while we're gone."

Arlan untied the lines and looked to shore.

"Hop in, Rookie. We're goin' huntin'."

* * *

Arlan suggested that they travel to Cooper Island to talk to Ray Samuels before heading down island. Captain Jay wasn't enthusiastic about the idea but agreed, and an hour and a half after leaving St. John, Captain Jay pulled alongside the dock on Cooper Island. Arlan tied the boat up and looked toward the familiar wood buildings with unpainted corrugated metal roofs a few yards off the beach. The largest building was an open-air restaurant and had a mix of wooden tables and wood and canvas chairs placed on the sand below its roof. Three small cottages had been built to the right of the restaurant, and Arlan knew there were another half dozen cottages he couldn't see up the hill behind the restaurant.

"Captain Jay, me son. And Rookie," Ray shouted from the kitchen in the back of the restaurant as soon as Captain Jay and Arlan stepped off the dock and onto the sugary sand. He walked out to greet them with a large toothy grin.

"Jesus. I thought only you called me that," Arlan said to Captain Jay as they trudged up the beach to the shade of the restaurant.

"Tis good to see yo two fine young men. But I know why yo come to see me," Ray said, his smile disappearing.

"You're right, Ray. We came to talk to you about Boiled Bob," Captain Jay said.

"And Lisa," Arlan added.

"Why don't yo bote spen de night. Der are no guests, and we can talk bout dis horrible ting done by Bob. I guess yo be go*in* after him?"

Captain Jay nodded and looked at his watch. He said, "Thanks for the offer, and we might take you up on it. We need to figure out what route he's takin' down island."

"He told me dat he go*in* across de Atlantic by way of Bermuda," Ray said.

"He's goin' down island, Ray. We all know that."

Ray frowned and said, "I suppose tis fo tru. I really didn't believe his story bout go*in* across the ocean. Tis hurricane season. Dat would be a foolish ting to do."

"We *are* talking about a *fool*," Arlan said and shrugged.

Captain Jay asked Ray, "Did you see anybody on the boat?"

"Saw a couple of people on de deck, but it was too far to see who de were. Bob came in by hisself. Bought some provisions and sailed away." Ray thought for a moment and added, "I wasn't sure at first, but de boat was de *Happy Hobo*. It looked different, dough. It had a different name too. Close to *Happy Hobo* but somethi*n* like Pappy Hobo." Ray shrugged and said, "It was far away." After a moment he smiled and said, "He was towi*n* a bunch of dinghies too."

"We know about the dinghies," Captain Jay said. "Whatever he did to the boat, it'll stand out like a sore thumb with that many dinghies in tow. He's gotta get rid of most of them before he tries to sail too far. We need to figure out where."

"That's fo tru," Ray said. "Yo gonna need to figure it out wit charts and maps."

Captain Jay looked at his watch again and said, "You got two rooms without rats and palmetto bugs?"

Ray let out a deep laugh and said, "Captain Jay, yo can have de room wit no rats or palmetto bugs, but yo gonna get mosquitos and scorpions. And I'll give yo a 10 percent discount. I'll give Rookie a clean room wit none of doz tings."

Captain Jay shrugged his shoulders with his hands out and palms up.

"He doesn't talk bad bout my hotel."

Captain Jay smiled and said, "Fine. But be sure to send all the women to my room."

"Yo can have all de women on de whole isl*an,*" Ray said, his arms spread wide.

Arlan looked up and down the empty beach and said to Captain Jay, "Looks like you'll be sleeping alone."

Ray laughed loudly.

Jay snorted and said, "I'm thirsty. How about a beer?" He then looked to Ray and said, "On you."

Captain Jay and Arlan spent the evening studying nautical charts, trying to figure out how far the *Happy Hobo* could have sailed, assuming Dominica was its intended destination.

"Why don't we just go to Dominica and wait?" Arlan asked.

"That dipshit and his stupid crew could hit a rock and sink before they get there. I'm gonna kill him before somethin' like that happens."

Arlan rolled his eyes and sipped his beer.

Chapter 7

DAY 6: OCTOBER 19

Early the next morning Captain Jay and Arlan sat at a heavy wood table in director chairs made of faded green canvas seats and backs tied to flimsy, wood frames. Calypso music drifted from a cheap radio Ray kept in the kitchen. Arlan struggled with the chair, trying to settle its pointed legs to dig evenly into the sand.

"You got ants in your pants?" Captain Jay asked, glancing at Arlan as he folded up the chart he'd been studying.

Arlan settled into a seat that listed slightly to his left and looked at Captain Jay, whose chair leaned forward, causing him to lean onto the table with his elbows. Arlan wondered how many patrons fell over into the sand when they allowed their chairs to settle on the back legs.

Ray brought out two plates of eggs and jonny cakes and put them on the table. He returned a minute later with glasses and a pitcher of juice. Arlan and Jay sat quietly and enjoyed their breakfasts as the Caribbean sun rose, its heat intensifying proportional to its azimuth.

Thirty minutes later Ray shouted from the kitchen, "Yo need to listen to dis."

Ray turned up the volume of the radio. The thin sound of a British-accented voice, mixed with static, repeated a BBC news flash.

> …Grenada Prime Minister, Maurice Bishop, and
> several of his cabinet members have escaped house
> arrest, where they'd been placed earlier this month by
> a hard-line military junta called the People's Revolu-

tionary Army. Tensions on Grenada continue to grow,
leading some to speculate that the US might get
involved if the political infighting becomes violent...

"Charlie was right. We might be heading into a shit storm," Arlan said.

"Damn, Rookie. You still don't know nothin'. Grenada's two hundred miles south of Dominica," Captain Jay said. He then stood, walked into the kitchen and handed Ray a wad of cash. He said, "Thank you for your help, Mr. Samuels. We gotta go."

Ray followed Jay out of the kitchen and said, "Take care of yoselves and don't be get*tin* into any trouble yo can't get out of."

"Don't worry about us. Worry about the other guys," Captain Jay said with a grin and walked to the dock.

Arlan smiled at Ray, shrugged and followed Captain Jay to the boat.

* * *

Captain Jay and Arlan left Ray Samuels and Cooper Island and in six hours, a third of the time a sailboat would have taken, they were a mile off the western tip of Anguilla and four miles north of St. Martin.

"What's that?" Arlan asked, pointing to a shape in the water a hundred yards off their port side.

Captain Jay looked in the direction Arlan was pointing and shrugged.

"It looks like a dog," Arlan said.

Captain Jay turned the boat toward the shape and a minute later both were laughing. A golden retriever was swimming toward Anguilla. Jay brought the boat next to the dog, and Arlan dropped the dive platform. Jay steered ahead of the dog and put the boat in neutral, waiting for the waves to push the retriever near the stern. When it was close, Arlan grabbed its collar and pulled it up onto the deck. It immediately licked Arlan's face and, when Arlan stood to raise and secure the dive platform, it trotted up to Captain Jay, who rubbed the dog's ears and pushed the throttle back into gear. Arlan found an old Folgers' coffee can in the gunwale used to throw chum in the water when fishing for yellowtail snapper. He filled it with fresh water and set it on the deck. The happy retriever lapped it up and then alternately nudged Arlan and Jay with its nose and wagged its tail.

"We should head to Road Bay on Anguilla and drop the dog off at the dive shop. The owner's a friend of mine. She may have heard about a missin' dog," Captain Jay said.

They skirted the north shore of Anguilla, looking carefully in the bays they passed for any sign of the *Happy Hobo*. Five miles up the coast Captain Jay slowed the boat and aimed its bow at a dock in the center of the horseshoe-shaped bay. Arlan jumped to the dock and tied the boat off, and they walked down the beach toward a wooden shack with a dive flag painted on its side. The happy golden retriever trotted behind them, acting like he was home.

They walked into the dive shop and were warmly greeted by a tall West Indian woman who hugged Captain Jay and introduced herself to Arlan as Myrtle. She then saw the golden retriever trot into her shop and shouted, "Tishna. Where you been?"

She bent down and Tishna tried to jump into her arms, almost knocking her over. Once Tishna had settled down, Myrtle explained that the dog's owners were from the island and had been sailing with friends for a couple of days around the island. Sometime this morning Tishna had disappeared, evidently having jumped, or fallen, off the boat. They hadn't noticed her absence until they were back in port.

"They are going to be so happy to see that Tishna has survived," Myrtle said. She looked at Captain Jay and asked, "What are you doing here, anyway?"

Jay explained. Tishna nudged Arlan's leg, and he squatted down to pet her.

"The owners are out on one of my boats now looking for Tishna. I'll need to radio them. But I'll tell you what they told me when they returned without Tishna. They said an ugly green and white yawl, towing several dinghies, sailed past them yesterday and looked to be heading straight for St. Marten."

Captain Jay smiled, looked at Arlan and said, "Told you, Rookie."

Arlan and Captain Jay thanked Myrtle and walked back to the boat. They motored around the west end of Anguilla, and Captain Jay then pointed the boat south to make the four-mile run to the crowded Dutch side of St. Martin. While there was light, they searched the bays on the west side of the island for the *Happy Hobo* before returning to Simpson Bay, near the airport, to find a place to sleep. Arlan knew they would have to be lucky to find the *Happy Hobo* without help. They needed to work closely with Forrest and his air search, but Arlan didn't want to bring up the obvious to Captain Jay quite yet. It was always best to let Jay come up with things on his own.

* * *

Ninety miles to the east-southeast of Cooper Island and four miles south of Anguilla, in the small bay to the west of Grand Case, Boiled Bob's crew was finishing up the paint job they'd started the previous afternoon. Earlier in the day, Boiled Bob and Maynard had taken the dinghies around the point to the dock in the center of Grand Case, having left one dinghy with the crew so they could paint the sides of the boat. Boiled Bob figured that if they sold them all they could get a ride back to the *Pappy Bobo* from one of the new buyers.

By late afternoon, having secured a buyer who'd told them he'd take all five but needed to go to his house to get the twenty-five hundred dollars and could return to the dock with the money in the evening, Boiled Bob returned to the *Pappy Bobo* to check on the crew's progress. He smiled as he rounded the point and could see the boat from a distance. Two wide green stripes had been painted along both sides of the hull. The new green stripes, along with the ugly green wood trim of the gunwale and the white-painted wood trim around the cockpit, gave the *Pappy Bobo* the look of a cheap fiberglass replica of the real thing. He was confident that they could sail anywhere, maybe even back to the USVI, and not be recognized. It didn't matter to Bob that he'd ruined a classic sailboat.

Boiled Bob arrived at the stern of the *Pappy Bobo*, shaking his head once again at the moniker LB had come up with. LB and Tricia were on the deck helping Pam and Mary who were in the dinghy putting the finishing touches on the green stripes. Bob climbed up onto the sailboat and asked LB, "What the hell is a Pappy Bobo, again?"

LB looked at his feet.

Boiled Bob smiled and said, "I'm just giving you shit. We've made a deal to sell all five dinghies." He looked at the companionway, then back at the crew. "How long before you finish?"

"Probably more than an hour," LB said. "And we'll need a dinghy to finish up."

"No problem. With the deal our buyer is getting I'm sure he'll give Maynard and me a ride back in this one," Boiled Bob said, in the happiest mood he'd been in since stealing the boat and kidnapping Lisa.

Boiled Bob went below deck. Fifteen minutes later Tricia ventured down the companionway, in spite of LB's warning not to.

Bob heard loud knocking on the door of the main berth, causing him to stop fondling Lisa, who was screaming through the gag he'd stuffed in her mouth.

"Bob, I need to speak with you," Tricia said in a shaky voice.

"Speak!" Boiled Bob shouted. "Then get the hell out of here."

"You need to leave Lisa alone. We need to take her to the island and let her go."

Bob laughed out loud and shouted, "Why would we do that?"

"Because we're all tired of you molesting her. This wasn't part of the bargain. We're not monsters. We don't hurt people," Tricia said with more resolve in her voice.

Boiled Bob shouted, "Bullshit!" but wondered if the crew was planning something against him.

He pulled his shorts up and opened the cabin door, knocking Tricia back a couple of steps.

"What I do with Lisa is my business, and if you interfere you'll regret it," Bob said. Spit landed on Tricia as he spoke.

Tricia backed up to the companionway ladder and climbed up to the deck. Bob followed and looked at LB.

"Are you part of this?"

"No, Boss. I mean…"

Bob looked over the rail at the two women in the dinghy and shouted, "How about you two? Are you part of this mutiny?"

The women shrank down into the dinghy.

LB said, "Boss, this isn't a mutiny. Tricia is just upset about Lisa, that's all."

Boiled Bob glared back at Tricia and said, "I'm going back to get our money and Maynard. You'd better straighten your attitude out by the time I return, or you'll be tied up down there too. I'll let Maynard have his way with you."

Boiled Bob pulled the dinghy to the stern and jumped in. He said to LB, "Keep an eye on Tricia," and sped away in the dinghy around the point and back to the dock at Grand Case.

* * *

Boiled Bob and Maynard stood on the beach next to the dock at Grand Case. The buyer of Boiled Bob's stolen dinghies had come to the dock with twenty-five hundred dollars to pay for all of the dinghies, save the dinghy Bob left with LB to finish up the work on the boat. When Boiled Bob asked the man, a stocky Frenchie who went by the name of Xavier, for a ride back to their boat he agreed with a smile. He'd just made a great deal. Each of the dinghies was worth four times what he paid for them. Boiled Bob was smiling too. The buyer never checked the two dinghies with the water-logged motors. A minute later Boiled Bob, Maynard and Xavier left the dock in one of the dinghies. Xavier drove while Boiled Bob and Maynard sat in the front of the inflatable Zodiac. In a couple of minutes they rounded the point into the small bay where the *Pappy Bobo* was anchored.

"Where's our dinghy?" Boiled Bob asked. "It's not tied to the boat."

"Maybe it's on the other side of the boat," Maynard answered. "They could still be painting."

Xavier joked, "Did you lose a dinghy? I have one I could sell you."

Boiled Bob turned and glared at Xavier, whose smile vanished as soon as he saw Bob's expression. Bob turned to look back at the boat but saw something on the beach, which was much closer to them than the *Happy Hobo*. He had to squint to make it out in the vanishing sunlight.

"Get us to the beach. Now!" Bob shouted at Xavier.

Two female figures had beached the *Pappy Bobo*'s dinghy and were climbing out. Xavier had turned his dinghy toward the beach and turned the throttle for maximum speed. Bob was sure Xavier had no idea what was going on and was too afraid to question his command. The girls' heads turned toward the fast-moving dinghy, and they ran toward the tree line and a small hill behind the beach. Xavier ran the Zodiac up onto the sand, tilting the motor as it exited the water so he wouldn't ruin the prop.

Closer, Boiled Bob could see whom he was chasing.

"That damned Tricia. She's somehow gotten Lisa loose," Bob said.

It would be close, but Bob was sure they could grab the women before they disappeared into the bush.

"Looks like you left the wrong man in charge," Maynard said.

Boiled Bob was first out of the dinghy with Maynard close behind. Tricia was first into the tree line and disappeared. Lisa tripped and fell as she entered the bush. Bob grabbed her wrist and brought her to her feet. Maynard gave chase to Tricia but returned in less than a minute.

"It's too dark in there. She could be anywhere," he panted.

Xavier had cautiously walked up to the two men and Lisa and saw that she was bruised and was not with these men consensually.

"What are you doing with her?" he asked.

Before Xavier could say anything else, Maynard stepped up to him and drove his knife under his ribcage and up into his heart. Xavier was dead as soon as he hit the ground.

Lisa cringed in Boiled Bob's grasp.

"Fuck, Maynard. What are you doing?" Bob shouted. "You're a fucking lunatic!"

"No choice," Maynard calmly replied, wiping his knife on the dead man's shorts. "He saw us, saw the boat and saw Lisa. He'd have gone to the police, and we'd be sitting in a jail cell in a few hours."

"We could have tied him up. He wouldn't have gotten free until we were well away from here."

Maynard flashed a humorless smile, grabbed Xavier's ankles and dragged him into the tree line.

Boiled Bob stood, still holding Lisa's wrist and stared at Maynard for a long time.

Lisa was first to speak. She tried to twist away from Bob and said, "You and your miniature sociopath are going to wish you'd never started this stupid venture. You're going to both pay with your asses when Captain Jay catches up with you."

Maynard snickered, held his knife up and said to Boiled Bob, "Control your play toy, or I will."

Boiled Bob wanted to kill Maynard and leave his body and his knife on the beach. Let the authorities ponder about what happened as he sailed away. But Maynard had the knife and was good with it. And Tricia had escaped and would likely run directly to the authorities. He saw no way out of this except to run.

"Tie the Zodiac to the Avalon. I'll hold onto Lisa while you drive," Bob said and dragged Lisa toward the two dinghies.

* * *

It was almost dark when Captain Jay and Arlan entered Simpson Bay, immediately south of St. Martin's international airport.

"Where are we going?" Arlan asked.

"The guy I buy electronics from has a boat slip near his store, which is near here. He also owns a guesthouse where we're gonna stay."

Arlan knew Captain Jay sometimes bought duty-free electronics from St. Martin to take back to sell to friends on St. John. He had no idea if it was a profitable business for Captain Jay. Most of his business ventures outside his dive business at the resort were not well thought out and usually resulted in Captain Jay owing somebody a lot of money.

"How do you know he's here, or that there are rooms available at the guesthouse? Did you call him?"

David Culberson

A jet landed as they idled through the harbor, its landing lights lighting the runway and its engines drowning out their conversation. After it landed and crawled toward the terminal Jay said, "Jesus, Rookie. He's here, and we'll get rooms."

Arlan rolled his eyes. *The eternal optimist*, he thought. Arlan had seen it dozens of times—Captain Jay shooting from the hip announcing that "we'll get what we want," often needing to change his want to the only available option. He would then smile with an expression that said "I told you so."

"You know this search is going to take forever without air support. Even then it might not be successful," Arlan said as they idled through the bay and into a cut that led to a crowded harbor, which was lit up by the lights of the multiple boat slips and businesses on its periphery. It also had the smell of stagnant water, like many unnatural harbors carved from land or shallow water that, in the short-term, seemed like a way to enhance the local economy or to beef up ancient naval dominance, but failed in its long-term environmental responsibility to properly flush or filter sediment and contaminants that inevitably seeped into the harbor from upland development.

Captain Jay didn't respond for a while, searching the harbor for the *Happy Hobo*. He then said, "As soon as we're in our rooms you're gonna call Tommy and figure out a way we can coordinate their air search with what we're doin'. This place is full of ugly boats. It'll be easier to spot it from the air."

Arlan tied the boat off in a marina slip, grabbed his bag and followed Jay across a deserted street to a guesthouse with few lights on. Arlan wondered why the town seemed empty and then remembered that it was off-season. The owner of the guesthouse was not around, but his manager recognized Captain Jay and gave him a warm welcome and led them to two small rooms. Thirty minutes later they walked to a restaurant a couple of blocks away where Arlan used a payphone to call Tommy while Captain Jay introduced himself to three local beauties who sat at the bar. A radio blared from a ceiling speaker near a hall that led to the restrooms where the phone was located, making it difficult to hear Tommy when he answered the phone.

Arlan told Tommy about the *Happy Hobo*'s disguise and of the dinghies in tow. He then told Tommy of their trip to Anguilla, finding nothing other than a dog swimming in the middle of the ocean. Arlan had to assure Tommy that they'd rescued the dog. While explaining, the overhead speaker spit out a news report from the BBC.

> ...Prime Minister Maurice Bishop and seven others were executed today in Grenada by the People's Revolutionary Army... a curfew has been put into place, and anybody caught out of their homes after dark will be shot on sight.

Arlan thought about that and suggested to Tommy that he and Forrest fly to St. Martin early the next morning so they could organize a wider search pattern. Unless he and Jay or the Black Ops caught up with the *Happy Hobo* soon, they'd be heading farther down island. Arlan had reservations about being anywhere near the political chaos on Grenada with Captain Jay, who'd recklessly storm into any tumultuous situation to catch Boiled Bob, with no fear or regard for his safety or those who followed him.

Arlan hung up and wondered if he should bail on the search but remembered what Captain Jay had said earlier—Grenada is two hundred miles south of Dominica. *Other than chasing an inept group of drug-crazed idiots around the Caribbean and into a war zone, what could go wrong?* Arlan thought and smiled at the ability of Captain Jay to find trouble. He walked to where Captain Jay sat and then stopped. He realized that it might be *himself* that always found trouble. That was troubling.

Arlan walked toward the bar and Captain Jay and the three young ladies, who were totally engaged with the charming captain. Arlan had no idea what he was telling them but was sure it was bullshit. Arlan smiled and introduced himself. It was going to be a long night.

* * *

As soon as Boiled Bob and Maynard tied the dinghies to the stern of the sailboat and Lisa was secured below deck, the anchor was raised, and Boiled Bob motored the *Pappy Bobo* due east from St Martin into the dark night. It was the wrong direction, but it was open ocean with no obstacles. They needed a fast getaway from the island, but the sail due south toward Dominica, particularly south of St. Martin, was full of rock outcroppings and small cays that were navigation hazards at night. They would turn back to the south once the sun was up, hoist the sails and be anchored off Dominica twenty-four hours later.

Boiled Bob sat in the cockpit, pissed off at both Maynard and Long Bill, never getting a clear answer from Long Bill as to how Tricia had escaped with Lisa, other than, "I don't know, Boss. I looked, and they were gone." Maynard's actions on the beach presented a totally different problem. Once Xavier's body was found and Tricia told the police her story, Boiled Bob would be wanted by yet another country's police force.

He needed to rethink his plan—and rid himself of Maynard once they landed in Dominica.

Chapter 8

DAY 7: OCTOBER 20 (Morning)

Early the next morning Captain Jay and Arlan sat with Pierre, the owner of the guesthouse and electronics store, in a small coffee shop a couple of streets from the guesthouse. Pierre was from the French side of the island but had a knack for retail business and realized a couple of decades earlier that he could make more money on the much busier Dutch side of the island. Arlan watched as Pierre and Captain Jay traded jokes and could see that their business relationship hadn't gone south—yet.

"What did you say the name of this boat is?" Pierre asked.

"It was called the *Happy Hobo*, but we have word that the name has been repainted to somthin' that sounds like it," Jay said.

"And this man, Boil Bob, he has your girlfriend?"

"It's Boiled Bob. He and a few of his drugged-out friends kidnapped her at gunpoint."

Pierre sat back in his chair and sipped his coffee. He then said, "This boat, why do you think it is here?"

Captain Jay answered, "Because he stole a bunch of dinghies, and he needs to unload them before he heads down island. We have a witness who saw the boat off Anguilla yesterday headin' this way."

"And how do you know he's going down island?" Pierre asked as he took a sip of his coffee.

"Jesus, Pierre, you a fuckin' detective or somethin'?"

Pierre smiled, leaned forward and asked, "Do you know that my brother-in-law is the chief of police on the French side? He's headquartered in Marigot. I'll tell him about your problem." He sat back and shrugged. "I don't know, though. There are a lot of sailboats in and out of here."

"We're gonna take a ride around the island. Ask around at the marinas. We'll have a plane in the air searchin' for the boat sometime this mornin'," Captain Jay told Pierre.

"I assume you'll need an automobile?" Pierre asked with a smile.

"You got one for us?"

"Yes. It should be at the guesthouse by now. It's my hotel vehicle, and for you I'll only charge half the going rate of an island rental."

"Bullshit, Pierre. I'll take it for nothin'. You've made enough from me with your high electronics prices."

Pierre smiled and said, "Maybe, if you ever pay me."

Captain Jay ignored Pierre's comment and said, "We'll check with you later. You gonna be at your store all day?"

"Oui."

"Pierre, don't give me that French shit," Captain Jay said.

Arlan waited for Pierre to stomp out of the coffee shop. Instead, he placed his hands on Captain Jay's shoulders and kissed each of his cheeks. He then stood back and said, *"Plus de francais, capitaine."*

Captain Jay laughed, and Pierre left the coffee shop.

Captain Jay looked at Arlan and asked, "What did he say?"

Arlan stood and said, "I think he said you're an asshole."

Captain Jay snorted and said, "Let's go, Rookie. What time did Tommy say they would land?"

Arlan looked at his titanium watch and said, "About now."

Arlan and Jay left the coffee shop and walked back to the guesthouse. The manager met them outside and handed Captain Jay the key to a van parked next to his office. It was a white van with "Pierre's Happy Place" painted on its sides in green and gold lettering. A cartoon likeness of Pierre's smiling mug was painted on the back doors.

Jay laughed and said, "Get in, Rookie. We got places to go and people to meet."

Arlan paused outside the van and looked up and down the street before getting in, glad that nobody on the island knew him.

Five minutes later they were at the airport to meet Tommy, Henry and Forrest, who'd flown the rented Aero Commander from Tortola to St. Martin.

The three men were easy to spot. They'd taken seats at an outdoor table at a café next to the parking lot at the airport and, as Arlan expected, all three doubled over laughing when Captain Jay pulled next to them in the ridiculous van. Arlan and Jay got out of the van and joined them. The discussion quickly moved from the van to how best to proceed with the search.

While Forrest talked about possible search routes, Arlan leaned toward Tommy and asked, "Were you able to check on Gallows Point and Frank yesterday?"

In a hushed tone, Tommy said, "Everything i-is fine. Frank's c-crew is working. B-Blake stopped by and was h-happy as hell. He told me to thank you f-for the dress."

Arlan didn't respond.

"Y-you bought him a d-dress?" Tommy asked with a grin.

"No. I bought his daughter a dress. She's entered in some kind of beauty contest this coming weekend."

Tommy paused, then laughed and said, "That dress m-must have taken th-the whole nine yards."

Arlan leaned back and listened to Forrest. Captain Jay looked impatient. It was obvious to Arlan that Jay was not happy about coordinating with the Black Ops, headed up by Charlie, who was still down island but firmly in control of the Black Ops. Besides losing some control of the search there was bad blood between Captain Jay and Charlie, whom Captain Jay used to work for before buying him out of the dive operation at the resort.

Arlan decided to lighten the discussion. He nodded to Henry and asked, "How did these two convince you to come along? I thought you were pretty busy opening up your liquor store."

Henry, an ex-mercenary from South Africa, was a son-in-law of Stu, the owner of the *Happy Hobo*. In his staccato Afrikaner accent, he said, "Forrest is going to need an extra pair of eyes."

Tommy laughed and said, "Henry's as b-blind as a bat."

"Some kind of degenerative disease, the doctor tells me. But I can still spot my father-in-law's boat, I'll tell you," Henry said.

"B-bull. It's all th-that damn rum you d-drink."

Henry smiled, raised his glass and said, "That too."

Tommy said to Arlan, "I'm c-coming with you g-guys on the boat. I want to be closer t-to the action when we c-catch up with Boiled B-Bob."

Arlan welcomed the addition. Captain Jay was impassive.

Forrest flashed his big smile and said, "We searched the British islands all day yesterday and saw no sign of the *Happy Hobo*. Tommy told us last night about the possible changes to the boat, so we decided to look around this morning before landing here."

"They're not there. We already know that," Captain Jay said.

"We flew around Anguilla—"

"We already checked there," Jay said. "They sailed here to St. Martin the day before yesterday. We have a witness."

Forrest kept his smile and said, "I was going to say, we flew around Anguilla this morning and didn't find the boat."

Henry added, "We then flew east and spotted a yawl. But it was heading south southwest, like it was coming into the Caribbean from the Atlantic."

"And it looked like a fiberglass replica of an Alden yawl. It was green and white with two big green stripes along the hull. Really ugly," Forrest said with a laugh. "We did a couple of flyovers, but it wasn't our boat."

"It could have been," Jay said.

"I don't think anybody could have done that much damage to the *Happy Hobo* in such a short time," Forrest said. "Besides, it had only two dinghies trailing behind it."

"Two?" Captain Jay said.

"That's not unusual," Henry said. "I've done it many times, especially on long passages."

"Maybe they sold all but two and sailed away," Jay said.

"And maybe they didn't," Henry said, looking perturbed at Jay.

Arlan said, "It doesn't make any sense for the *Happy Hobo* to be that far east. I think Forrest is right."

Captain Jay stood and said, "We're gonna check around the island by land today. We'll stop and ask questions about the dinghies. He's had to have sold them here. Somebody saw somethin'." Captain Jay started to walk toward the van, then turned and said to Forrest and Henry, "You should fly south and look for that green and white yawl." He then nodded to Arlan and Tommy and said, "You guys comin'?"

Forrest stood, pulled something from his shirt pocket and handed it to Captain Jay. "You might need this," he said.

Jay walked back to the table, and Forrest held out his hand.

Captain Jay took what Forrest offered and asked, "Where'd you get this?"

"I asked around the island for a photo of Boiled Bob the day I found out about the kidnapping. One of his pissed off followers who left him a year ago gave that to me. She was really mad," Forrest said with a smile.

Arlan looked over Jay's shoulder and saw a photo of Long Bill, Boiled Bob and Maynard standing shoulder to shoulder on a beach in the shade of a palm tree. Long Bill, a head taller than Boiled Bob and towering over Maynard, had a broad grin. Boiled Bob wore a smirk and Maynard a sneer.

Perfect, Arlan thought.

* * *

Captain Jay, Arlan and Tommy took the van back to the guesthouse, walked across the street to the marina where Jay had left his boat and asked a few sailors about a green and white yawl. They knew nothing about the yawl, and when Jay showed them the photo they shook their heads. After walking up and back down the harbor front, with no recognition of anybody in the photo, they decided that the next place they should check was the Philipsburg, with its crowded harbor and commercial center.

Captain Jay drove the van east, away from the crowded harbor and up a mountain with a spattering of homes that had panoramic views south to the Phillipsburg harbor and a peek of St. Barts, fifteen miles farther to the south. The van descended the mountain and entered Phillipsburg on the narrow main street that ran one block parallel to the mile-long beach. Shops, bars and restaurants lined both sides of the street. Jay drove the van to the far side of the beach near a marina and cruise ship port and parked in the nearest parking space.

Arlan exited the van and looked back up the beach.

"This is going to take some time. There are a lot of places local sailors could use as a hangout," Arlan said.

"Damn, Rookie, don't be so pessimistic. We'll start with the first one, then move on to the second," Captain Jay said and walked toward an open-air bar near the parking space.

Three hundred feet and five establishments later, the trio entered an outdoor café attached to a large provision store. Arlan noticed that there weren't many people out and about—not as many as he'd seen along this touristy strip during previous visits. A couple of dozen tourists sauntered slowly along the beach, sometimes stepping in and out of shops. Some sat at cafes and mingled with the spattering of locals.

So far they'd seen a couple of sailors who looked disinterested enough with their surroundings to be locals. The sailors weren't too keen to answer questions about a green and white yawl that may have passed through or about dinghies being offered for sale. One man refused to look at the photo of Boiled Bob and his companions. Captain Jay called him a jerk and stomped toward the next café.

"M-maybe you should t-try a better bedside m-manner," Tommy said as they walked to the outdoor café that was attached to a large provision shop. As they walked closer, Arlan could see that the store sold hardware as well.

Two men and a woman, all of whom looked as though they'd attended Woodstock in the late 60's and hadn't changed their clothes or haircuts since, sat at the table nearest the beach. The only other patrons in the café were three large men who sat a couple of tables away, talking loudly and drinking shots of something. They were quintessential tourists, probably having chartered a bareboat that was anchored nearby. It wasn't yet noon, and Arlan smiled, knowing they would be passed out by mid-afternoon, especially if they ventured out of the cafe to the beach where the intense Caribbean sun would bake their inebriated brains in no time.

Captain Jay introduced himself to the shaggy group of aging hippies and sat at the table next to them. Arlan and Tommy did the same, nodding at the trio as they sat. Once they learned that Captain Jay and his two friends were residents of the Caribbean they became more talkative, occasionally glancing over to the table of belligerent men, obviously annoyed at their loud behavior. The woman had a European accent, maybe Dutch. The two men were either American or Canadian.

"We're looking for a sailboat," Captain Jay said once he deemed the perfunctory niceties to be over with.

The woman laughed, pointed out into the bay and said, "Take your pick."

Captain Jay forced a laugh.

Tommy said, "You l-look like sailors. Do you know of the *H-Happy Hobo*, the Alden y-yawl out of St. J-John?"

The greyer of the two men, who'd introduced himself as Dave, said, "I know the boat. Been on it once about five years ago. It's always here during race week. It's a hell of a nice boat."

"It w-was stolen last w-week, and we think it's h-heading this way."

"Wh-what d-did h-he s-say?" a loud voice boomed from the table across the café where the three tourists sat, all laughing and looking toward Tommy.

Tommy didn't laugh and, to Arlan's surprise, didn't walk over to confront them.

After an awkward moment, Captain Jay said, "We think that the people who stole the *Happy Hobo* have disguised it. Some of the bright work has been painted over, and the name on the stern has been doctored." He paused and then said, "And it's towin' five or six dinghies stolen from Cruz Bay."

"Th-they also kidnapped a friend of ours and w-we think she's on the b-boat."

"Wh-what b-boat are y-you t-talking about?" one of the tourists shouted while his friends laughed.

Tommy looked at Arlan and said, "He's looking to get his ass kicked."

Arlan and Jay looked at each other. Tommy hadn't stuttered. Things were going to get rough real soon for the three men making fun of Tommy.

Everyone stared at the tourists for a moment. Then Dave said, "I think I saw that boat two days ago. Didn't know then it was the *Happy Hobo* but thought it looked familiar. Came in the morning, and two men brought a bunch of dinghies to the dock." He pointed to a dock a hundred yards farther down the beach. "I was curious. You don't see many Alden yawls around anymore. I checked with Adrian, the owner of this place, and he told me that the shorter of the two men with the dinghies came in and told him he was selling five of them at a price too good to be true."

"How much?" Arlan asked.

"I think something like five hundred dollars each. Anyway, I walked to the dock to look at them. They were in great shape. All inflatables. Two Avalons and three Zodiacs. I'd have bought one if I'd had the cash."

Captain Jay pulled the photo from his pants pocket and showed it to Dave.

"Didn't see the tall one, but the other two look a lot like the men trying to sell the dinghies."

Captain Jay looked out into the bay.

"They're not here," Dave said. "After an hour or so the man with the scraggly beard in your photo walked away and came back with a box. Adrian told me later that he came in and bought a few gallons of green paint and some brushes, rollers and tape. Anyway, both men towed the dinghies back to their boat and left. Looked to be sailing north, not south."

"D-did you see the n-name on the stern?" Tommy asked.

"Sure did."

"D-did y-you s-see th-the n-ame on th-the s-stern?" came a reply from across the room.

Tommy stood and walked toward the three men. Arlan and Captain Jay didn't bother to follow. Tommy didn't need their help. Not for just three men.

The lady with the European accent said, "Those men are assholes."

Dave said, "I think your friend might need some help."

Arlan said, "No. It's the other way around." He and Captain Jay both smiled.

Arlan asked Dave, "What was the name on the boat?"

Tommy walked within inches of the men at the table and said with no stutter and no anger, "You need to apologize."

All heads turned to the table across the room.

The men stood, their laughs turning to frowns. Each was taller than Tommy, which probably gave them a boatload of confidence. It wouldn't matter.

"Go fuck yourself," the man on the far side of the table said.

Tommy stepped away from the table to allow the three men to bunch together. He then said, "I don't care for that kind of language. You need to apologize twice."

Dave and his friends were uneasy and squirmed in their chairs. Dave stood. No small man himself, he said, "If you aren't going to help your friend, I will," and started toward the other side of the café.

Captain Jay reached out, grabbed his arm and said, "Don't. Tommy will be fine. You'll only get in his way. It'll be over in a minute."

Dave looked to Arlan, who smiled and shrugged. He sat back down.

Across the room the man closest to Tommy on his right shouted, "Fuck you, you pussy!" and tried to shove Tommy.

Tommy grabbed the man's left wrist with both hands and twisted it behind his back and up so high everyone heard a loud pop. The man tried to use his right arm to grab at Tommy, but Tommy held him at bay by applying more pressure. The man yelped.

Tommy said, "What is it you don't understand about apologizing?"

The man to Tommy's left moved behind Tommy. Tommy took his left hand from the first man's wrist, placed it behind the man's neck and, with a strong upward pull with his right hand, an equally strong push with his left hand and a kick to the man's knees, Tommy brought the first man's head down onto the table, breaking his nose. Tommy then quickly snapped his left elbow back and into the second man's throat. The man immediately reached for his throat with both hands and dropped to the floor.

Arlan and Jay smiled. Their new friends at the next table recoiled at the sudden and decisive violence. With two of the three tourists out of the fight, Tommy looked at the third, who kept his distance on the opposite side of the table.

Tommy smiled and nodded to the man still standing, who backed away with his hands up and said, "Sorry, man. We didn't mean it to make fun of you."

"You n-need to apologize," Tommy said.

The man looked confused until Tommy took a step forward. He then said, "Okay. Sorry for me and my friends. We didn't mean anything by it."

Tommy looked at the two men on the floor and said, "C-consider the n-nose and the throat t-tourist souvenirs."

Dave and his friends stood to leave, afraid of Tommy or maybe worried the police might show up. Dave leaned toward Captain Jay and Arlan and said, "If I ever see you guys again remind me not to cuss." He smiled and then said, "By the way, *Happy Hobo*'s new name is *Pappy Bobo*."

Arlan laughed. It took Captain Jay a moment to respond.

"What the fuck's a Pappy Bobo?" Jay asked.

Arlan shrugged.

Dave laughed and said, "Some other guys and I have been wondering about that since the boat left the bay. None of us could figure it out."

Tommy came back and sat in his chair while the three men who'd challenged him put cash on the table and walked from the café to one of the dinghies on the beach—one choking and another leaving a trail of blood.

Tommy smiled and said, "Those g-guys were rude."

"We know that, Tommy," Arlan said.

Captain Jay stood and said, "Let's go. We've got a name and a better description. We need to return the van to Pierre and get in contact with Forrest. He needs to fly south."

"How do you know they're going down island?" Arlan asked. "Dave told us they headed north."

"They're headin' south, Rookie."

"Even if they are heading south there are a lot of islands where they could stop on the way. Or they could sail west of the islands to who knows where."

"He's close, Rookie, and we're gonna catch that son-of-a-bitch," Captain Jay said, more determined than ever.

"You mean we're going to find Lisa."

"Yeah. That's what I said."

Chapter 9

Day 7: OCT 20 (Afternoon)

Captain Jay, Tommy and Arlan returned to the guesthouse where Pierre's Happy House manager came out of his office and told Jay that Pierre had an important message for him from his brother-in-law, the police chief.

"What is it?" Captain Jay asked.

"Something about an American lady in Grand Case, on the French side of the island. Pierre told me to call him as soon as you showed up. He's on his way from the electronics store."

A minute later Pierre half-walked and half-ran toward the guesthouse from around the block where his store was located.

"Captain Jay, I called all around the island looking for you. A friend who owns a cafe in Philipsburg told me that you'd beat up some tourists and left in my van."

Captain Jay laughed and pointed to Tommy, who'd slid the side door open and was reclining in the back seat. "He did it."

Tommy sat up and offered his hand through the open sliding door. "N-nice to m-meet you. I'm Tommy."

Pierre shook Tommy's hand and stood back, confused. "My friend told me that three big tourists left his café pretty beat up."

Tommy grinned and said, "Only t-two had injuries."

Pierre looked at Jay and then Arlan. Both smiled and shrugged.

Pierre looked back at Tommy. He then shook his head and said to Captain Jay, "My brother-in-law told me that a crazy American lady came into the police station in Grand Case last night with a story about kidnapping and stealing a sailboat and dinghies. She told him where she had escaped from the stolen boat and where it was anchored. The officer told her that he would send somebody to check the bay in the morning, when it was light. He then sent her away, thinking she was on drugs."

"What was her name?" Arlan asked.

"The officer didn't write it down and couldn't remember. But, this morning a policeman was sent to the bay west of Grand Case to see if the boat she claimed was stolen was still there. It wasn't, but there was a dead man in the bush behind the beach."

"Who's the dead man?"

"It seems he's a local. My brother-in-law doesn't know if it's related but asked that you drive there to meet him."

"Where's the crazy American lady?" Captain Jay asked.

"The police found her this morning on a bench near the dock in Grand Case. She told them she had no money and no place to go and, after repeating her story, they took her back to the station. She's there now."

Captain Jay looked over at Arlan, then to Tommy. "Let's go." He then looked back at Pierre and said, "You comin'?"

"No. I must get back to my store. My brother-in-law is expecting you. His name is Philippe."

Jay paused and looked at Tommy and Arlan, then sheepishly asked Pierre, "How do I get there?"

Pierre laughed and said, "It is an island. Take any road. You can't get lost."

Both Arlan and Tommy laughed. Arlan remembered Captain Jay telling him the same thing the first time he got on the ferryboat to St. Thomas to use Jay's old Willys Jeep to find provisions.

Captain Jay slapped his hands down on the steering wheel and said, "Jesus, Pierre. What is the shortest way to get there?"

"Oh, *le raccourci*?"

"Dammit, Pierre. Stop the French shit. This ain't France."

"But I am French and French territory is less than one mile from here. You're heading into the middle of it. If you spoke a little of our language you would be better liked, you know."

"How the fuck do I get to Grand Case, see voo play?"

Pierre laughed again and said, "Turn left at the corner and follow the signs to Marigot. Keep going until you get to the next town. You should be there in less than thirty minutes."

A squall, with its almost horizontal rain, hit the van as soon as they turned the corner. It passed them by in a minute, leaving behind hot, steaming humidity that rose from the watered-down, sun-baked concrete roads and buildings. Sweat dripped from Arlan's forehead.

The drive was over relatively flat terrain with no elevated views of the sea and other islands, but as they entered Grand Case, they could see north out into open sea and saw another squall line heading west.

"This w-weather is going t-to keep Forrest from s-seeing too much," Tommy said.

Arlan looked at his watch and wondered what they'd do if Forrest didn't spot the *Happy Hobo*. They had no idea if Lisa was alive, and they had no clue where to search next. It was mid-afternoon, and depending on what they found out in Grand Case, if anything, they'd have little daylight left to continue their search. Arlan didn't look forward to blindly heading south in search of the *Happy Hobo* with the weather worsening.

* * *

The tiny police station in Grand Case was easy to find. Captain Jay parked the van next to a black police truck, garnering a smile from a tall, hatless man wearing a dark-blue police uniform who stood outside the passenger side of the vehicle listening to two shorter policemen gesticulating and speaking their native French language. Arlan noticed that the two shorter policemen wore no jackets and that their light-blue dress shirts had perspiration spots under their armpits that extended to their waists. Captain Jay, Arlan and Tommy stepped out of the van at the same time a man who had been sitting in the driver's side of the truck got out with his hand on the hilt of the firearm he wore in a shoulder holster.

"Calm down, Luis," the tall man said in French accented English. The driver relaxed, and Philippe walked toward the van.

"I'm Commandant Creque, but you can call me Philippe," he said. "You must be Pierre's friends." He looked at the van's moniker and smiled. He then said, "How do you like driving around in Pierre's Happy House van?"

Captain Jay said, "I feel like I'm a driver for a whore house."

"Or a ch-children's nursery," Tommy said.

Philippe laughed and said, "At least you had no problem at the border?"

"No. We were waved through," Arlan said.

Philippe said, "Everybody knows Pierre, and he is welcomed on both sides of the island with no hassles." He paused a moment and said, "I've already heard of your exploits on the other side of the island. I just want to remind you that, on this side, you will call the police before taking matters into your own hands."

Arlan thought that they might be in hostile territory but saw the brief smile Philippe flashed his driver after his warning to the Americans.

"Gentlemen, it is hot out here. Let us go inside and talk in the shade."

Philippe turned and spoke to the two short policemen in French. They walked to a nearby black and white sedan and drove away. The driver of the black truck turned on the engine and sat in the air-conditioned interior. Philippe stepped aside and swept his arm toward the entrance to the police station.

"After you, gentlemen," he said, paying particular attention to Tommy.

The station's interior was painted yellow and was sparsely furnished, with a countertop-high front desk that divided the room and a wooden bench against the entry wall. A glass-walled conference room with a table that could seat at least eight people was to the left of the entrance. There were two doors behind the front desk. A large man dressed in the same style as the two policemen who left in the sedan had come through one of the doors, and Arlan could hear the last throws of a toilet's flush as he closed the door behind him. He saluted Philippe.

"Sergeant," Philippe said to the large man. "How is the American woman?"

The sergeant glanced toward the other door and said, "She is fine, Commandant."

Philippe turned and said to Captain Jay, "I've guessed that you are Captain Jay, based on Pierre's description." He then nodded to Tommy and asked, "What is your name, may I ask?"

"I'm T-Tommy. Tommy L-Lowell," Tommy answered with a grin.

Philippe nodded and then said, "And then you are the rookie, according to Pierre?"

"Arlan. Arlan O'Brien. Captain Jay calls me Rookie, though I have no idea why. I'm a seasoned veteran of countless adventures he's dragged me into. And I'm still alive—so far."

Philippe laughed and said, "Let us hope you survive this one as well."

Philippe pulled a small notebook from his front pocket, opened it and silently reviewed his notes. He then said, "It seems we have a bit of a mystery. Perhaps you can help us solve it?"

Philippe waited a moment and continued. "What we know is that one of our residents is dead of a knife wound. We found him near the beach in the small bay just west of here. A Zodiac dinghy was found on the beach. The dead man's wife told us that a couple of Americans had brought several dinghies to the dock yesterday, and her husband had made a deal to buy them. He left his house in the evening with the money to pay for the dinghies and never returned. She reported him missing this morning. We found him only because the sergeant sent one of his men to check out the American woman's story about a boat theft and kidnapping and her escape on the same beach where we found the dead husband. We also found four dinghies tied to the dock and none of the locals know who they belong to. The American woman claims to have no idea about the dead man but has some very interesting things to say that might be related to your search."

Philippe nodded to the sergeant, who stood, walked to the second door and opened it. Tricia came out and was escorted to the conference room. She kept her gaze on the floor all the way. Captain Jay, Arlan and Tommy recognized her as one of Boiled Bob's followers.

Philippe said, "I can assume that you know her?"

"We know her," Captain Jay said. "Let's see what she's got to say."

Once they were all settled around the table, Philippe asked Tricia to repeat her story. Without looking up from the table, Tricia told them the entire story, from the planning of the theft to the robbery and kidnapping. She confirmed that Lisa was alive and being held hostage by Boiled Bob, leaving out any reference to his treatment of her. She also told of the *Happy Hobo*'s disguise and name change. When asked about the body of the local man, she repeated that she'd taken Lisa off the boat to the nearest beach and that Boiled Bob and Maynard and a man she'd never seen had come around the point from Grand Case in a dinghy and given chase. She and Lisa made it to the beach and tried to run to the tree line. She made it and Lisa fell. That's all she knew, except that she thought she heard the third man shout at Boiled Bob and Maynard.

When finished, Tricia looked up, crying. She apologized to Captain Jay several times for being part of Boiled Bob's plans. Philippe had Tricia removed and taken back to the room she'd been held in.

"What are you going to do with her?" Arlan asked Philippe.

"I don't know. I tend to believe her story, but there is no sailboat freshly painted green and white and named *Pappy Bobo* in the bay or anywhere else that we've looked on our side of the island. I've checked with my counterparts on the Dutch side, and they've found nothing either. So, we have no evidence of a crime she's committed in our country. I'll make a call to the USVI about the dinghies, but we have no reciprocity or extradition laws. I'll probably let her go."

"What about the murder? It sounds a lot like Maynard's work," Arlan said.

"Tell me about Maynard," Philippe said.

Captain Jay said, "He's an asshole Frenchie from St. Thomas."

There was an immediate silence in the room.

"No offence, Commandant," he added.

"None taken," Philippe said with a smile.

Arlan and Tommy told Philippe all they knew of Maynard, and Philippe said that he'd call on his St. Thomas Frenchie friends to fill in the blanks.

Philippe said, "As of now, I have no solid leads about a boat called the *Pappy Bobo*. Philippe hesitated and then asked, "By the way, what is a Bobo? Is there something in your English language that I have not heard of?"

Arlan laughed and said, "The name seems to have everybody wondering."

Captain Jay stood, pulled a hundred dollars from his wallet and handed it to Philippe. He said, "Give this to Tricia. She should be able to get to St. John with this."

Philippe frowned and said, "That is quite generous. I would have thought that you would want her arrested. But, of course, I just told you I'm not inclined to do that."

"She gave us enough information for me to find that bastard, Boiled Bob."

Philippe cocked his head and said, "And to find your girlfriend, this Lisa?"

"Yeah, that's what I said," Captain Jay said and walked out of the building.

* * *

Based on what Tricia had told them, Captain Jay wanted to leave immediately for Dominica. Arlan and Tommy convinced him to wait until they'd met with Forrest and Henry to find out if they'd seen the *Happy Hobo* from the air. Jay agreed and drove the van though a rain squall to the airport, where they parked and ran into the terminal. They found Forrest and Henry having drinks in the airport bar.

Forrest flashed his toothy smile and said, "The weather has us socked in. We couldn't see a thing by mid-afternoon and decided the best thing to do was come back for a drink or two."

"It s-seems you've been s-socked in for a while," Tommy said, nodding to the empty glasses on the bar.

"This bartender is awfully good looking, but she doesn't seem to be in a hurry to wash glasses," Forrest said and finished his drink, placing the empty glass next to the collection of empty glasses on the bar.

"What's the weather forecast? When can you get back up in the air?" Arlan asked.

Henry raised his glass, spilling some of its contents and said with a slur, "Not today."

"Did you find out anything?" Forrest asked and then listened as Tommy, Arlan and Jay told them what they'd learned.

Both Henry and Forrest were visibly relieved that Lisa was alive.

"We're leavin' tonight," Captain Jay announced.

"Are you sure he's going to Dominica?" Forrest asked.

"Either there or Grenada," Jay said.

"If the boat we saw early this morning was the *Happy Hobo*, it would be halfway to Dominica by now. But it still makes no sense why they were that far east," Forrest said.

"Sure it does," Captain Jay said. "They had to get away as soon as Maynard killed the local guy and Tricia escaped."

"We don't know it was Maynard who killed the man," Arlan said.

"Bullshit, Rookie. It was Maynard and that damned Boiled Bob. You heard Tricia. The man was probably givin' them a ride back to the boat after buyin' the dinghies. They killed him as soon as they caught up with Lisa, who I'll bet didn't go along peacefully. Couldn't have him go to the cops."

"Tricia went to the cops," Arlan said.

"Yeah, but they didn't believe her at first. That bought them some time."

"Why go east? There's nothing there until they reach Africa," Arlan said.

Henry, the most experienced sailor in the group said, "Because there are too many navigational hazards south of St. Martin. They probably motored east until sunrise, when they could turn south and set sail."

Looking at Captain Jay, Arlan asked, "Aren't there too many navigation obstacles for us if we leave tonight?"

"It's different, Rookie. We've got LORAN."

Arlan rolled his eyes. LORAN was an antiquated navigation system invented during WWII, and Captain Jay's ability to use it was suspect ever since he ran his dive boat up on some rocks outside Caneel Bay while returning from a birthday bash on Tortola late at night a few months earlier.

Arlan started to protest but knew it was useless. He was surrounded by men who lived for adventure and cared little about the risks. He wondered if he was heading down the same path. Since he'd known Captain Jay, he was off to a good start.

"It's two hundred miles to Dominica," Henry said. "Assuming they don't stop in Antigua or Nevis or Guadeloupe or a number of other islands between here and there, they could reach Dominica by early afternoon."

The conversation stopped while that set in. Arlan hoped the silence was Captain Jay rethinking his plan.

"They're goin' to Dominica," Captain Jay said. "And that's where we're goin'."

"Th-there's a lot of o-ocean between here a-and there," Tommy said.

"We're leavin' tonight, Tommy. You comin'?"

Tommy smiled and said, "W-wouldn't miss it."

Henry shrugged and said, "If we can fly in the morning we should spot the boat before they get to Dominica and have a little time to search a couple of other islands along the way." He paused, looked at Jay and said, "Just in case."

Captain Jay ignored him.

Henry said, "Depending on the weather, you could be there by mid-morning. If you're lucky you might stumble into them on your way. If neither of us sees the boat by the time we get to Dominica, then it has stopped somewhere else or could be sailing farther down the island chain."

Henry stopped talking for a moment, and then said, "If they're going to Dominica, the likely place for them to pull in would be Portsmouth. But they could bypass Portsmouth and sail to a bay farther down the island. There are several. With the seas as big as they are from the east, it's unlikely they'll land on the north or east side of the island."

"Is Charlie still on Dominica chasing Dreads and weapons?" Arlan asked.

"He is," Forrest said.

"He's sure to have a network of locals under his control. He can put the word out to watch for the boat in all of the likely entry points."

"I'll make the call," Forrest said and walked to a nearby payphone.

Ten minutes later Forrest returned to the table and said, "Charlie is in Portsmouth. He'll send word to his contacts around the island to watch for the disguised *Happy Hobo* and will wait for you to arrive in Portsmouth sometime tomorrow."

Captain Jay stood and said to Arlan and Tommy, "You guys comin'?"

They stood, and Captain Jay tossed the keys to the van to Forrest. "You can give us a ride, then use the van and our rooms at the guesthouse tonight."

Forrest and Henry followed. Arlan glanced at Tommy, who looked at Arlan and shrugged. They were inching closer to Charlie's shit storm, and Captain Jay didn't seem to be paying attention to anything beyond punishing Boiled Bob.

As they walked to the airport exit Arlan said to Forrest, "We'll need Charlie's phone number."

Chapter 10

Twice in the last twenty-four hours Boiled Bob had seen the same twin-engine, upper wing aircraft fly overhead, each time doubling back for a second flyover. The first time was the morning after they'd hastily departed St. Martin. Boiled Bob had estimated that they'd motored about thirty miles east in the dark before setting sail to the south. They were east of the normal sailing route through the islands, and Boiled Bob had been surprised to see the plane. His surprise had turned to fear as he watched the plane fly over, return and fly over at a lower altitude before disappearing to the west. The second time he'd spotted the plane was twenty-four hours later just north of Dominica. The pilot of the plane seemed more interested, but, lucky for Boiled Bob, a squall line had hidden the boat before the plane could make a third pass. The *Pappy Bobo* reached Dominica by noon. Boiled Bob skirted the main port of entry of Portsmouth and sailed to Roseau, twenty miles to the south, on the eastern side of Dominica, and hadn't seen the plane again.

Boiled Bob had avoided Maynard as much as possible during the long sail to Dominica, having Long Bill take the helm whenever he rested below deck. While they sailed, Bob talked little, his thoughts occupied by what to do next. His plan to relocate his crew to a different island and live a more utopian life had changed dramatically. Maynard had to go, that was for sure. Boiled Bob's brain was also mired in the Lisa problem. He couldn't keep her as a hostage, and he couldn't kill her and risk being hunted for the foreseeable future by the Black Ops.

He'd decided he'd talk to her when they were on Dominica and try to make a truce so he could get her to cooperate while he planned his next move, which might be to let Lisa go. But he needed to find out if the Dreads could protect him if Lisa went to the authorities on Dominica.

Boiled Bob looked at the shoreline of Roseau and the mountainous backdrop. It was a beautiful setting. The mouth of a river made up the point that was the center of the town, with a mile of structures along the mostly rocky shoreline in both directions. A few docks jutted into the bay, and a larger shipping port was to the north. Maynard told Boiled Bob to steer to the south and anchor close to shore, near a small dock where a few other boats were at anchor.

Once anchored, Boiled Bob sent Maynard to shore to contact his Dread friends. Two hours later Bob saw the dinghy speeding back toward the *Pappy Bobo*, carrying Maynard and three menacing Dreads. Long dreadlocks flew in the wind as the three Dreads turned their heads to scan the shoreline and the other boats in the bay, settling on the *Pappy Bobo* when they were within a few feet of the boat. The dinghy slowed just in time to lightly bump the sailboat, and Maynard stepped to its bow and tossed the line to Boiled Bob, who tied it off to a cleat near the stern. When all four were aboard, Maynard made the introductions. There were no handshakes. All three Dreads went by Ras—Ras Lyon, Ras Joseph and Ras Renk. They pushed past Boiled Bob and his crew, not waiting for permission to check out the boat. Ras Renk smelled like a combination of marijuana, sweat, urine and dirt. Boiled Bob had to breathe through his mouth as he passed by. The other two Dreads smelled like marijuana.

When they were out of hearing range, Boiled Bob cornered Maynard and whispered, "What the fuck are you doing? I don't want those guys on the boat. What about Lisa?"

Maynard said, "They wanted to see the boat. They have a proposition for us."

Ras Lyon walked to the bow. The other two Dreads went below.

Ras Lyon walked from the bow to the stern. After leaning over the stern, he walked to where Boiled Bob and Maynard stood and from the bow said, "Bad bwai, you be teif*in*."

Boiled Bob turned to Maynard and asked, "What the fuck did he say?"

Maynard smiled and said, "He thinks you're a bad man and that you stole this boat."

"How would he know that?"

Ras Lyon smiled and asked, "Yo fadder was a fool?"

"What?" Boiled Bob asked and looked at Maynard.

"Bobo means 'fool' in their patois," Maynard said. "Pappy is universal."

Boiled Bob looked at Long Bill, who'd stood near the stern and shrugged. He then looked back at Maynard and asked, "Did you know this?"

Before Maynard could answer, Ras Joseph, who popped his head up from the companionway, said, "Di is not yo boat an yo have beef below."

Boiled Bob looked to Maynard again.

Maynard said, "He knows this isn't your boat."

"I got that part."

"And you have a pretty woman tied up below deck."

Boiled Bob glared at Maynard and said, "So, you've told them everything? Even about Lisa?"

"They want to use the boat. They had to know who's on board and why."

"Why?" Boiled Bob asked. "And why do they want to use *my* boat?"

All three Dreads were below now, and Boiled Bob and Maynard followed. By the time Boiled Bob climbed down the companionway Ras Lyon had come back to the galley from the forward berth with a grin. Boiled Bob fumed. The space below deck was hot, crowded and smelled like Ras Renk.

"Dat woman in de front wit de rag in her mout is yo dawta?" Ras Lyon asked Boiled Bob.

"What?" Boiled Bob said, understanding nothing of the Rasta's dialect.

"He's wonder*in* de beef is yo girlfriend," Ras Renk said.

Boiled Bob turned and looked at Maynard, who shrugged.

"She doan look like a will*in* guest," Ras Renk said with a wide grin.

Boiled Bob threw his arms up and climbed back onto the deck. Maynard followed. Before the Dreads appeared topside, Boiled Bob asked Maynard, "What do they want?"

"I told you. They want to use the boat."

"For what?"

"You'll see," Maynard said. "They want us to follow them to shore."

Boiled Bob took a step back.

The three Dreads climbed from below deck and walked toward the stern.

Maynard said, "I thought you wanted to help them."

"I did. I mean, I do. But I don't want them to take over the boat. It's mine."

"Let's see what they have to offer," Maynard said. "It might even be profitable."

Boiled Bob glanced at the Dreads, who looked like they'd have him for dinner if he refused. He nodded and stepped toward the stern to untie the dinghies.

The three Dreads climbed into one of the two dinghies behind the *Pappy Bobo* without saying a word to Boiled Bob. Ras Lyon started the engine and headed to shore. Boiled Bob told LB to watch Lisa while he and Maynard climbed into the other dinghy.

Pam spoke up and said, "Mary and I want to go along."

Boiled Bob had noticed the two women looking longingly at the three Dreads while they were on board.

"We need some time on land," Mary said.

Boiled Bob shrugged and motioned for them to come along. Pam and Mary stepped into the second dinghy, and the four followed the Dreads to shore.

On the way, Boiled Bob turned his head sideways and shouted to Maynard, "What deal have you made with these guys?"

Maynard shouted back, "Don't worry. They know the boat is stolen and that Lisa is a hostage. They like that. They want to deal with you because they know you have no regard for the law."

Boiled Bob felt a sense of pride and relaxed a little.

"Okay. But why do they want the boat?" Bob shouted.

"They want us to go to Grenada and bring back weapons. That's why they wanted to come on board to check out the boat. They wanted to see how much space there was below deck."

"How many weapons do they want to load onboard?"

"I don't know. They've been being supplied by a Cuban naval boat from Grenada, but they told me that the Cubans are worried about a US invasion of Grenada and have stopped moving shipments around the Caribbean until this thing blows over."

The Dreads landed their dinghy on a pebble shore near a parking lot that was empty except for two rusted, grey and white vans. Boiled Bob pulled onto the beach next to the Dreads. Five minutes later the group loaded into the two vans, their drivers leaving the parking lot and driving north through Roseau. They then turned inland and drove up a valley between two mountain ridges for a few miles before heading up a steep, rocky road that took them into thick jungle. They eventually parked the vans in a clearing next to an encampment of old wooden shacks that had been built at the base of what looked to be steps carved into a steep rock outcropping that rose sharply upward where they were enveloped in the thick vegetation.

Boiled Bob leaned toward Maynard and asked, "Where the hell are we?"

"Trafalgar Falls," Maynard mumbled. "It's one of two camps the Dreads use. Last time I was here they were all at a camp called Jaco Flats."

A few beat-up trucks sat haphazardly around the camp. A fire smoldered in the middle of the camp, and a few Dread men and women milled about, sharing joints that looked to be rolled in banana leaves. The fire was mostly embers, and the smoke that wafted through the camp was from the marijuana. The men were shirtless and lean, just like the three Dreads that came aboard the boat. The people in the camp stopped whatever they were doing and scowled at Boiled Bob, Maynard and the two white women after they exited the vans. When a tall Dread with long, grey locks stepped from a shack and warmly greeted Maynard, the crowd went about their business of rolling and smoking joints.

"Bredren, wa gwan?" he said to Maynard.

"Ras Kabinda. Irie. Bwai, ya done know seh mi deya gwaan easy," Maynard replied.

"Yes I, a so it go still. Not'n na gwaan, but we a keep di faith, nuh true?" Ras Kabinda said.

Maynard looked around the camp and said, "I don't see Ras Paul."

"All good tings must end. I and I and my bredren parted wit him. He tink he can hide out from Babylon. He can't. Dey will come fo him. Dey will come fo all of us in time. Dat is why I and I will trow de first stone."

Boiled Bob had no idea what they were saying, but it was clear they knew each other well.

Maynard introduced Boiled Bob, Pam and Mary to Ras Kabinda, and he nodded with a smile. Ras Lyon stepped onto the shack's stoop and conferred with Ras Kabinda for a minute before both retreated into the shack. Ras Lyon and Ras Joseph followed and motioned for Maynard and Boiled Bob to do the same. Ras Renk led Pam and Mary to the fire, where they sat on logs and were offered joints from several of the men around the camp.

The inside of the shack was dark and musky, the only light coming from small windows on three of its four walls and the door they had walked through. Several AK-47 rifles were stacked on shelves in the back. Boxes of ammunition sat on the floor next to them. A few mismatched chairs were strewn around the room, and there was a large table against one wall.

"Many tanks Maynard fo de bring*in* deez weapons a to us a while back back. It seems dat you ready to do it again fo I and I," Ras Kabinda said, dropping much of the rasta speak.

Ras Kabinda looked at Boiled Bob and said, "I understand yo are wit us because yo want to live amonks de chosen?"

Boiled Bob took a moment to sort out what Ras Kabinda had said and answered, "We want to help with your fight against the oppressors here on Dominica."

"Tis as brudder Maynard tell I and I." Ras Kabinda paused and then said, "I and I want to take yo boat to Grenada to pick up mo weapon fo I and I." He pointed to the AK-47s stacked against the back wall.

"You want to take my boat to Grenada?" Bob asked.

"The Cubans are afraid of Babylon and doan want to bring dem weapons across de water to I and I anymore. Dey tink der will be a big fight wit Babylon in de days comin on Grenada. I and I need yo to take yo boat to go to come back wit mo weapons."

Boiled Bob was confused. He heard Maynard say that they wanted his boat. Now they say they want him to sail the boat for them. "You want me to sail to Grenada and to bring back more weapons like those?" Boiled Bob asked and nodded to the AK-47s on the shelves.

"Dat tis what I'm aksin you."

Bob, not sure where to go next with this bizarre conversation, asked, "Why don't you take a boat to Grenada and get the weapons yourself? Not that I don't want to help."

"Because yo are a bald-head," Kabinda said. He then frowned and said, "Because yo look like a tourist and with all of de Babylon warships in de area yo won't look suspicious. A nice boat sailed by a group of Dreads would be a problem."

"How much do I get paid to do this?" Bob asked.

Ras Kabinda frowned. Bob looked around the room and saw the other Dreads glaring back.

"I tought you wanted to help I and I wit the oppressors here on de island," Kabinda said.

This wasn't going as planned, but Boiled Bob didn't dare argue. He was confused and hesitated before answering. He wasn't going to make money, but maybe this was an opportunity to get rid of Maynard.

Bob said, "Okay, the tall man who is still on the boat and I will sail to Grenada. I'll need to know who to meet and where."

"I and I gonna send Skandar wit yo. My bredren spent his youth as a fisherman wit his fadder and knows the oceans well."

"What?" Boiled Bob said. "I don't need help sailing my boat to Grenada."

A moment later a muscular, shirtless man with cold eyes walked through the open door. He was just about as tall as Long Bill, and his dreadlocks hung down past his bulky shoulders.

"Dis is bredren Ras Pyter," Ras Kabinda said. "But he goes by his Babylon name, Skandar."

Skandar looked even meaner than Maynard.

"I know the seas here too," Boiled Bob said, not wanting to protest too much and anger the Dreads.

Ras Kabinda sighed and said, "Yo gonna leave tonight. It gonna take a night and a day and anodder night to get der. If der is gonna be military trouble on Grenada, yo need to go to come back fast."

"But..."

"And bredren Skandar know de Cubans on Grenada. De Cubans know him. Dey doan know you."

Boiled Bob thought for a moment. He heard Pam and Mary laughing and deeper laughs came from some of the Dread men out by the fire. They would probably be okay hanging out with the Dreads for a while. But how was he going to get rid of Maynard? And how would he slip Skandar and continue to sail past Grenada and farther south? And what about Lisa?

Boiled Bob took in a deep breath and said, "I'll take Skandar, but I want Maynard to stay here."

Ras Lyon and Ras Joseph protested. Maynard's hand slipped to the waistband of his shorts.

Ras Kabinda smiled and asked, "Why?"

"Because he's already killed a person on this trip and has caused us a world of trouble," Boiled Bob said.

Maynard took a step toward Boiled Bob, but Ras Kabinda's hard stare stopped him.

"He's a risk," Boiled Bob said.

Maynard's hand shot down his pants. The Dreads watched Maynard's reaction with indifference.

Ras Kabinda said to Maynard, "I and I doan need anudder dead white man to tro away down de falls. Last one gone floatin all de way to de ocean. Babylon come to accuse I and I of killin he."

Boiled Bob sensed that Ras Kabinda knew Maynard was a problem and said, "We may not return with your weapons if he comes along. We'll probably be in jail and the boats and weapons confiscated."

Maynard, not taking his eyes off Boiled Bob, said, "I know the Cubans better than Skandar."

"Dey know Skandar," Ras Kabinda said. He looked at Boiled Bob and said, "Der are many dog heart amonks I and I."

Boiled Bob frowned and shrugged his shoulders.

Ras Kabinda then repeated what he'd said in a way Bob could understand. "Maynard has a cruel heart. Dat's fo true. Sometimes tis good fo I and I. Not dis time. We need dose weapons. Time is runn*in* out fo de Cubans."

After useless protests from Maynard it was agreed that Skandar and Boiled Bob would be driven back to the beach and depart for Grenada that night and that Lisa and Long Bill could stay on the boat. Maynard would stay with the Dreads. When Pam and Mary were asked what they wanted to do they giggled through heavy marijuana smoke and said that they wanted to stay in the camp. The Dread men around them smiled.

Convinced that the Grenada invasion was a hoax, Boiled Bob rolled his eyes and left. In reality, given the way things had been going, he was glad to be shedding his crew. Maybe he and Long Bill could sail the boat to Venezuela, sell it to one of the many modern-day pirates he knew lived there and disappear to Uruguay or Chile. But he had Lisa to deal with and now Skandar, the big Dread with reptilian eyes.

* * *

Charlie's paid contacts around Dominica were on the alert, and one, a fisherman from a small village north of Roseau, spotted the ugly green and white yawl as it passed his village. He followed it in his fishing boat and saw it anchor close to the beach in Roseau. He took his boat to a nearby dock and watched as a small white man took one of the two dinghies tied behind the boat and sped to shore. The fisherman didn't see where the small white man went, but a couple of hours later, two old vans arrived and parked near the beach where the man from the boat had left the dinghy. Three Dreads and the small white man exited one of the vans, dragged the dinghy into the water and sped back to the anchored yawl. Thirty minutes later the Dreads took one dinghy from behind the boat and returned to shore. The small white man, joined by another man with a scraggly beard and two attractive white women, took the other dinghy and followed the Dreads. Both dinghies were pulled up onto the beach, and everybody climbed into the two vans and sped away. By the time the sun set, the fisherman had returned in his boat to his village and called Charlie to tell him what he'd seen.

What he didn't see was the man with the beard and a large Dread return to the yawl later that night, weigh anchor and sail south.

* * *

Twenty-four hours after they departed St. Martin, and about the same time Boiled Bob and part of his crew were climbing into the vans with the Dreads, Captain Jay, Arlan and Tommy arrived in Portsmouth, Dominica. Bad weather and rough seas had caused them to duck into St. Johns, Antigua in the middle of the night. After getting as much sleep as they could, they continued to Dominica in the morning under slightly better weather conditions.

Charlie had been waiting for Captain Jay and his crew in a house he kept on a hillside above the beach that commanded a view of the entire bay. A little after sunset, and a few minutes after having received word from the fisherman who'd spotted the disguised *Happy Hobo* in Roseau, Charlie saw Captain Jay's dive boat round the point to the north of Portsmouth and cruise into the bay.

Arlan and Tommy had just finished tying the boat off when Charlie pulled up and parked his borrowed Land Rover on the beach next to the dock.

Tommy and Arlan walked to the end of the dock and greeted Charlie with grins and handshakes. Captain Jay followed and nodded at Charlie, continuing his act as the young wolf waiting for his chance to overthrow the alpha. Arlan didn't think Charlie cared one way or another.

The big, beady-eyed man with the military crew cut and gravelly voice, said, "We found the *Happy Hobo*."

"Wh-where is it?" Tommy asked.

"They pulled into Roseau earlier today and have anchored there for the night."

Captain Jay turned back toward the dock and said, "Let's go."

"Not so fast," Charlie said. "They left the boat and got into a van with a bunch of Dreads."

"Big deal," Jay said.

Charlie stared at Captain Jay for a moment, shook his head, then smiled and looked to Tommy and Arlan. He asked, "How was the trip?"

"Rough," Arlan said.

Charlie looked to Captain Jay and said, "The Dreads have two camps in the mountains, one at Trafalgar Falls and one at Jaco Flats. They almost always use Jaco Flats, which is far more remote. It's hard to get there in the daytime. In the dark it's almost impossible."

"There aren't any roads?" Jay asked.

Charlie still had a smile, but his eyes told Arlan that his patience with Captain Jay was running out.

Charlie said, "Part of the way."

Captain Jay said, "You've got a car. Let's go."

Charlie shook his head and started to walk back to his Land Rover. After a few steps he turned and asked, "You coming?"

Captain Jay said, "How far is it?"

Charlie asked, "How far is what?"

"The Dread camp."

"You'll find out tomorrow."

Captain Jay asked, "What's this tomorrow bullshit?"

Tommy seemed to be enjoying the contest between Jay and Charlie. Arlan, trying to diffuse the tension said, "Shouldn't we at least retrieve the *Happy Hobo* or *Pappy Bobo*, whatever it's called now?"

"Fuck the boat. I want Boiled Bob," Captain Jay said.

"Wh-what about Lisa?" Tommy asked.

"Yeah, her too. But she's with Boiled Bob. We know where they are. Let's go."

Charlie said, "The Dreads are armed to the teeth. They won't like it much if a bunch of outsiders show up at their camp at night. During the day we have a chance to get in and out alive."

Captain Jay started to protest, but Charlie cut him off and said, "I'll call a couple of friends and ask them to get the *Happy Hobo* in the morning. They can sail it back up here, and we'll call Forest to bring down a crew to sail her back to St. John as soon as this weather clears up. We'll leave for the Dread camp first thing in the morning."

Charlie stared at Captain Jay for a moment and then said, "You can stay on your boat or at my place. Your choice."

Arlan looked at Tommy and shrugged. They grabbed their gear and followed Charlie. Captain Jay climbed into the Land Rover a couple of minutes later. Nobody spoke during the ten-minute drive to Charlie's borrowed home.

Chapter 11

DAY 9: OCT 22 (Morning)

Just before daybreak the next morning, Arlan heard a vehicle pull up to Charlie's house. A car door slammed shut, and thirty seconds later he heard Charlie greet somebody at the entrance of the house. Arlan got out of his bed, pulled his shorts and shirt on and walked into the great room. He met Tommy and Captain Jay in the hall, and they walked into the great room where Charlie was having a conversation with a local of medium build dressed in sharply creased beige pants and a white, short-sleeve dress shirt.

Charlie smiled and asked, "What did you bring for us, Winston?"

Winston looked toward Arlan, Tommy and Jay before resting the heavy duffle bag he carried into the house on a dining table near the kitchen. He looked to Charlie.

Charlie nodded and said, "They're okay. They're the guys I told you about."

Charlie said to his house guests, "This is Winston. He works for me."

Winston nodded with a hesitant smile, unzipped the bag and pulled out several identical weapons, placing them loudly on the wooden table. They were compact submachine guns that Arlan guessed were Uzis, but he wasn't sure. He'd only seen one Uzi, popularized in Hollywood, in real life.

Tommy stepped to the table, smiled and picked up one of the weapons.

"M-MAC 10?" Tommy asked Charlie.

Charlie said, "It's a MAC 11, a more compact version of the MAC 10."

Arlan had never heard of a MAC 10 or 11.

Captain Jay stepped to the table and picked up one of the weapons. He didn't comment but inspected it with the familiarity of somebody who'd handled that type of weapon before.

Charlie handed one to Arlan, who had no idea how it operated. Charlie took one and handed the last MAC 11 to Winston. What seemed to be normal to everybody else in the room was surreal to Arlan. This was the Old West. Strap on your guns and ride into trouble.

Charlie handed each an extra clip loaded with ammo and said, "You need to wear baggy shirts. We don't want to march into Jaco Flats announcing that we're armed."

Arlan looked down at his tight T-shirt and said, "I don't have a baggy shirt."

Charlie asked Winston, "Can you pick up a large dress shirt someplace?" He then looked to Tommy and Captain Jay and said, "Anybody else?"

Tommy said. "I-I'm good."

Captain Jay, wearing a Polo shirt that hugged his chiseled torso, said, "I'll need one too."

Winston nodded and walked out of the house.

Arlan toyed with the MAC 11, trying to figure out how it worked while not wanting to look like the rookie that he was. It was very small—no more than ten inches long but heavy enough that he wasn't sure the elastic waistband on his shorts would hold it in place.

Tommy asked Charlie, "What's th-the plan?"

As Charlie explained the Dread location, Captain Jay walked over to Arlan and took the MAC 11 from his hands. He took the clip out, pulled the forward bolt back, slid a safety slider from the trigger and then aimed out the window and fired. Arlan heard the click of an empty chamber. Captain Jay then smiled at Arlan, slid the two safety mechanisms back into place, popped the clip back in place and quietly said, "You got that, Rookie?"

Arlan nodded.

Arlan listened as Charlie explained where they were going and what they should expect. Fifteen minutes later Winston returned with two heavily starched, white dress shirts and handed them to Arlan and Captain Jay. Arlan took his T-shirt off and buttoned up the dress shirt that was three sizes too large but hid the MAC 11 well when he stuffed it into the waistband of his shorts. He took one step, and the weapon slid through his waistband and down to his crotch, the barrel peeking out of his right pant leg. Arlan pulled the MAC out of his shorts and set it on the table. He readjusted the drawstring in his shorts and placed the MAC 11 back into his waistband, where it stayed.

Five minutes later the five men loaded into Charlie's Land Rover and headed south on a road that hugged the west coastline of Dominica.

* * *

Sailing south, safely offshore on the Caribbean side of the Windward Islands, Boiled Bob could see the mountains of St. Lucia to the east. They'd sailed far to the west of Martinique as the sun rose and would be well to the south of St. Lucia by noon. If the weather held, they'd land in Grenada the following morning.

Skandar and Long Bill stood near the bow talking in animated tones. Long Bill had been trying to befriend the Dread soon after he stepped onto the boat. He seemed to be making headway.

Boiled Bob decided it was a good time to approach Lisa. He called for LB and told him to take the wheel and then climbed down the companionway and to the forward berth where Lisa was held. She was no longer handcuffed or gagged. This far from shore, there was no need.

Boiled Bob hesitated outside the narrow wooden door to the berth and then knocked.

"What do you want, dickless?"

Boiled Bob paused, letting his anger pass before pushing the door open. Lisa sat on the edge of the bunk, ready to fend off Boiled Bob's advances. Boiled Bob closed the door behind him and leaned back against it, making no move toward Lisa.

After a full minute, Boiled Bob asked, "How are you doing?"

Lisa looked perplexed and then said, "Well, let's see. I was kidnapped at gunpoint, held against my will on my father's stolen boat and raped by you—or so you say. But I have to tell you, if you raped me, it must have been with a twig because it sure doesn't feel like anything has been inside me for a while."

Boiled Bob fumed but remained silent. He stayed by the door and, after another several seconds, said, "I'd like to make a deal with you."

"Fuck you."

"I can't keep you as a hostage. We've been commandeered by the Dreads from Dominica to run weapons from Grenada and back to Dominica."

Lisa frowned.

"It's something Maynard set up. I think he's been helping them for a while."

Lisa said nothing.

Boiled Bob said, "Look. I'm done with all of this. As soon as I can ditch the Dread I want to sail to South America."

"On my father's boat?"

"It's insured. And I need it to get away from here."

"Where are the rest of your sociopathic friends?"

"Maynard, Pam and Mary stayed on Dominica. I didn't want that bastard Maynard around anymore anyway. Tricia… well, you know about Tricia. She's somewhere on St. Martin," Boiled Bob said, not mentioning the man Maynard had killed.

"Tricia's probably at the police station," Lisa said with a smile.

Boiled Bob ignored her and said, "Like I said, I want to make a deal with you."

"What kind of deal?"

"I want you to cooperate by not screaming or trying to run away when we get to Grenada. In return, I won't use the handcuffs or a gag anymore, and you can have the run of the boat." Boiled Bob paused and then said, "Stay away from the radio, or I'll ask Skandar to restrain you. He's not friendly."

"Skandar is one of the big men with dreadlocks, I assume?" Lisa said.

Boiled Bob nodded and said, "A different one, but from the same tribe. I don't know the arrangement in Grenada, who we'll be meeting or where, but when the time is right, I'll let you go."

"When will the time be right?" Lisa asked with a smirk.

"When I know I can get away before you can contact the authorities. But I'm not really worried about that. There is a rumor that the US is about to invade Grenada, and the islanders are probably running around going crazy. Nobody will care too much about a silly white woman who claims to have been kidnapped."

Lisa looked confused, and Boiled Bob filled her in on Bishop's arrest and execution and tensions that had grown between Grenada and neighboring islands.

"Will you cooperate?" Boiled Bob asked Lisa.

"We'll see," was all she would commit to.

Boiled Bob left the berth and climbed back on deck. He had no idea if he could trust her not to scream and run as soon as they were in a safe harbor, but he also had no idea where they were going and if anybody there would give a damn that Lisa was his hostage.

* * *

After thirty minutes of driving along the winding coastal road on the east side of Dominica, Charlie turned inland into the mountains and toward the center of the island. Arlan had taken his MAC 11 out of his shorts and placed it on the seat next to him, tired of the weapon bouncing on his crotch. He double-checked one of the two safety devices Captain Jay had demonstrated to make sure it was on. He couldn't remember the second safety mechanism and didn't want to ask Captain Jay. He hoped he wouldn't need to use the weapon in a firefight.

Charlie pulled off the road and parked the Land Rover in a clearing at the base of a steep hillside covered with thick vegetation. He said, "We walk from here. Keep your weapons hidden, and let me do the talking when we get there."

"Where are we goin'?" Captain Jay asked Charlie.

"Jaco Flats," Charlie answered and continued to walk up the trail.

Arlan looked at Captain Jay and Tommy. They both shrugged.

"What's Jaco Flats?" Arlan asked.

Charlie glanced over his shoulder and said, "It's an old slave village. The Dreads started using it as a hideout about ten years ago when the government passed a law making dreadlocks illegal. The law only lasted a couple of years, but the Dreads keep the camp as a base to operate."

"Operate what?" Arlan asked.

"There are two factions of Dreads at Jaco Flats. One doesn't like the government but only wants to be left alone. The other is violent and wants to overthrow the government. They've been receiving weapons from Grenada that we know are being supplied by the Cubans."

"Didn't some racists from the South try to take over Dominica a couple of years ago?" Arlan asked.

Charlie didn't respond. The trail was steep, and the jungle that enveloped it was stifling. Charlie's silence could have been because he wanted to conserve energy, but Arlan believed otherwise. He'd heard of an attempted coup of Dominica two years earlier by a cast of bumbling characters, seemingly very similar to Boiled Bob and his crew. Part of the rumor was that Charlie was in the thick of it, as he was with most things in the Caribbean that US intelligence agencies were concerned about.

In the 60's and 70's and early 80's, the world was full of mercenaries, both active and retired, who were available for hire on a moment's notice. Surplus weapons were as cheap as candy, and there was a crowded field of financiers who dreamed of owning third-world countries, particularly those countries with unstable governments and an abundance of natural resources. The bizarre thing was that most of these third–world countries were predominately populated by Africans or those who descended from Africa, while those who wanted to take over were white racists. Why racists would want to live as a minority amongst the people they despised was perplexing.

The group that wanted to take over Dominica included a Canadian mafia lieutenant and a group of KKK members funded by a racist lawyer from a southern state. Their leader was an idiot who claimed to be ex-Special Forces and a mercenary. He was neither. He and his fifteen-member army and their weapons didn't make it out of the US before an undercover agent herded them into a windowless van in a parking lot near Lake Pontchartrain, Louisiana, where they were surrounded and captured by CIA, FBI and DEA agents.

Twenty minutes later Arlan asked, "How far is the camp?"

"Another half hour," Charlie shouted over his shoulder.

"Why the hell would Boiled Bob be up here?" Captain Jay asked, clearly tired of the hike.

Charlie didn't answer.

Arlan said, "You said that there are two factions of Dreads. Do they both use this camp?"

Charlie said, "We've had no intel that they've split up. This will be a good opportunity to find out."

"What's that mean?" Arlan asked.

"We knew they had a dozen or so AK-47s a month ago, but they may have built up their arsenal. I need to know what we're going to be up against when we come back to take the weapons."

"H-have you been t-to this camp?" Tommy asked.

Charlie didn't say anything for a while and then answered, "We had somebody in the camp until a couple of weeks ago. We found him floating near the mouth of the river with a deep machete cut in his neck."

Arlan shook his head, wondering if he'd just walked onto a movie set. This adventure was becoming more surreal every step.

Forty minutes later Charlie led the group into a clearing with several wooden shacks and a dozen or so local men and women with long dreadlocks milling around. None were alarmed, and people went about their business with little regard to the newcomers.

"Mr. Kline," a voice called from the doorway of the farthest shack. "We knew you were coming since you parked your vehicle down the hill. White people have an odor, you know."

A tall Dominican with long, grey dreadlocks and beard walked out onto the shack's porch. He had a large smile filled with bright, white teeth. He asked, "How can we be of help to you today?"

"Ras Paul. Irie. Where are Ras Kabinda and his group?" Charlie asked, looking around the camp.

"They are not here," Ras Paul said.

"I can see that. Where are they?" Charlie asked.

"We split up a couple of weeks ago. He and his followers do not believe in Jah and Jah's word of peace. They want to bring only bad things to our island."

Charlie waited a moment and asked again, "Where are they?"

"I don't think it is a good thing to be telling the CIA where my brethren have gone," Ras Paul said.

Charlie smiled and said, "You've heard that an invasion of Grenada is coming?"

"I've heard the rumors," Ras Paul said. He then pointed to Charlie's waist, smiled and said, "I see you have weapons under your shirts. Have you come to invade us?"

Charlie returned the smile and said, "If you're stockpiling weapons from the Cubans your camp will be invaded. Not by us. Not today. But it'll happen."

"Then I will ask again, how can we be of help to you today?"

"We're looking for a lady."

Ras Paul laughed and said, "You've come to the wrong place. The women here are all spoken for."

"We're looking for a white lady who was kidnapped by a man whose name is Boiled Bob."

Ras Paul shook his head and said, "Don't know anybody named Boiled Bob, and I haven't seen a white lady here at Jaco Flats for years."

"Boiled Bob has a man with him named Maynard. He's a short Frenchie and likes knives."

Ras Paul raised an eyebrow. He said, "I know of this man, but I have not seen him for a few months. He is Ras Kabinda's friend."

"And where is Ras Kabinda?"

"As I told you, it would not be appropriate for me to tell you the whereabouts of our brothers."

Charlie said, "Ras Kabinda has been getting weapons from the

Cubans. You know that as well as I. You might have some of the weapons here in your camp."

"We aren't armed," Ras Paul said.

"We're going after those weapons. If anybody gets in the way, they're going down."

A younger, clean-shaven Dread with short-cropped locks stepped from the dark interior of the shack onto the porch.

Arlan recognized him and said, "Slim?"

The younger man looked at Arlan and smiled.

Arlan said, "You're a friend of Norman Doway. I brought the Bob Marley cassettes a few months ago. I met you when you and some of your friends came to pick Norman up in his village."

"I remember. Arlan? Right?"

Arlan nodded.

Slim smiled and said, "Tanks, mon fo de music."

Charlie, Tommy and Captain Jay looked toward Arlan.

Arlan shrugged and said, "It's a long story."

Slim said something to Ras Paul, who thought for a moment and said, "I don't like you or your CIA, but I like Ras Kabinda less. I don't want his violence and badness on our island." Ras Paul leaned toward Slim and said something Arlan couldn't hear.

Ras Paul's smile disappeared, and he said, "They've set up a camp at Trafalgar Falls."

Charlie stared hard at Ras Paul for several seconds and then said, "I hope you're not jerking me around."

"It's true," Ras Paul said, then added. "Kabinda took his weapons with him. I didn't want them in our camp. That's why he left."

Charlie asked, "How many weapons did he have?"

"A few. But one is too many. He was expecting more to arrive soon."

Charlie nodded and backed away to the trail, motioning the rest to follow.

On the way down the trail Captain Jay said, "This was a fuckin' waste of time. We're farther away from Boiled Bob than when we started. We should've left last night."

Nobody commented.

A few minutes later Arlan said, "Ras Paul had no Rastafarian accent. He had no West Indian accent either. He sounds like a British gentleman."

Charlie smiled and said, "He's from here but was educated in England and has a doctorate degree in mathematics. He only uses the Rasta speak when needed."

"H-how far to the next p-place?" Tommy asked.

"We'll be there in a couple of hours," Charlie answered. He then said, "Be prepared for a fight."

Arlan asked, "Why are you sure there'll be a fight?"

"Paul and Kabinda have been at odds for a year or more. Kabinda is violent. Paul and his group aren't killers. They stick with thefts and an occasional kidnapping for ransom. Paul has been able to keep Kabinda in check, but we knew there'd be trouble if Kabinda went out on his own."

"Ras Paul must know about de weapons shipments," Winston said. "Why didn't you aks how de weapons got here?"

"Did you see Ras Paul's face when Maynard was mentioned?"

"I did," Arlan said. "He knows Maynard."

"You th-think Maynard h-has something to do w-with delivering w-weapons?"

"I would say there's a good chance we'll find Lisa, Boiled Bob and the rest of the crew with Kabinda," Charlie said, which caused Captain Jay to walk faster.

Farther down the trail Charlie asked Arlan, "What's with the Bob Marley tapes?"

Arlan shrugged and said, "Norman needed a tourist to sneak them into the country. They're illegal here. He knew they wouldn't check through my bags at the airport. Hell, Norman must have bought all of the Bob Marley cassettes on St. Thomas. The bag was heavy, and he made enough money to pay for my trip."

Tommy laughed. Charlie smiled and continued down the trail.

Captain Jay snorted and said, "Jesus, Rookie. That was illegal. I'm hangin' out with a crook."

"Are you kidding?" Arlan said, thinking about all of the sordid activities he'd seen Jay involved with.

Captain Jay laughed.

Arlan shook his head and followed the group down the steep trail.

Chapter 12

DAY 9: OCT 22 (Afternoon)

It was well past noon when Charlie's Land Rover drove through the tiny mountain village of Trafalgar and parked on the side of a gravel road a hundred yards past the village.

"We walk from here," Charlie said.

"You sure you know where you're goin'?" Captain Jay asked.

Charlie stopped, looked at Captain Jay and then up the gravel road. He said, "You see any other road?"

Captain Jay huffed and started walking up the road, which led into a valley with steep slopes on either side that were covered with impenetrable Caribbean bush.

Charlie watched Jay go by and said, "Keep the noise down, and don't get shot."

A few minutes later the road came to a dead end. A couple of vans were parked in an area of the bush that had been cut. Beyond the vans was a clearing. In the center of the clearing was a large, smoldering campfire. A half dozen old, unpainted wooden shacks with rusted corrugated metal roofs made up the periphery of the clearing. Marijuana wafted throughout the camp. The few Dread men and women who milled around the camp were taken by surprise when four white men and a local walked into the clearing. Charlie, Tommy and Winston naturally spread out, widening their target area if the Dreads were looking to open fire. All had their hands ready to pull the weapons from their shorts. Arlan and Captain Jay looked over at the two familiar white women who sat on short logs near the campfire, staring slack-jawed at the group of white men.

"Those women were part of Boiled Bob's group," Arlan quietly told Captain Jay. "I've seen them around the island."

"I know them," Captain Jay said and then raised his voice and asked them, "Where's your idiot boss?"

Two Dreads came out of the nearest shack followed by Maynard, whose hand rested lightly on the waistband of his shorts.

Winston looked to the shack and said, "Ras Kabinda. Wha yo do*in* up here near de falls? I tought yo and Ras Paul were friends."

The tall man with grey dreadlocks nodded at Winston, scanned the group and said, "Yo bring yo dogs wit yo everywhere you go?"

"We're looking for a woman. An American woman," Charlie said.

"Der are two of dem over der," Ras Kabinda said and pointed to where Pam and Mary sat. "Take dem wit yo if you want dem, Mr. CIA mon."

Charlie looked toward Tommy and Winston and, with a smile, said, "I'm getting tired of being called a CIA man."

"I and I know you, CIA mon. Yo come to make badness fo I and I?"

"We're looking for a woman today. Not either one of those women. You can keep them."

Captain Jay had heard enough. He stepped toward the shack and said, "Maynard, you little piece of shit. Where are Boiled Bob and Lisa? I don't see that tall stupid fuck Long Bill around either."

Arlan saw movement inside the shack and heard the metal on metal sound of a round being chambered into a rifle. Maynard stepped off the porch and pulled a large knife from his shorts.

"They're not here," Maynard said.

"You dumb little fuck," Captain Jay said. "You think you're pretty good with that knife, don't you?"

"Y-you left a dead man b-back on St. Martin?" Tommy asked, stepping in front of Captain Jay.

Maynard looked surprised and then said to Tommy, "I-is th-that r-right?"

"That's right. You're going to have to answer for it too," Tommy said.

Arlan looked at the others. They all knew what was coming next.

Charlie and Winston reached for their weapons. Arlan saw the barrel of a rifle poke out of a window in the shack. He and Captain Jay reached for their weapons a second later.

Maynard lunged at Tommy with the knife. Tommy sidestepped Maynard and grabbed at Maynard's knife hand. Maynard was fast, and prepared. In one fluid motion, he tossed his knife to his left hand, crouched down and swung the knife at Tommy's legs. Tommy was caught off guard for a moment. He stepped back, still holding onto Maynard's right hand. Before Maynard could take another swing with the knife, Tommy stepped into Maynard's body, blocking Maynard's left arm before it could gain speed. Tommy then let go of Maynard's right hand, grabbed Maynard's knife hand and twisted it palm down, forcing Maynard's arm to straighten and twist at an odd angle. The knife dropped to the ground. Tommy then slammed his left elbow down onto the back of Maynard's twisted arm. A sickening crunch reverberated through the camp, and Maynard fell to the ground, his left arm bent backward.

In the three seconds it took Tommy to disarm and break Maynard's arm nobody moved. The camp went still, except for Maynard, who rolled away from Tommy, whimpering.

Two Dreads appeared on the porch behind Ras Kabinda. Both held assault rifles.

Charlie waved his MAC 11 and said, "We have more firepower than you. If anybody else comes out of the shack with a weapon, we're going to rain bullets down on your ass."

Ras Kabinda looked from right to left and saw four sophisticated mini submachine guns pointing in his direction, then turned to see the two Dreads who stood behind him with assault rifles. Only Tommy hadn't taken his weapon from his shorts. Arlan could imagine Ras Kabinda wondering how these white men and Winston appeared from nowhere and had gained the advantage within a few minutes.

During the standoff, Arlan glanced at the MAC 11 he held and checked to make sure the safeties were disengaged. One was and one wasn't. He lowered the weapon and, as discretely as possible, slid the cover from the trigger guard before raising it again.

"As I told you before," Charlie said, "We're looking for an American woman and a scraggly-haired white man who is called Boiled Bob."

"I and I know dis mon, Boiled Bob. He gone. He and de tall mon, dey go last night. I and I doan no a ting bout de beef."

"What the fuck does that mean?" Captain Jay asked.

"It means that your girlfriend is dead, and so are you," said Maynard, who'd risen to his knees and then screamed and lunged at Tommy with the knife in his good arm, the knife he'd grabbed from the ground when he rolled back toward the shack.

Arlan was ready to fire. Tommy stepped in close to Maynard again and, ignoring Maynard's dangling left arm, used both hands and his thumbs to grip Maynard's hand that held the knife. He didn't try to disarm him. Instead, he made sure Maynard's hand was tightly wrapped around the knife's handle and twisted Maynard's wrist and the knife toward Maynard's torso. He then let Maynard's momentum carry the knife into his body, just below his sternum. Maynard's stare froze as Tommy let his body drop to the ground.

Arlan braced for the firefight, aiming at the two Dreads on the porch as did Charlie, Winston, Captain Jay and Tommy, after he was able to pull his weapon out.

Ras Kabinda raised his hand and shouted, "Nuff dis badness.

"Okay, Mr. CIA. I and I doan have anudder white woman and doan care if dis white mon has been keeled by anudder white mon," Kabinda said, looking down at Maynard's body. "Dat is one less white mon on dis eart."

Captain Jay shouted toward Pam and Mary, "Where is Boiled Bob?"

Pam, who'd hidden behind the log she'd been sitting on a couple of minutes earlier, said, "Long Bill and Lisa stayed on the boat. I don't know where Bob is. He left last night."

Ras Kabinda said, "I and I doan know where Boiled Bob and de beef go to."

"That's a load of crap," Charlie said.

What was a tense situation became more intense. Arlan was surprised nobody had fired a weapon yet. He wasn't going to unless things went to hell in a handbag and it became a matter of survival.

Ras Kabinda looked to Winston and said, "I and I tink it tis time fo you to go bock to Babylon. Dis is no place fo yo and yo dogs."

Charlie let out a deep breath and lowered his weapon. He started to back away, never taking his eyes from the Dreads on the porch. Winston turned, weapon held high, and surveyed the rest of the camp. Nobody moved. He then followed Charlie. Tommy, Arlan and Captain Jay did the same.

"An doan be comin bock," Ras Kabinda shouted.

"Fat chance," Charlie said under his breath, causing Arlan and Tommy to laugh.

As soon as all five men were out of sight from the camp they turned and walked quickly to the Land Rover and drove back down the mountain to Roseau, where they would turn north and retrace their steps to Charlie's house in Portsmouth.

"Why'd we leave?" Captain Jay asked. "We could've taken them down."

Nobody answered. Arlan was happy to have gotten out of the camp without firing his weapon. He was pretty sure that, other than Captain Jay, the others felt the same.

Charlie looked in his mirror at Tommy and asked, "Are you okay?"

"I'm f-fine."

Charlie then answered Captain Jay by saying, "Why take the risk of being shot? I know where they are and that they probably have a lot more AK-47s than they showed. We'd have been in a lot of trouble if they'd had a chance to arm themselves. They made a mistake not to post a lookout down the road." Charlie then added, "I'll send a team in to take them out in a few days—after we find Lisa."

"Do you think Boiled Bob and Lisa weren't there?" Arlan asked.

"Yeah. We'd have seen them. There was no place to hide," Charlie said.

"What about the *Happy Hobo*?" Captain Jay asked. "They could've sailed last night."

Nobody answered.

Before turning north to Portsmouth, Charlie stopped in Roseau. The *Happy Hobo* was not in the bay. He made a call from a pay phone, and Arlan could tell from Charlie's body language during the short call that something was wrong.

Charlie returned to the Land Rover and said, "My guys told me the boat wasn't at anchor when they got there this morning."

"I told you we should've gone there last night," Captain Jay said and spit out of his window. "Get us back to my boat. We're goin' to Grenada."

"How do you know they're going to Grenada?" Arlan asked.

Captain Jay said, "They're headin' to Grenada, Rookie. That's where the weapons are, and that's where they're goin'."

Ten minutes farther up the coastal road to Portsmouth, Winston said, "I tink dat's right. Maynard was deal*in* wit de Dreads before, runn*in* guns from Grenada. I tink Kabinda sent your sailboat wit a crew to Grenada to pick up more weapons. De Cubans doan wanna be runn*in* guns in der boats wit the US Navy in de area."

"Fuck your guns," Captain Jay said. "I want Boiled Bob."

"And Lisa," Arlan said.

"Like I said," Captain Jay said with a shrug. "We need to leave as soon as we get back to my boat."

Charlie said, "We'll leave early tomorrow morning. The weather's bad, and it's going to be a wet ride. I've got access to a bigger boat with a dry cabin."

"I'm gonna leave tonight," Captain Jay said.

"We only have an hour or so of daylight. We're taking my boat in the morning. Winston will prep it while I make some calls," Charlie said.

Captain Jay shouted, "Bullshit!"

Charlie sighed and said, "The *Happy Hobo* has been sailing for twenty-four hours and will be in Grenada by mid-morning. Even if you left tonight you wouldn't beat them there." Charlie paused and then said, "You don't even know where to look. It's a big island."

"Bullshit," Captain Jay said again. "We can get Forrest to fly down and search by air."

"Listen to me. Besides trying to find a needle in a haystack, there's an invasion coming with a whole lot of firepower. Even if the weather was good, the US military isn't going to let anybody fly around the island, and the Navy will be checking every boat in the area, especially power boats that look like they can run guns. If you get by the US navy, which is unlikely, you'll have Grenada boat patrols to deal with. If you want to see the *Happy Hobo* again you better come along with me."

"Why you?"

"Because I've got connections you've never dreamed of."

Arlan saw Tommy smile. Arlan didn't feel like being the referee between the two alpha males. He was still digesting all that had happened in the past few days, particularly the last few hours. He kept quiet. Captain Jay didn't say anything the rest of the drive. Nobody did.

After parking the Land Rover in the driveway, Charlie said, "Leave your weapons with Winston, and get some sleep. I've got a few calls to make."

"I wanna keep mine," Captain Jay said. "We're goin' into a war zone."

Charlie smiled and said to Captain Jay, "That's why you're not taking weapons—especially you." He turned and walked into his house.

Arlan and Tommy stood next to the Land Rover and looked at Captain Jay, who grinned and said, "What are you two gay boys lookin' at?" He then handed his MAC 11 to Winston and followed Charlie into the house.

Arlan looked at Tommy, who shrugged, handed his weapon to Winston and followed Captain Jay.

Arlan did the same.

Chapter 13

DAY 10: OCT 23

It had taken the *Pappy Bobo* a night, all the next day and another night to sail the passage from Dominica to Grenada. The weather was bad, but the trip was uneventful—other than being shadowed and then dwarfed by a US Navy destroyer.

Boiled Bob had been at the helm and had struggled to see anything during the moonless night. He'd asked both Long Bill and Skandar to stay on the bow and watch for navigation hazards. An hour before daybreak and a few miles north of Grenada, the *Pappy Bobo* was violently hit with bright lights, so bright they blinded Bob, who'd had to turn his head away and squeeze his eyes shut until his vision returned, fuzzy as it was. He'd looked to the bow and saw Skandar and Long Bill shading their eyes with their hands. A loudspeaker had crackled through the bright light, blasting out a radio frequency that the captain of the sailboat was to tune in to on his marine radio so that the sailboat captain could answer a few questions. Bob had had no idea what kind of vessel was near him or who'd requested the radio conversation. The bright lights had prevented him from seeing anything except the brilliant glow of everything on his boat exposed to the light. He'd thought about shouting to whomever was behind the light and telling them to fuck themselves but had sensed that the speaker was attached to something very large. He'd climbed down the companionway, turned a knob on the radio to the requested frequency and climbed topside with the microphone, which was tethered to the base unit with a long, coiled cord. During the long sail from Dominica he'd practiced a made-up story in case he was confronted. His story was that he and his crew were returning the *Pappy Bobo*, which was a charter boat, back to its home port in Trinidad after having completed a charter that required them to drop their guests off on St. Martin, where they could catch an international flight back to the US.

Boiled Bob had stood on the deck near the companionway so he could hear the radio's speaker, which hung on a wall in the galley. He'd had to look away from the blinding light as he'd listened to the commander of the other vessel introduce himself and ask where the sailboat was from, where it was headed and who was on it. Bob had heard the words *destroyer* and *US Navy* and lost some of his swagger. He'd tried to picture what was behind the light, but couldn't. He'd shakily answered the commander's questions and told his made-up story. After a long pause, Bob had started to think his story wasn't working and wondered if he could slip away from the other vessel. What he hadn't known was that the destroyer had inched closer to the *Pappy Bobo* during their conversation.

As abruptly as it had appeared, the light, just as abruptly, had disappeared, leaving a glow in Boiled Bob's brain that had, momentarily, caused him to lose all perception of distance and shapes. His eyes had needed time to adjust. When they did, Boiled Bob looked to where the light had been and jumped back and had almost fallen over the rail and into the sea. He'd glanced to the bow and had seen Skandar and Long Bill still crouched down, their eyes open with shock.

Boiled Bob had turned his head back toward the navy destroyer. All he saw was grey. He couldn't see the sky or the sea or anything to either side of the mass of steel a few yards off his port side. As the destroyer began to move, the commander had used the loudspeaker to thank the sailboat captain for his patience and told him to have a safe sail. Boiled Bob had then watched as the five-hundred-foot vessel slid by for what seemed like an eternity, until it had finally vanished into the dark.

An hour later, just as the sun pushed a grey haze ahead of its appearance, Boiled Bob looked back and saw specks on the edge of the northern horizon. Maybe he was being too paranoid, but he was pretty sure he was looking at a fleet of ships.

* * *

Well after sunrise, and still shaken by the abrupt presence of the US Navy destroyer, Boiled Bob sailed along the west side of Grenada, glancing behind him every few minutes. The nautical chart that he kept under the cushion of the seat just behind the helm was out, and he reviewed the anchorages on the lee side of the island. The aerial view of Grenada reminded him of a tiny Greenland, which reminded him of a fat tadpole with a short tail. In Grenada's case, the tail at the bottom of the island curled to the west, as opposed to Greenland's tail, which curled to the east. He looked toward the island as the boat traveled south, comparing the chart with what he saw on land. The mountainous tropical forests that spilled onto beaches and rocky shores were occasionally interrupted by villages near the ocean with colorful shacks and houses built along the beach. The chart showed him just two dimensions and offered little of the three-dimensional, real-life graphics. A couple of coastal villages were built on relatively flat land where the beaches tended to be longer, which allowed homes and shacks to be built close to the shoreline. These villages were linear, and it was hard to tell from sea level how deep into the island they spread, if at all. Villages built where mountains ended at the beach were much more vertical, with houses stacked up the mountain behind each other until the slopes became too steep to carry the construction materials needed to build roads and homes.

Bob would have normally pulled into Grenada's main port of entry, St George's' Harbor, on the southwest side of the island, but Skandar insisted they sail past St. George's, around the southwest tip of the island and into one of many deep, narrow bays on the south side of the island.

As they sailed around the tip of Grenada's tail, called Point Salines, Bob could see the controversial nine-thousand-foot runway that was being built by several hundred Cubans. The almost completed runway ran east-west and hugged the south shore of the point, its western tip having been built out into the sea on fill. A multitude of military and construction vehicles were on the runway, and many more were grouped near warehouses on the distant eastern end of the airstrip. Some of the construction vehicles were abandoned, apparently on purpose, while others, mostly front-end loaders and dump trucks, deposited boulders and construction debris up and down the runway. Bob didn't know much about military tactics but was pretty sure the workers were attempting to make the runway useless to invading aircraft. Bob smiled and wondered if any of them knew the size of the fleet that was coming for them. All the boulders on the island wouldn't stop it. There was going to be a slaughter—one that he'd be far away from. He had no plans to stick around once Skandar left the boat.

An hour after passing the new runway, Skandar pointed to a deep bay and said, "Dat's where we go. Take da boat all de way to da back of de bay. Der is a dock der. Tie along de back side of de dock."

Long Bill dropped the sails and Boiled Bob started the engine. It took fifteen minutes to navigate through the dozen boats anchored in the bay. Several homes and shacks lined the slopes on either side of the bay, but the only commercial structure was a warehouse on the shore behind the dock, which had been built east-west and took up half of the narrow back of the bay.

After tying alongside the inside of the dock, Boiled Bob could see that the *Pappy Bobo* was hidden from the entrance of the bay by the dock, which made him smile for the first time in three days. With increasing cloud cover and hidden by a dock, he was confident he wouldn't be spotted by anybody chasing him, not that that was possible with the US military hovering nearby. His problem now was how to ditch Skandar and get the boat back to sea before the invasion started.

* * *

Just before sunrise Arlan was awakened by Charlie greeting Winston at the front door of his house. It took him a moment to remember where he was and then thought back to the previous night and trying to sleep while listening to Charlie making preparations for their journey from Dominica to Grenada. Through the thin walls of the house, Arlan had heard Charlie make several calls from the living room. One call was to Forrest. He could tell from Charlie's end of the conversation that Forrest and Henry were still on St. Martin. Charlie had told them that, weather permitting, they should leave early in the morning and search the waters north of Grenada for the *Happy Hobo*. He had then added that they would likely run into a US carrier group and should steer clear, though he'd make some calls to ensure Forrest's plane was recognized as a friendly. He had then told Forrest that the only functioning airport on the island, Pearls Airport, was closed, and he'd need to return to St. Martin after his flyover.

Arlan had then heard Charlie call Winston and tell him to take a team up to Trafalgar Falls after dropping them off at the boat the next morning to retrieve all of the weapons Kabinda had in his camp. After a pause Arlan heard, "Take them out if you have to."

During the next call Arlan had heard Charlie describe a boat and the route they'd be taking to Grenada. He'd then heard a lot of "Yes, sir" and "No, sir."

He remembered, just before falling asleep, thinking that he was way over his head in this adventure and wondered what made Charlie, Tommy and Captain Jay so confident that they would not only survive, but thrive, during the next few days. Maybe they were able to tune out the risks. Not ever having gone through anything close to an invasion, Arlan had no idea what the risks were. His last conscious thought had been that he'd find out soon enough.

* * *

Winston drove Charlie and his crew to the dock in Portsmouth where Charlie's borrowed boat, an old wooden trawler, was tied along the dock. It was a clunky, fifty-foot-plus boat that made Arlan smile.

It will be dry, he thought.

"What the fuck is that?" Captain Jay said with a laugh as they walked toward the dock.

Charlie said, "It's a down island freight boat. It'll blend in."

"I'd like to get there this year," Captain Jay said.

Charlie stepped onto the boat and said, "Don't worry. It's been retrofitted with a new engine and keel. It's a lot faster than your boat. It also has the best navigation and electronics of any boat in the area."

Captain Jay snorted and stepped onto the boat. He looked back to Arlan and Tommy and said, "Come on. We're gonna get Boiled Bob."

"What about Lisa?" Arlan asked.

"Yeah. Her too," Jay said with a shrug. He then smiled and said, "We're gonna shoot some Cuban beaners too."

Arlan looked at Charlie, who rolled his eyes.

"W-we don't have anything to sh-shoot with," Tommy said with a grin.

Captain Jay flicked his hand and snorted. He then said, "No big deal. We'll find somethin'."

Charlie smiled, shook his head and said, "Untie us."

The retrofitted trawler made good speed over the rough seas. They put two hundred miles behind them in the next ten hours and would be in Grenada by nightfall if they kept that pace. Eight hours into the trip, Charlie, who sat alone at the controls in the pilot house, slowed and started a garbled dialogue on the radio that Arlan and the others, who sat in the cabin a few feet below Charlie, couldn't make out. Charlie then turned the boat to starboard.

"Who did you call?" Captain Jay shouted up to Charlie.

"You'll see."

Ten minutes later the trawler was lit up by a powerful spotlight. Arlan peeked through a porthole to find the light's source and was momentarily blinded. A loudspeaker called out, "Mr. Kline?"

Charlie pulled the throttles back, and the boat rocked in the heavy seas. He then opened the door of the pilot house and stepped onto the narrow deck that surrounded it on three sides. Holding onto the rail, he held a megaphone to his mouth and shouted, "Tell that son-of-bitch commander of yours to turn that damn light off and offer an old man some hospitality."

The light dimmed, and Arlan could see the outline of a very large naval vessel towering over their trawler.

"Charlie is picking a fight with the navy," Arlan said.

"Shit, Rookie, the fun's just startin'."

A new voice came over the loud speaker and said, "Charlie, what the hell you doing out here twiddling your dick in the middle of nowhere on that godforsaken ugly boat?"

Charlie laughed and answered, "You going to let us board? Or are you going to leave me out here to twiddle my dick all night?"

"I don't know. Are you housebroken yet?" the voice replied.

Tommy asked, "D-do you know th-this guy?"

Charlie shouted down to Tommy, "Yeah. I know him. We got shot up on a beach in the Pacific together as seventeen-year-old marines."

"Isn't th-at too y-young to be in th-the marines?"

"Yep."

Twenty minutes later they were aboard the "USS *Trenton*, a transport ship and part of the Twenty-Second Marine Amphibious Unit, or "our floating hotel," as Colonel Faulkner described it when he welcomed his old friend Charlie and the others to his command center. Charlie and the colonel embraced, and Charlie introduced Arlan, Tommy and Captain Jay.

"Maybe Charlie told you, but we go back a long time. We met as young leathernecks in the Big War. We were dumb enough to storm a beach that was being peppered by Japanese snipers. We both got shot, and the damn medics threw us back on the steel landing crafts. The snipers loved that. They'd shoot into the landing craft, and their bullets would ricochet around for a while. Hell, I got hit two more times from one of those bouncing bullets," the colonel said and smiled at Charlie, who said nothing.

"Charlie and I took different paths after the war. I stayed in to fight the good war overtly. Charlie took a more covert turn, chasing spooks around," the colonel said and slapped Charlie's shoulder.

Charlie smiled but didn't respond. Arlan could tell he wasn't happy about having his history discussed. Most who knew Charlie well, if that was possible, had surmised that he worked for the CIA or some other covert group. He tried to hide. The events of the past couple of days were good proof, but the colonel had just confirmed it.

"It's too rough to tether your bathtub of a boat to our ship, so I put a crew on her until you're ready to leave," the colonel said and then added, "But I suggest you stay the night if your destination is Grenada."

Charlie didn't commit. Instead, he asked, "How'd you find us?"

"I got a message from a mutual friend last night to look out for you. He gave me a description of your boat. We've been tracking you for a few hours. What's this about a stolen boat and a kidnapped woman?"

Charlie took five minutes to explain their situation. When he was finished, he handed the photo Forrest had found of Boiled Bob, Long Bill and Maynard to his friend and said, "The short one is no longer a problem."

The colonel raised his eyebrows and looked at Charlie but didn't question him. He said, "And you think these two are on Grenada with a stolen sailboat and a kidnapped woman?"

It was more a statement than a question.

He didn't wait for an answer. He said, "If you don't mind, I'll copy this and pass it along to some of the other commanders. I'll send it to Bragg and have them give copies to some Rangers who'll be going in the same time we do."

He passed the photo to a subordinate with his instructions. He turned back to Charlie and said, "I wouldn't put too much faith in our ability to find these people, or the boat you're looking for. We've got higher priorities at the moment."

Charlie smiled and said, "I understand. But we're going to shore, and I'd appreciate what you can tell us about your plan. We'd like to stay away from any hotspot, if possible."

"Bull. I've never known you to shy away from hotspots, Charlie. If your friends are anything like you, you'll all be in it up to your elbows before it's over," the colonel said and laughed.

Arlan wanted to raise his hand and volunteer to the colonel that he wasn't at all like Charlie.

The colonel said, "I'll tell you what I know because, frankly, we could use some help."

Arlan looked around at all of the high-tech equipment and the no-nonsense uniformed professionals going about their business and wanted to laugh at the colonel's statement.

"How well do you know the island of Grenada?" the colonel asked.

Charlie glanced at the others and said, "Pretty well. We've all spent time there, and some of us have been diving around the island."

The colonel looked at everybody in the group, seemingly measuring what he'd say next. He then said, "Here's the deal, Charlie. You know the history of this thing, right?"

"Mostly, but my friends don't know as much. You might as well bring them up to speed, as long as you're in a talkative mood, that is," Charlie said with a smile.

"Prime Minister Maurice Bishop shopped his new airport at Pont Salines to the US a few years ago, telling them that a bigger airport was needed on the island to compete for tourism with other Caribbean islands. The US refused to fund it, so Great Britain did. But Castro provided the labor and equipment, and, with Cuba's involvement, the US figured that the nine-thousand-foot runway would be used to land Soviet planes and that Castro would have another foothold in the Caribbean."

The colonel paused while one of his officers approached and whispered something to him. The colonel nodded, and the officer walked away.

"Anyway, Bishop was executed by members of something called the People's Revolutionary Army, which, evidently, has the support of Grenada's official military."

"Are they a threat?" Arlan asked.

The colonel shrugged and said, "Who knows. It's politics. We don't get involved with politics, right, Charlie?"

Charlie barely stifled a laugh.

"It doesn't matter. The neighboring islands, headed up by Prime Minister Eugenia Charles of Dominica, have called for our help. They don't want Castro or the Soviets in their neighborhood. And, besides killing Bishop and scores of island residents, the new government on

Grenada has imposed a twenty-four-hour curfew—shoot to kill any violators."

Captain Jay asked, "What's that have to do with squat?"

The colonel smiled and asked Charlie, "Where'd you find this guy? He cuts to the chase quickly, doesn't he?"

Charlie shook his head and said, "You don't know the half of it, my friend."

The colonel continued and said, "There is a medical school on that island, and about six hundred of its students are American. That's the president's angle for going in. This is a rescue mission first and a mission to restore democracy and keep Grenada out of Castro's hands second." The colonel looked thoughtful for a moment and then said, "Or maybe it's the other way around."

The colonel paused and read a note handed to him by one of the dozen or so people running around the room. After reading it he stuffed it into his pocket and said to nobody, "This thing is at risk of going south."

Nobody said anything and waited for the colonel to continue.

The colonel turned his attention back to his guests and said, "We've had two days to plan this thing. You heard about that bombing of the military barracks in Beirut a couple of days ago? Killed more than three hundred people? Two hundred forty were US Marines." The colonel paused and said, "Well, that's pissed everybody off, and the president is loaded for bear. Our carrier group, the Guam, was on its way to the Mediterranean when we got the call to divert to an area near Dominica to await orders. Another carrier group, the Independence, is on its way as well."

"That's a lot of firepower," Charlie said.

"Hell, once the word got out that we're going to pick a fight with a little island, everybody wanted in—the navy, the army, air force and us. It's a big cluster fuck with a lot of talk but precious little island knowledge."

The colonel reached for a pamphlet on a nearby desk and handed it to Charlie. He then said, "This is our reconnaissance—a tourist map. Oh, and we have a nautical chart based on a 1936 British reference chart, and it has no grid lines. We have no eyes on the ground, no topography maps and no idea what beaches we can land on and which ones are blocked by coral reefs."

Charlie grabbed the tourist map, glanced at it and passed it to Captain Jay, who snorted and handed it to Tommy, who then handed it to Arlan. Arlan smiled. All four of them knew more about Grenada than what was on the tourist map.

Charlie said, "This is all you have?"

"Yes, sir," the colonel said with a laugh. He then asked, "You plan to go in tonight?"

"We were planning to be there tonight, but…" Charlie glanced at the tourist map, "…I guess it wouldn't hurt to start our search in the daylight."

"Good. If you're all hell bound for glory to find your sailboat and the kidnapped woman you'll need to know a few things. We can help you with that. You can help us with intel. We'll set up some bunks for you and secure your boat until the morning. But I'm going to give you a warning," the colonel said. "If you don't find the people you're looking for by nightfall, you'd better hunker down the next morning for a while and let the dust settle."

The colonel moved them to another room that was just as busy as the one they were just in. In the center of the new room was a vertical glass panel about eight feet tall and five feet wide and accessible from both sides. A fairly detailed depiction of Grenada had been drawn on it, and cutouts of small boats, planes and flags grouped in varying colors were stuck to the glass with some kind of sticky substance. They were placed around the island as though they were ready to pounce. St. George's, on the southwest side of the island, was depicted with labels and arrows that pointed to Fort Rupert, the Government House, a prison, Grand Anse Beach just to the south of the city and a few other landmarks that Arlan wasn't familiar with. Most of the toy cutouts were bunched off the shore of St. George's. A flag with the name "Independence Group" stuck out from one of the toy ships.

The new runway being built at Point Salines was drawn on the map with an arrow pointing to the medical school campus at the east end of the runway. Other villages around the island had been noted, along with the old Pearls Airport and the village of Grenville on the northeast part of the island. Three battleships had been placed off the coast of Grenville, and a flag with the name "Guam Group" had been placed on the largest ship. Rows of marker-scribbled humps, depicting mountains, had been drawn on the glass in the center of the island, with no real relevance to their actual locations or elevations.

"This is what the island should look like about zero five hundred hours on Tuesday, about thirty-four hours from now. You see anything out of place?"

Charlie asked, "You planning a beach assault?"

"Up here at Pearls Airport and..." the colonel pointed to the south of St. George's, "...down here on Grand Anse Bay. My marines are going into Pearls Airport. The Rangers are going in down here at Point Salines. We've got SEALs and Delta doing some of the dirtier work like taking over the radio station for PSYOP people."

The colonel saw the confused looks and explained, "That's the psychological warfare part. They want to secure the airwaves to make sure they can send messages out that we're coming with good intentions and all that bull. We plan to bring in a battalion of Rangers first. They'll leave from Hunter Army Airfield in Florida during the night and land on the new airstrip at Pont Salines before dawn. It's protected by about seven hundred Cuban construction workers and a couple of hundred Grenadian troops. Our info is that they have Cuban-supplied anti-aircraft weapons and some mortars. Nothing big."

Charlie grunted and said, "I'm more worried about your amphibious assaults. There are significant reef formations off the coast in both locations. Depending on sea conditions you may not get to shore by boat. You should be ready for an assault by air. The weather around here hasn't been very cooperative lately. After all, it's still hurricane season."

"I'll recommend we send in a SEAL recon tomorrow night to check that out."

Charlie then said, "Be prepared for a fight with the Cubans. I'll guarantee you that those Cuban construction workers are all trained military."

Arlan looked around the room at the technical equipment that was unlike anything he'd ever seen. He smiled as he thought that, if there was some dramatic background music, he'd be convinced he was playing a part in a war drama.

The colonel paused while they were offered beverages by a very good-looking woman in a navy uniform. Captain Jay smiled when she approached him, followed by a whispered comment that Arlan couldn't hear. Arlan kicked Tommy's toe and nodded toward Jay.

Tommy smiled, leaned toward Arlan and said, "And I th-thought he was in a h-hurry to find Lisa."

"Right now he's in a hurry to get laid."

The colonel and Charlie continued their discussion with the colonel saying, "Once we've secured both airports we'll fan out to rescue the students at the True Blue Campus near Point Salines, then to St. George's to rescue the governor-general, Sir Paul Scoon and his family, then off to round up the bad guys—those that are left alive."

"Are there any friendly troops on the island?" Charlie asked.

"Not that we're aware of. This isn't a civil war. The police, a local militia, the People's Army and the Cubans all support what's called the Revolutionary Military Council. It's the men at the top who have been having a turf war. With Bishop dead and his main opponent, Deputy Prime Minister Bernard Coard, either gone or dead, a general in charge of the military, named Austin Hudson, seems to have come out on top."

"Where do the people of the island stand?"

"We don't know whose side they're on. I guess we'll find out soon enough."

Arlan, still trying to digest that they were in the middle of what was probably classified information said, "Excuse me... sir. But are we supposed to be listening to this? I mean, isn't this for military people only?"

The colonel smiled, put his hand on Charlie's shoulder and said, "Charlie's family. And he's got clearance. You wouldn't be with him if you weren't worth your weight in salt. So I have no problem sharing this info with all of you. Like I said, you'll likely be in this up to your ass, and you'll either help us with recon or you'll run. My guess is that none of you run from much anything."

Maybe not, but I can swim pretty fast, Arlan thought.

The colonel said, "I don't know if there still is a curfew, and I don't know how you plan to get around the island, but I'm going to leave some equipment on your boat so you can do some reconnoitering for us, if you don't mind."

Charlie said, "No problem. And we'll have no problem getting around the island—or the curfew. I have contacts."

"Again, I suggest you find what you're looking for tomorrow and get the hell out. But if you get stuck, contact Lieutenant Colonel Hagler with the Ranger's 75th Infantry. He'll be first in at Point Salines and will let you know when it's secure. His name is on one of the radios I left in your boat. My group will be up north securing Pearls Airport and the surrounding area. But I want you to keep in touch with me so I can relay info, especially tomorrow as you run around the island looking for the woman. Tell me what you see."

"Anything else you can say we should watch out for?" Charlie asked.

"Yes. The Grenada Police have three British-built patrol boats. My men on your boat tell me that you're equipped to see them before they see you. Stay clear of them. I don't think they have much firepower, but you have none—that I'm aware of."

Charlie smiled and said nothing.

The colonel nodded to the pretty officer who'd served them beverages, who'd been waiting nearby, and said, "Lieutenant, see these men to our guest quarters." He then looked around at his guests and said, "I assume you haven't changed your mind and will be staying on board tonight?"

Arlan looked at Captain Jay, who was swooning over the lieutenant. Charlie and Tommy noticed, and Charlie rolled his eyes. He said, "I guess we're staying."

"Good," the colonel said. "We have a commander on board. His name is Butler. He sailed recreationally around Grenada a few years ago and went to shore a few times. I'd like for him to meet us for dinner so we can further discuss the terrain we'll be up against." He picked up the tourist map and said, "We need something a lot better than what the government handed us."

The colonel turned to talk to another officer, then turned back to Charlie and asked, "By the way, are the Cubans sending weapons up to Dominica?"

"Yeah, but we've got a handle on that. And, if you do *your* job, it's unlikely that any more will make it up there," Charlie said. He then looked around the busy room and seemed to notice all of the activity for the first time. "Does this operation have a name yet?" he asked.

The colonel smiled and said, "It's called Operation Urgent Fury."

"Sounds appropriate," Arlan said under his breath.

Chapter 14

DAY 11: OCT 24

Boiled Bob woke up to the sound of an argument on the dock in broken Spanish and West Indian Creole. He took a moment to shake the sleep from his brain and remembered that, after having docked the *Pappy Bobo* in Prickly Bay the day before, Skandar had left. Boiled Bob approached Long Bill and told him to prepare to cast off. He'd planned to leave Skandar and Grenada behind. Long Bill had argued, and by the time Boiled Bob had decided to make the preparations himself, Skandar had returned in a military truck with a machine gun mounting and two Cubans wearing orange construction vests. Skandar had walked out to the boat and said that they would stay there overnight. Boiled Bob had started to argue, but Skandar's menacing stare stopped him.

The Cubans, Skandar and Long Bill had stayed onshore near the end of the dock talking for most of the night, and Boiled Bob had heard Long Bill and Skandar return to the boat after midnight and the Cubans drive away a few minutes later. He'd fallen asleep listening to Long Bill and Skandar talking and laughing topside. It seemed that Long Bill had found a new friend.

Fully awake, Boiled Bob climbed from his bunk and strained to make out the words of the argument that continued at the end of the dock. He decided to check on Lisa before going topside to see who was arguing about what. He stepped toward the forward berth and lightly knocked on the door.

"What, fucknuts?"

"How did you know it was me?" Bob asked through the door.

"I wasn't sure. But you just confirmed it by answering to your name, fucknuts."

Boiled Bob seethed. He wasn't sure he could go through with getting Lisa off the boat, even if it was for his own good. He sighed and said, "Listen. Skandar's got some Cuban military types watching over us. Or maybe they're holding us prisoners…"

"Welcome to the club, fucknuts," Lisa said.

"I think we need to get off the boat. Let's go up top and see how we can get you out of here."

The door opened, and Lisa pushed past Boiled Bob and made her way topside. Boiled Bob followed. Nobody was on the boat, but they could see Long Bill and Skandar on the end of the dock arguing with what looked like the same two Cubans he had seen the previous evening. The same military truck was parked nearby, this time with a machine gun mounted on it. What looked like a teenager wearing a uniform a few sizes too large, stood with one arm draped over the mounted machine gun. The two men Boiled Bob had seen the night before still wore orange construction vests but now had assault rifles hanging on their shoulders.

Long Bill looked up and saw Boiled Bob and Lisa. He walked toward the boat and said, "It looks like we may have to stay a while, Boss."

"I thought those guys were construction workers."

"I guess they are, Boss—until they aren't."

"Why is it that you think we have to stay?"

Long Bill smiled and said, "Skandar says that the Cuban's commander is preparing for a fight. I think they're going to let us fight with them. That's what Skandar's arguing with them about."

"Us?"

"Well, that's what you wanted, isn't it? To come to a new island and fight the war against oppression?"

"Jesus, LB? Have you gone nuts?" Boiled Bob turned to Lisa and said, "We need to get you out of here. I'll ask the guys talking to

Skandar if they can take you to a hotel."

"So, just like that, you're letting me go? What about my father's boat, jackass?"

"I thought my name was fucknuts," Boiled Bob said with a smile.

"That too. Along with dickless. They all fit."

Boiled Bob saw Long Bill smile.

"I need the boat. Your father has insurance. I told you I would let you go when we got to Grenada. We're here. It's time for you to leave." He then looked at Long Bill and said, "Get this boat ready to sail. We're leaving too."

Long Bill hesitated. Boiled Bob stepped off the boat and walked toward Skandar and the Cubans.

"Skandar, get the weapons onto the boat, we're leaving. And I want to know if these men can take Lisa into St. George's to a hotel."

The Cubans stared at Boiled Bob. One took the rifle off his shoulders and pointed it in Boiled Bob's general direction.

"Yo not goin to go anywhere, except wit us," Skandar said.

"There's an invasion coming any hour. I don't want to be here when the bombs fly. You shouldn't either."

"I taut you wanted to help I and I wit de revolution," Skandar said sarcastically.

"Things have changed. I didn't plan to fight the US Navy."

"Yo tall friend, LB. He wants to fight fo us."

"He's stupid."

"Don't matter. Yo and yo beef will be comin wit us. Once de American are gone we gonna take de weapons back to my country. I can't be havin yo sail away while we wait fo Babylon to go away."

"Fuck your Rasta-speak bullshit. I'm leaving."

The Cubans pointed their rifles at Bob.

Skandar shouted to Long Bill, "Tall mon, get de beef and come wit us!"

Boiled Bob looked back toward Lisa and shrugged.

Long Bill led Lisa to the truck and helped her into the back. Bob climbed in, followed by Long Bill and Skandar. The two Cubans wearing orange construction vests got into the cab. The truck drove up over a ridge and down the other side to a warehouse near the east end of the new airstrip, no more than a half mile from the *Pappy Bobo*. Lisa glared at Boiled Bob the entire way. Boiled Bob looked at the bed of the truck. He had nothing to say to her. She had it right... they were both hostages now.

* * *

Captain Jay was late for the transfer back to Charlie's boat. When he did show up he was red-faced and uncharacteristically sheepish.

"I-is that a h-hickey?" Tommy asked, nodding to Captain Jay's neck.

Captain Jay looked around and flashed his Elvis grin.

"Who th-the hell gets a h-hicky anymore?"

"He does," Charlie said. "That's his Purple Heart. Let's get going."

As the group gathered on the destroyer's stern and prepared to leave the USS *Trenton* on a small tender, the colonel arrived and said, "Late last night I put the word out throughout the two fleets to look out for your stolen boat. It turns out that a navy destroyer stopped a yawl named *Pappy Bobo* and had a conversation with its captain," the colonel told them.

"When?" Charlie asked.

"Just before sunrise yesterday. The boat's captain told them that they were heading back to their home port, Trinidad."

"That's bullshit," Captain Jay said.

The colonel smiled and then told them that the sailboat wasn't boarded, and there was no way to tell who might have been below deck, but two tall men were topside with the captain, one red-headed white man and the other black with long dreadlocks."

"Sounds like Long Bill," Arlan said. "Wonder who the Dread is."

"Who knows? Let's get to Grenada," Captain Jay said.

Nobody argued.

The colonel wished them luck and left for the bridge. Two hours later, Charlie and his crew tied the trawler to a dock in Grand Mal Bay, a couple of miles north of St. George's.

"What are we doin' here?" Captain Jay asked.

"We're picking up a friend," Charlie said, offering no more.

Arlan looked around the stereotypical island village. There were dozens of wooden shacks with unpainted corrugated metal roofs. The wood siding on the majority of the shacks, once painted with bright colors, had faded over time, giving parts of the village the look of pastel Caribbean landscapes. Mixed with the faded wooden shacks were newer block and concrete constructed homes in various stages of completion, their yards littered with rusted rebar, plywood and old concrete blocks. Grass and weeds grew up around the unused construction materials. Chickens strutted throughout the village. Nervous, skinny dogs gathered around the two dumpsters visible from the beach. One chased a mongoose into an old, round metal downspout and waited for it to come out—something it would regret if it was there when the mongoose decided to exit the downspout. A few rusted vehicles were strewn around the village on sandy roads. Children played soccer in an open field in the middle of the village. Four weathered old men, wearing long pants and dirty, white tank tops played dominoes near the open field. They drank Vitamalt, a ubiquitous syrupy-sweet beverage Arlan saw on every island he'd visited. He had tried it once, and that was enough. A heavyset woman lazily hung clothes on a line strung across her porch, taking a minute or more to hang each article of clothing. Nowhere was the urgency of a pending invasion or the worry of an island in the midst of political upheaval. Arlan took it all in and smiled.

A few minutes later a van drove up to the dock, and a tall West Indian man dressed in sharply creased pants and a white, collared, short-sleeve shirt got out of the van and walked down the dock toward the trawler. He furtively looked in every direction, like a man used to a covert lifestyle. The morning sun made the white shirt somewhat translucent, and Arlan could clearly see a large-caliber handgun tucked into the man's waistband. When the man was closer he smiled and nodded to Charlie, who nodded back and said, "Welcome aboard, Desmond."

"Tanks, mon," Desmond said and stepped onto the boat with a broad smile and a handshake for everybody as he introduced himself.

"What do we know?" Charlie asked Desmond.

"De curfew is lifted. But dat wouldn't have boddered us anyway. I know most of de soldiers. We can go wherever we need to go."

"What about the Cubans?"

"Dey could be a problem. Dey won't let us near the new airport or der camp at Calivigny, a few bays to de east of de airport."

"The US military will take care of that soon enough," Charlie said.

"Can't be too soon, mon. De people hate dem."

"The locals support an invasion?"

"Fo true."

Charlie pulled out the photo of Boiled Bob and handed it to Desmond. He said, "We're looking for the one in the middle. He's probably with the tall one. His name is Boiled Bob. The tall one goes by the name Long Bill."

"What about de short mon. He's got cold eyes. Looks like a killer."

"Not anymore," Charlie said with a grin and glanced toward Tommy.

Desmond started to comment but stopped, giving Tommy a long look. He then studied the photo for several seconds and frowned. He said, "Dis mon, Boil Bob. He looks mighty familiar." Desmond cocked his head and said, "I cannot place it, but I've seen dis mon."

"Lately?" Captain Jay asked.

"No. Sometime in de past."

Charlie shrugged, described the *Happy Hobo* and told Desmond of its changes and new name. Desmond continued to study the photo. Giving up, he shrugged and shook his head. He handed the photo back to Charlie.

Charlie waved him off and said, "You keep the photo." He then said, "We need to do a visual of all the bays that are deep and calm enough for sailboats to anchor. Will the patrol boats be a problem?"

"Dey are all in de port in St. George's. I tink de police are afraid to go out to sea."

"All right. Let's get moving. Desmond, take this radio and one of my guys. Show the photo around to your contacts. The rest of us will look for the *Happy Hobo* by boat. It won't be on the north or the east side of the island. The seas are too rough. It won't take us more than a few hours to check St. George's and the bays on the southern side of the island. We'll rendezvous at noon."

Arlan was sure Captain Jay shouldn't go with Desmond. He would be too unpredictable if they found Boiled Bob. Tommy would probably be the best choice.

Charlie interrupted Arlan's thoughts with, "Arlan, you're going with Desmond."

Arlan was about to ask why when Charlie added, "You'll keep your wits about you if you run into trouble. These two brutes…" Charlie said, nodding toward Tommy and Captain Jay, "…will probably get themselves shot."

Captain Jay and Tommy shrugged in agreement.

Arlan left with Desmond for a three-hour tour of the southwest and most populated part of the island. They stopped at many places during their drive through St. George's to ask about the *Happy Hobo* and the men in the photo. Nobody knew about the boat. A few frowned and had the same reaction Desmond had had when looking at Boiled Bob. All, after a moment, shrugged with resignation.

One local said, "I doan know. All dem white young men look deh same." He then looked to Arlan and said, "Sorry, mon."

Arlan laughed it off, wondering how Captain Jay would have responded had he been there. He'd probably tell one of his off-color racial jokes—one that he could get away with on St. John.

After three hours searching around St. George's and the neighboring bays, Arlan said, "This is like looking for a needle in a haystack. Boiled Bob could be anywhere."

"I tink it tis time to call Charlie to report."

Desmond used the radio to call Charlie, and Arlan could tell from Desmond's side of the conversation that Charlie and his group had seen no sign of the *Happy Hobo*. Charlie wanted to do some reconnaissance for the US Marines on land, where they could continue their search. Arlan imagined he'd taken dozens of photos while searching for Boiled Bob by boat. At the end of the conversation, Desmond suggested that

Charlie pull his boat into Prickly Bay and tie it to a bulkhead deep in the bay near a boatyard owned by his cousin.

Fifteen minutes later, Desmond and Arlan arrived at the boatyard in the back of Prickly Bay. Arlan looked out into the bay and saw Charlie's boat approaching the dock at a couple of knots. Arlan watched the boat navigate through several anchored boats and turned his attention to a dock attached to the west side of the bay, extending east about three hundred feet and jutting a third of the way across the back of the bay. He focused on an ugly green and white yawl with a beige sail cover.

Arlan pointed to the dock and asked Desmond, "Can I get to that dock from here?"

Desmond looked to the dock, then pointed to a short fence that ran around the boatyard and said, "Jus climb dat fence over der and walk around de bush. You'll be der in five minutes."

A few scratches and many mosquito bites later, Arlan walked onto the dock. The sailboat's stern pointed toward him, but a smaller vessel blocked his view of its moniker. He passed the smaller boat and saw the name, *Pappy Bobo*, sloppily painted on the stern of the green and white sailboat. Arlan glanced toward the bay and saw Charlie's boat a hundred feet away heading toward the boatyard. He was undecided if he should shout for them to turn to port and tie off at the dock where he stood. Two dinghies were tethered to the boat, but that didn't necessarily mean anybody was onboard. He walked to the boat and listened for a minute, hearing nothing from inside. He then leaned over and knocked on the wood deck. Nobody came topside. Arlan shrugged and whistled toward Charlie's boat. Tommy and Captain Jay were already on deck with bow and stern lines, ready to tie the boat off at the boatyard's bulkhead.

Tommy knew Arlan's whistle from the countless times he had called his dog back to the Gallows Point office after giving chase to birds, lizards, brave dogs that stupidly trespassed onto her turf and goats—except the billy goat. She never attacked the billy.

Tommy looked over to the dock they'd just passed and to where Arlan stood. Tommy's head cocked to one side, and he squinted. Two seconds later, Arlan heard Tommy shout to Charlie to change course.

Arlan waited for Charlie's boat to nudge the dock. Captain Jay tossed him the bow line and jumped onto the dock. Tommy waited for Charlie to reverse the engines and bring the stern close enough to the dock so he could make the jump and tie his line off. Arlan had to tie his end of the boat off and could only watch as Captain Jay stormed onto the *Happy Hobo*. By the time Arlan, Tommy and Charlie made it to the sailboat, Captain Jay had gone below deck and returned topside with an exasperated expression.

"Nobody's home," Captain Jay said.

Charlie shouted to Desmond, who was still standing on the boatyard's bulkhead a hundred yards away, and motioned him to come to the dock.

Desmond climbed the fence and took the same route Arlan had taken.

He walked out onto the dock and said, "Dis is de boat?"

All heads shook in the affirmative.

"Tis an ugly boat. Maybe once it was a beautiful boat?"

Charlie said, "Get a couple of your men to watch this boat. They're not to let the boat leave this dock. If Boiled Bob or the tall man comes back, your men are to hold them here. If Lisa is with them, they're to take her and explain the situation. Let her stay wherever she wants until we return, but make sure she's comfortable."

"Understood," Desmond said.

The group spent fifteen minutes going through the boat, looking for anything that might give them a clue as to where Boiled Bob and Lisa were. They confiscated two small handguns but found nothing unusual, other than a pair of handcuffs that hung from a wooden rail above the bunk in the forward berth and a couple of mostly empty rolls of duct tape on the bunk. Captain Jay's face flushed, and Arlan was sure he'd kill anybody who said anything at that moment. He didn't say a word. Nobody did.

"Let's just get the son-of-a-bitch," Captain Jay said as he climbed back to the deck and stepped onto the dock.

Charlie asked Desmond, "How long before you can get some men here?"

"I will go to come back. Tirty minutes."

"Okay. We'll wait."

Desmond retraced his steps back to the boatyard. Charlie stepped back onto the boat.

"What are you lookin' for?" Captain Jay asked.

"We're going to disable the boat. I'll take care of the engine. You guys take the winch handles and as much rigging as you can without cutting the lines. They'll be needed when the boat's sailed back to St. John."

Forty-five minutes later Desmond pulled his van into a parking lot near the dock. A small, foreign-made boxy car followed and parked next to Desmond's van. Two large West Indians climbed out, causing the car to rise a half foot.

"I th-think they'll d-do," Tommy said with a grin.

"Let's drive around the area and see what we can find out," Charlie said.

They climbed into Desmond's van and left the two big locals to watch the *Happy Hobo*.

"I want to get closer to the new airport," Charlie said as soon as they left the parking lot.

"Okay, mon. We can go as close as de Cubans let us go."

Arlan saw Charlie pull a miniature camera from his shirt pocket and start to take photos. The camera was small—too small to be a commercial model. It was the size of a cigarette lighter and looked like something from a James Bond movie.

Desmond drove north to a busier road and turned west for a few hundred yards. He then turned south, completing three sides of a rectangle. They could see the east end of the airstrip and some warehouses from their elevation. They also saw a roadblock set up by armed Cubans a couple of hundred yards farther down the road, preventing access to the airstrip. Desmond stopped, letting Charlie out to take photos with his miniature camera.

"I can't see the other side of the landing strip. I'm going for a walk up that hill. Turn the van around and wait for us."

Who's us? Arlan wondered.

"Arlan, you're coming with me."

Arlan gave Charlie a confused look, and Charlie said, "You're more nimble than these two brutes. I'll need you to go up a tree to get photos of the entire airstrip."

"Oh," Arlan said and turned to look at Tommy and Captain Jay, who both smiled.

Captain Jay said, "Don't fall, Rookie."

Arlan and Charlie walked through thick, thorny brush and came to a large genip tree near the crest of the hill. Grenadians called the large fruit-bearing tree a *skinup* tree. It was easily forty feet tall and had many branches and handholds, making it an easy climb. Arlan only wished the tree was full of the clusters of sweet, grape-sized pulpy fruit with thin, leathery skin it was famous for. But they'd ripened in mid-summer and were long gone.

"What's happening down there?" Charlie shouted up to Arlan.

"There's a lot of military people and vehicles moving in and around construction workers and bulldozers. Looks like an ant colony," Arlan shouted back.

"Are they parking equipment on the paved runway?"

"Yeah. They don't have snipers down there, do they?"

"An invasion will come from the sea. They'll be pointed that way, not up here."

Pointing out the obvious didn't make Arlan feel any less exposed.

Charlie shouted, "Take pictures from east to west and come on back down." As an afterthought Charlie shouted, "Take a shot of the warehouses below us too."

If the camera had a zoom lens, Arlan would have seen Boiled Bob, Long Bill, Lisa and a few Cubans standing in a fenced area connected to one of the warehouses two hundred yards below the tree. He saw people but, at that distance they were the size of bugs. Had he looked up the next hill to the north he'd have seen anti-aircraft guns being set into place, pointing to the airspace above the new runway.

Arlan and Charlie walked back to the van, and the group spent the rest of the day looking for Boiled Bob and Lisa, with Charlie taking every opportunity to take pictures of everything he thought important.

Desmond drove them to every restaurant, bar and boat provisioning store he could think of. He also showed scores of locals the photo of Boiled Bob. Most shook their heads with no recognition. Some frowned and said that he looked familiar. One woman said, "I know dis mon. He was in de newspaper a few years ago. I tink."

"Tanks," Desmond said and drove on.

"A lot of people seem to recognize Boiled Bob but not Long Bill. Those two are inseparable. You'd think that, if they spent a lot of time here, Long Bill would be the more memorable," Arlan said.

"I don't think Boiled Bob has spent a lot of time on Grenada. I know he takes boats down island, but he and his group of turds are always on St. John. The locals must be mistakin' him with some other skinny white boy with a beard. We all look alike, don't we?" Captain Jay said and slapped Desmond's shoulder.

Desmond hesitated and then let out a loud laugh. "All you white guys look de same," he said. "Smell de same too."

Captain Jay feigned smelling his armpits and said, "Not me. I'm beige."

Desmond laughed louder.

Charlie said, "It's almost dark. Let's get back to the boat. We can send Desmond's men home and watch the *Happy Hobo* ourselves."

Charlie used one of the radios to contact the colonel on the USS *Trenton* to tell him what they'd seen at Point Salines.

Charlie said, "You may have a tough time landing. They're parking all kinds of equipment on the runway." After a thirty-second pause Charlie said, "I hope you'll be jumping in the dark. They'll be gunning for your troopers as soon as they leave the plane."

After a few more seconds of truncated dialogue Charlie signed off.

"What is the plan for tomorrow?" Arlan asked.

Charlie smiled and said, "We wait—and duck."

Chapter 15

Day 12: October 25 (Morning)

BOOM! Boom! Rat-tat-tat –tat! Boom! Rat-tat-tat!

"What the fuck?" Arlan shouted.

He bolted upright in the bunk he'd slept on, looked through the porthole and saw that the sky was dark, with just a hint of daylight in the east. He heard Charlie stomping around on deck giving orders to Desmond. Tommy and Captain Jay had stayed the night on the other side of the dock on the *Happy Hobo*. Captain Jay was there to jump Boiled Bob if he returned, Tommy to jump Captain Jay if his anger got out of control while jumping Boiled Bob.

Within a minute all were on the dock watching the sky above the Point Salines airstrip, over the hill to the west. Even in the dark grey sky they could see the black puffs of anti-aircraft ordnance exploding several hundred feet above the runway. Mixed with the booms of the anti-aircraft fire was intermittent automatic gunfire from AK-47s, which were useless against an onslaught of US aircraft but could pick off paratroopers as they jumped.

BOOM! Rat-tat-tat-tat! BOOM!

Arlan strained to see the planes they could hear coming in from the west.

"We've got to get closer," Charlie said.

"Why?" Arlan asked.

Charlie ignored him.

"Desmond, is there anything between us and the other side of that hill?" Charlie asked and pointed west.

"Just a couple of homes and bush. From de top yo can see de airport."

"Stay here to watch for Boiled Bob. Whoever wants to come with me, let's go."

Charlie walked toward the hill. Tommy and Captain Jay followed. Arlan looked at Desmond, who shrugged and said, "You go ahead. I'll watch fo Boil Bob."

Arlan nodded and followed the others up the hill.

The sky had lightened by the time they arrived at the top of the hill and found a clearing that allowed them to see the airstrip. The east end of the runway was below them and about eight hundred feet away. The far end of the runway seemed to Arlan to be a couple of miles away. To their right, several hundred yards away, they could see a bank of three or four anti-aircraft guns firing into the sky above the runway. The runway had scores of bulldozers, trucks and other vehicles parked randomly along its entire length. Below them, near the warehouses Arlan had taken photos of the day before, soldiers fired rifles into the sky above the western end of the runway.

Charlie punched his handheld radio and made contact with the colonel. After listening for two minutes Charlie said, "John, I know you're busy with your own invasion up north, but can you relay my report to the USS *Guam*?" He paused and then said, "I know we don't have maps with grid lines or coordinates, but you need to strafe the hillside to the north of the east end of the runway. That's where the anti-aircraft guns are. You should send in your Cobras before you drop paratroopers. They'll be sitting ducks if you don't."

Thirty seconds later Charlie signed off.

Arlan heard distant bombing that must have been closer to or in St. George's, three miles to the north.

"Wh-what's going on?" Tommy asked Charlie.

"The colonel spread the news of what we saw yesterday but, with so damn many chiefs involved with this fiasco, they sent Army Special Forces and the Navy SEALs in for a look see. The seas were too rough, and some of the men died in the water. Rangers were sent from Florida on transport planes at three this morning, expecting to touch down on that runway before dawn."

"T-that's not going to h-happen."

The sky lightening, they watched as two helicopter gunships engaged with the anti-aircraft guns to their north. They also saw the first transport carrier fly in from the sea at about five hundred feet elevation, dropping dozens of paratroopers, who fell out of the plane in a constant rhythm. Their chutes opened seconds before impact and they were immediately fired on from the warehouse area and the hills above them to the north. Arlan noticed muzzle flashes coming from the beach on the south side of the runway, closer to the western tip.

Charlie clicked his mike and said into it, "The warehouses at the east end of the runway. Small arms fire aiming at the paratroopers. Looks like more is coming from the beach to the south."

Charlie listened for a while and signed off. Nothing happened until two more transport planes dropped their paratroopers. Finally, two fixed, upper-winged planes with four engines came in low from the west. One flew directly at the warehouses; the other peeled off and flew at the beach. Both showered their targets with a hailstorm of lead.

The noise was deafening, and the concussions of bombs caused Arlan to pinch his nose and blow out, just as he would do while descending on a dive. He saw the others do the same.

"I'd hate to be where those beaners are about now," Captain Jay said.

"Th-things are pretty r-rough down there. Wh-what's going on with the r-rest of the invasion?" Tommy asked Charlie.

"John's up on the northeast side of the island securing Pearls Airport. He says they don't have much resistance up there. All he can do is relay what I tell him to the Guam group…" He pointed out to sea to the northwest. "Somewhere out there. The dickheads in the army didn't believe our report of vehicles and debris on the runway. Instead of landing at night, like they'd planned, the Rangers had to fly in a holding pattern and get everybody geared up to jump. That's why they jumped in daylight. The first pilot saw where the anti-aircraft guns were and reported them about the same time we did."

"Might have saved them some headache if they'd listened to you and the colonel," Arlan said.

Charlie shrugged and said, "It's the military. Lots of ego involved as you get higher up. Everybody wants to be the hero."

Most of the paratroopers had landed and were grouped on the west side of the runway, fanning out on either side, moving east. The lead units took out resistance while other units started to move vehicles from the airstrip. Those that were disabled and wouldn't start were pushed to the side. Arlan saw some of the Cuban bulldozers come to life and move down the runway, operated by American troops. They pushed parked vehicles out of the way and used the big steel dozer blades to protect troops that gathered behind them from small arms fire still coming from the east end of the runway.

Within an hour all of the resistance on the beach died down, and most of the runway was cleared. An hour later several hundred Rangers had pushed the Cubans back to the warehouses. A hundred or more surrendered. Arlan saw scores of Cubans and local militia run up the hill to the north trying to escape. It was just after nine in the morning. The stiff resistance for Point Salines had lasted about two hours.

Charlie said, "Let's go."

They walked back down the hill to the dock where they found Desmond talking to the two men who'd watched the boats the day before.

Desmond said, "I aks dese men to come back to watch de boats so I can take you round de island to look fo Boil Bob. I know which roads we can take to stay out of de way of de Grenadian military and de Cubans. De phones still work*in*, and I've been in contact wit my friends around de island all morn*in*."

"Okay. First, take us back to the airport," Charlie said. He then used the radio to contact Lieutenant Colonel Hagler, who was in charge of the Rangers who had just secured Point Salines.

* * *

BOOM! Boom! Rat-tat-tat!

Boiled Bob was jolted out of his cot when the first anti-aircraft shells exploded. He stood and then ducked when the sound of very close AK-47s started firing. He looked over at Lisa, who'd slid off her cot and was huddled in a corner of the small room. Long Bill and Skandar were gone. The room they'd slept in had two doors, one that led to the warehouse interior and another that led to a fenced warehouse yard full of beat-up construction and military equipment, some with Russian labels in large block letters painted on the sides. Others had Spanish labels painted on them. Boiled Bob made his way to the door that led to the warehouse yard and opened it. It was dark with the sky just beginning to lighten. He could see nothing from that side of the building.

Rat-tat-tat-tat-tat! BOOM!

"What the hell is going on?" Lisa shouted.

"Don't know. Sounds like a war out there."

Boiled Bob closed the door and felt his way to the door that led into the warehouse area. He cracked it open to see if the guard that had been stationed there the previous night was still at his post. The room was dark, the only light coming from one dim overhead light that allowed Boiled Bob to see that there was nobody in the warehouse.

The sky brightened a little, and Boiled Bob turned toward Lisa. He said, "Don't worry. I'll get you out of here."

He heard Lisa snicker and say, "Right."

BOOM! BOOM!

"We're definitely in a war zone," Boiled Bob said.

Lisa said, "I hope you're the first casualty, asshole."

Rat-tat-tat! BOOM!

"Thanks for bringing me to a first-row seat of a war," Lisa said. A moment later she added, "Along with stealing my father's boat and holding me hostage. Do you have any more fuckups in mind today?"

Bob said, "You're pretty mouthy for someone who's stuck in this warehouse, surrounded by Cubans and *me*."

"You're the least of my worries."

Boiled Bob fumed but had no intention of wasting time arguing with Lisa. He wanted to find Long Bill, get back to the boat and sail the hell away from this crazy place. He walked to the door that led into the warehouse and opened it. The sound of gunfire was louder and more frequent. Distant shells erupted every few seconds, shaking the metal building and causing Boiled Bob to duck. He half-crawled to an exterior door and looked out. The eastern end of the runway was a hundred yards away. Between Boiled Bob and the runway were a couple of hundred armed Cubans. Many were in sandbag defense bunkers, some manned machine guns and most were running from other warehouses to take up defensive positions nearby.

The sky had brightened a little more, and Boiled Bob could see a large plane fly in from the west, dropping things from the rear of the plane. As the things fell close to the ground, parachutes opened. The things were paratroopers. Within seconds Boiled Bob saw muzzle flashes and heard bullets hit the warehouse. The Cubans fired back. The cacophony of the sounds of war was deafening. Boiled Bob retreated into the warehouse just as the first shell hit near the doorway where he'd been standing. He hit the floor as pieces of the building were ripped apart. Within moments he heard and felt several more shells explode throughout the Cuban defenses. Boiled Bob ran to the small room where he'd left Lisa. She was gone. The door to the yard was open, and Boiled Bob could see through the doorway that half the yard and the surrounding fence had been obliterated. He took a last look to the front of the building and wondered if he should try to find Long Bill. *Fuck him*, he thought as he ran through the destroyed warehouse yard, up the hill and toward the dock in the bay that he knew was on the other side.

Boiled Bob made it about fifty yards up the hill when he spotted the first group of armed Cubans behind him. He ducked under some brush. They passed him going the same direction—up the hill and away from the action. He didn't know if they were looking for other Cubans trying to flee the battlefield or if they were fleeing themselves. He was about to crawl out of the bush and continue uphill when a trio of Cubans, stragglers from the first group, hiked up the hill. After they passed, Boiled Bob rose and cautiously climbed the hill, ducking for cover every time he heard voices.

It took Boiled Bob hours to sneak to the top of the hill and start the easy climb down to the dock.

* * *

Arlan sat in the back of the van as Desmond retraced his route from the day before when he had driven Charlie to get a closer look at the Point Salines runway. Sporadic gunfire echoed through the hillsides behind them. The Caribbean's blue sky was filled with white, billowing clouds and whispery-black smoke from exploded ordnance. Heat inside the van, combined with the acrid smell of exploded ordnance was nauseating, and Arlan was glad that the ride was short. The Cuban-manned roadblocks he saw the previous day were now manned by American soldiers. Charlie used the radio the colonel had given him to contact the lieutenant colonel in charge of the Rangers who'd taken the airport and told him that they'd be arriving in a white van. After a brief discussion amongst themselves on one of their radios, the soldiers manning the roadblock told them where to find the lieutenant colonel and let them pass. The van zigzagged along the side of the runway, which was cluttered with construction debris, overturned vehicles and equipment that had been shoved off the runway by American soldiers on Cuban bulldozers.

A huge Hercules transport plane touched down on the cleared runway, and two others landed in the time it took Desmond to zigzag another hundred yards. A Hercules transport plane that had landed earlier was already offloading Jeeps, trucks, motorcycles and hundreds of boxes that were being moved by a dozen olive-colored forklifts.

Arlan looked back down to survey the scene they'd just driven through. It was busy. He then looked farther to the west and saw tents being erected near the edge of the runway. Coils of concertina wire had been hastily stretched out in a large rectangular shape. In it were a hundred Cuban and Grenadian prisoners. Dozens more prisoners were being led from the east in groups of two or three by armed soldiers. All were handcuffed with plastic ties, and belts or clothing had been used to wrap the prisoners' upper torsos just below their shoulders.

A hundred yards farther down the runway Desmond parked the van near the temporary command post for the 75th Ranger Regiment, where the group was welcomed by the commanding officer, who introduced himself as Lieutenant Colonel Hegel. Charlie introduced himself and the others.

"Sorry I can't roll out the red carpet, but we're kind of busy," Lieutenant Colonel Hegel said, with a smile. "Sounds like you've been busy as well. John called me last night and told me to expect your radio call. He also told me a little of what you've done for us in the last day or so. We appreciate it."

"Too bad you had to jump in the daylight," Charlie said.

"Yeah. Well, as John probably told you, this operation has more ego at the top than brains. I wouldn't be surprised if there are more medals passed out after this is over than the number of participants."

A bullet hit the top of the tent post behind them a full second before the sound of the sniper fire could be heard. Arlan ducked. Nobody else did.

Captain Jay leaned toward Arlan, smiled and said, "Too late. Once you've heard it the bullet's long gone, or in your brain. You'd have been dead and wouldn't have known it."

Arlan looked at Captain Jay and said, "Thanks for that info. I'll keep that in mind next time I go with you on one of your adventures where there are snipers."

"Did John secure Pearls?" Charlie asked the lieutenant colonel.

"Took him about two hours. No casualties. Wish I could say the same here."

Arlan glanced down the runway toward the concertina wire and the prisoners. Two very tall prisoners were being led to the temporary prison by two much shorter soldiers. Both prisoners were handcuffed and secured around their torsos. One was a wide black man with dreadlocks. The other, only an inch or so taller but much thinner, was a white man with red hair and a large nose.

Arlan squinted and asked, "Isn't that Long Bill?"

Everybody turned and looked to where Arlan pointed and smiled, except the lieutenant colonel, who looked confused.

Charlie said, "We know that man. He's one of the guys we've been chasing for a couple of weeks."

The lieutenant colonel nodded and asked, "Is he American?"

Charlie nodded.

"Then he could be in deep shit. Firing on US troops is treason."

"Do you mind if we talk to him?"

"No. But you better get all of the information you can from him now because he'll be going away for a long time," the lieutenant colonel said and shouted for the men leading the prisoner to hold up.

Long Bill had a look of surprise when he saw the men from St. John approach. He then smiled and asked, "What are you guys doing here?"

"Are you really asking that?" Tommy said, then stepped close to Long Bill and punched him.

Skandar took a step back. Long Bill went down holding his nose. Blood ran between his fingers. One of the soldiers escorting the two tall prisoners stepped forward with his weapon ready, but the lieutenant colonel shouted for him to stand down.

For the next few minutes Long Bill told everything he knew up until he was captured. He had no idea where Boiled Bob and Lisa were, only that they'd been in one of the warehouses at the east end of the runway in the construction camp before it was destroyed.

The lieutenant colonel, who'd stepped closer to the group, said, "We've pretty much cleared that area. The bodies we've found are Cuban, so far. No females. We've not been able to move the debris for any bodies underneath yet. But we'll be getting to that next, if you want to wait around."

Another sniper shot resounded through the command post, causing a few to duck, including Arlan. Captain Jay snorted and said to Arlan, "Too late again, Rookie."

"Why don't you get yourselves some grub while we sort this out," the lieutenant colonel said. "We've got rations and coffee in the back of my tent."

Charlie looked at the others, who all shrugged. What else could they do? Charlie told Desmond to drive back to the dock to check and see if Bob and Lisa had somehow stumbled back to the boat. They then spread out on boxes under the tent and drank bad coffee and ate mush from tins.

An hour later, after a few more sniper rounds and multiple landings and take-offs of large transport planes, the airfield started to look like a circus that had come to town. People milled everywhere. More prisoners were rounded up and placed inside the concertina wire. Bombing was heard in the distance, and smoke rose from over the mountain to the north. Arlan thought once again of a Hollywood set. If it wasn't for the acrid smell of the smoke that hung in the air, mixed with jet fuel from the busy airstrip and sweat that permeated the air close by, he would have thought he was having a dream.

The lieutenant colonel rejoined the group and said, "We haven't cleared all of the debris from the warehouses yet. It's slow going because we have to check for explosives as we go. We've got the students from the True Blue Campus. They'll be flown back to the US on our transports."

"Any resistance?" Charlie asked.

"Minimal. Strange thing is that there were only a couple of hundred students. We were told there were six hundred American students at the medical school."

Charlie looked surprised and said, "There are. But there are a couple of campuses on the island."

"What?" the lieutenant colonel said and immediately called for his radio.

"There's another campus just south of St. George's at Anse Bay," Charlie said. "We found out yesterday. I have pictures of it on this camera." He pulled the miniature camera from his shirt pocket.

The lieutenant colonel alerted his commander on the USS *Guam* about the second campus, and all hell broke loose. The lieutenant colonel, his radio up to his ear, straightened his back as if coming to attention. Arlan heard more "Yes, sirs" and "No, sirs" during the next five minutes than he'd heard in the past five years.

"If you don't mind, I'll take your camera and get it out to the *Guam* by chopper. We'll have the photos in a couple of hours."

Charlie handed him the camera and said, "There's a lot more on there besides the other campus. Some of it should be useful as you move inland."

172

The next thirty minutes were spent listening to the lieutenant colonel make and field radio calls to the command ship and to some Special Forces that had already infiltrated the St. George's area. He then walked to an adjacent tent.

"The 82nd Airborne has arrived," Charlie said, pointing down the airstrip at a second command post being set up nearby.

"I-its getting crowded a-around here," Tommy said with a smile.

Arlan could tell the others were getting antsy. Sitting and waiting was not something they did well.

Captain Jay stood, puffed out his chest and said, "Fuck this. This isn't a war. It's a brawl. David and Goliath bullshit. Let's find fuckin' Boiled Bob." He looked for support. He received frowns. "And Lisa," he added.

The lieutenant colonel returned to tell them that no other bodies had been recovered from the construction camp. "The people you're looking for are not among the dead, and we've not seen anybody alive or wounded that meets their descriptions."

He waited a moment and said, "I have a crazy lead for you, though." He sighed and said, "It seems we bombed a mental hospital by mistake in St. George's."

"Bad shit happens in war. What's that have to do with us?" Charlie asked.

"Well, you know that photo you gave to John and he passed along to some of us? The photo of the man you're looking for?"

They all shrugged as if to say *So?*

"It seems that he's in St. George's."

"No way," Captain Jay said.

"We're a little busy up there. Your man is not one of our priorities. Hell, he wouldn't even be on the radar if not for John. The people we have up there are Special Forces. They don't make mistakes. They're sure it's him."

The lieutenant colonel paused and said, "It turns out we're going that way. You want to come along?"

The mood instantly brightened, and everybody stood and followed the lieutenant colonel.

The lieutenant colonel turned and smiled at the men following him. He said, "You'll see things that aren't in the tourist brochures."

Charlie and Tommy smiled. Captain Jay licked his lips like a lion ready to pounce. Arlan tried to think of an excuse not to be flown by chopper into a war zone.

Lieutenant Colonel Hegel paused long enough to tell an assistant to make room for four more passengers and then said, "Let's go. I'll fill you in on the way."

Charlie tried to radio Desmond but couldn't get a response. He looked at the radio and frowned.

When Lieutenant Colonel Hegel saw Charlie's frustration, he said, "We started to have radio communication problems earlier this morning. Hell, some of the new troops aren't even using the right frequency. That's an organizational problem. But something's going on in the atmosphere because my radio works only about half the time. I'm surprised you were able to reach me. Are you trying to reach the man who brought you here?"

"Yes. I need to tell him we're heading north."

"I'll leave word here with my assistant to look out for him if he returns. He'll fill the man in."

They walked across the airstrip, which was bordering on chaos. Helicopters were landing and taking off like insects. The noise was deafening. Arlan saw a line of people his age, most dressed in shorts and flip-flops, being loaded onto a transport plane. The lieutenant colonel pointed out that they were the American medical students from the True Blue Campus being airlifted to the US.

The lieutenant colonel led them to a helicopter that could easily seat ten people. The pilot and co-pilot saluted from their seats in the cockpit, and a crew member handed the lieutenant colonel and his guests headphones as they sat on hard benches in the cabin. The headphones were all attached to a small box screwed to the roof of the cabin, creating a mess of spring-coiled communication lines that hung from the ceiling to each man's head. The lieutenant colonel nodded to the pilot once everybody was seated, and the helicopter's rotors began spinning. Arlan was glad to have the headphones. As the rotation of the rotors increased, so did the noise.

Arlan looked down to the commotion on the runway as the chopper ascended. The scene wasn't what he'd pictured in his mind as a war zone. He'd only known what the movies had depicted—organized troops either lined up or marching in cadence with solidarity of uniforms and equipment and a somber mood that enveloped the immediate area. What he saw was troops in multiple styles of uniform mixed with locals dressed in bright colors and sandals, who, out of curiosity, had managed to skirt the US military roadblocks and come to the airport as spectators. Prisoners wore a mix of construction vests and camouflage shirts, and feral dogs darted from tent to tent in search of food scraps.

When the helicopter reached a higher altitude and the runway below him was temporarily out of his sight, Arlan looked to the south and saw a beach with medium-sized blue waves rhythmically collapsing on the white sand. He then looked north to the lush, steep mountains. Leaves of jungle trees reflected the bright sunshine. Only the black and grey smoke from exploded ordnance marred the tropical scene.

Chapter 16

Day 12: Oct. 25 (Afternoon)

Boiled Bob cautiously stepped from the bush at the base of the hill and onto the graveled parking lot next to the dock where he'd left the *Pappy Bobo*. A van and a small boxy car were parked in the lot. An old wooden trawler was tied to the dock opposite the *Pappy Bobo*. He waited ten minutes and saw no activity. With a shrug, he walked onto the dock as casually as he could. At first, he was worried that his torn T-shirt and cuts on his arms and legs from the thorny bush would stand out. He then realized that he was in a war zone. Who'd notice? His caution gave way to confidence.

He approached the *Pappy Bobo* and was greeted with, "Well, if it isn't Major Asshole, Boiled Bob."

Lisa raised herself from the companionway with a broad smile and said, "You look like shit. But then, that's what you are."

Boiled Bob nervously glanced around the dock. Lisa looked fresh and wore clean clothes. *Why was she smiling?* He looked to see if she held a weapon and saw nothing.

He said, "You seem pretty happy, bitch. What I don't understand is why you came back here to my boat."

"It's my father's boat," Lisa said and smiled.

Boiled Bob looked from bow to stern and said, "What if I don't want you on the boat anymore?"

"It's my *father's* boat, asshole. And I don't want you on my *father's* boat anymore."

"A lot you can do about it," Boiled Bob said and started to step over the rail and onto *Pappy Bobo*'s deck.

He turned when he heard the rush of footfalls from the trawler a few feet away. "What the f…?" Boiled Bob grunted as two large West Indian men tackled him to the dock, taking his wind away.

"Looks like you've been caught, asshole," Lisa said with a laugh. "Guess who's come to see you?"

Boiled Bob was lifted to his feet with a large arm that locked around his neck.

Lisa said, "No answer? Want to guess?"

Boiled Bob wanted to answer Lisa but couldn't. His windpipe was choked off.

"I'll give you a hint. Your worst nightmare," Lisa said. "Have you guessed yet?"

Boiled Bob was about to pass out when he heard a shout from behind him, telling the men who held him to stand down. The man who held him loosened his grip but not before placing him face-first on the hard dock.

Bob turned his head to the side and shouted, "I was going to let her go. We had an agreement. Ask her."

The two men tied his thumbs behind his back with a plastic tie and lifted him to his feet.

A third man stepped onto the dock from the trawler and smiled at Boiled Bob.

Lisa smiled and said, "Meet my new best friend, Desmond. He's Charlie Kline's right-hand man here on Grenada. That's Charlie's boat behind you. Do you want to know who his crew is?" Lisa asked and smiled.

Boiled Bob grunted and struggled with the men who held him. One of them slapped the side of his head, knocking Bob off balance.

Lisa said, "Come on Bob, ask who the crew is."

One of the men slapped Boiled Bob, who finally asked, "Who… bitch?" which brought him another slap.

"Let's see… There's Arlan O'Brien…"

"So."

"Oh, and there's Tommy Lowell."

Bob didn't respond.

"And, somebody who you know really well..."

Bob snarled.

"Come on, Bob, you don't want to guess?"

Bob turned his head, not wanting to give Lisa the pleasure of seeing his anguish.

"Captain Jay has come, in person, to thank you for the wonderful way you've treated me as your guest on this excursion."

Boiled Bob looked out into the bay and to the sea to the south, the direction he'd hoped to have been sailing by now. Explosions and small arms fire filled the air to his right and behind him. The bright-blue sky, crowded with white cumulus clouds, was polluted with whiffs of black and grey smoke drifting with the trade winds. The sight and the sounds, his handcuffed thumbs and the woman he'd kidnapped comfortably laughing at him were too much.

"I was going to let her go. We'd agreed. She can go now," Boiled Bob cried.

The men dragged him back into the trawler and tied him to a rail in the cabin.

Boiled Bob collapsed onto the hard deck wondering how this could have happened. He took a deep breath and felt that he might black out. He went slack against his restraints. He wasn't sure if he'd blacked out or not. He had no perception of time and wasn't sure how long it had been before he'd heard Desmond talking to Lisa. He'd told her that his radio wasn't working, and he hadn't been able to contact Charlie to let him know she was safely onboard and that Boiled Bob was captured and secured. Desmond had told Lisa that he'd drive back to the US command post at Point Salines to find Charlie. Bob then heard fading footsteps on the dock and a car start and drive away. One of his three captors was gone. He felt a surge of adrenaline. He might get out of this yet.

* * *

As the helicopter rose and soared away from the command post at Point Salines, a loud click followed by static crackled through the headphones, separating Arlan from his thoughts on the bizarre scene below them.

Charlie's voice crackled through the headset. Arlan looked over at him and saw that he'd twisted a small arm on the side of his headset to a position in front of his mouth. Arlan had no idea the headsets were two-way radios. He felt for the arm on the side of his headset and pulled it down close to his mouth, just in case he had anything to say. He couldn't imagine what that would be.

"Where are we going?" Charlie asked.

"We'll fly past St. George's and let you off at Grand Bay. That's where John and his marines are landing to relieve the Special Forces in St. George's. There's still resistance from Fort Rupert and the prison. A Delta Force team was working near Fort Frederick, which is next to the mental hospital. In the aftermath of the bombing of the hospital all hell broke loose. Those patients not killed in the blast escaped into St. George's. A nurse approached the Delta team with three patients and told them they needed to care for them, then stomped away, leaving two large, black female inmates and one bearded, skinny male inmate in their care. The male is white and has an unmistakable likeness to your man."

The lieutenant colonel pulled a grainy paper copy of the photo of Boiled Bob, Long Bill and Maynard from his shirt pocket and unfolded it. "This is the copy I got from John. We thought John had lost his mind, combining a personal mission with Operation Urgent Fury. But when word got out what you'd done to help us with intel…" He looked out the window of the helicopter, then back to Charlie and added, "…and your service to our country. Well, we, most of us anyway, decided to help you if we could."

"Are you sure it's him?" Charlie shouted. "He has no business in a mental hospital in Grenada. He was in Dominica two days ago and on St. John a couple of weeks ago. How the hell could he be in a mental hospital? Not that he doesn't deserve to be there."

The lieutenant colonel shrugged and said, "I can't answer that, but our guys up there are pretty good at what they do and think it's him."

* * *

Boiled Bob knew as soon as he heard the man named Desmond tell Lisa that he couldn't reach Charlie that nothing would happen to him until Charlie and the prick, Captain Jay, returned to the boat. When he heard the car leave he knew there were only two men on the boat guarding him, and they weren't in the cabin. He just needed to find a tool to free himself, and then he could get off of the boat, off of the dock and onto the island, where he could blend in until he found a way to South America.

His hands were tied together and to a rail, but his feet were free, and his toes were nimble and dexterous. He looked around the wooden deck of the cabin and saw nothing that could help him escape. A cabinet below the countertop in the center of the cabin was tantalizingly close. By lying on his back and thrusting his hips upward, resting his body weight on his right shin, he could reach the thumb knob that held the cabinet door closed with his left foot. He used his left big toe and the longer toe next to it to turn the knob. The cabinet door opened toward him, blocking his view of the inside of the cabinet. Frustrated, he kicked the door, which slammed into the cabinet's face frame and fell off the hinges. He froze and waited for his guards to come crashing into the cabin. They didn't. He listened for a while and heard only the gentle sound of the sea lapping against the boat's hull, interrupted by the distant thunder of bombs, the staccato of small arms fire and the chopping of helicopters as they flew through the skies just over the hill.

Boiled Bob felt around the inside of the cabinet with his toes and hit pay dirt. He found a screwdriver and pulled it toward him with his toes.

Now what? he thought.

* * *

Lieutenant Colonel Hegel's Blackhawk helicopter flew off the coast and was passing St. George's when three pings hit the helicopter. All on board instinctively looked around the craft for damage.

"Small arms fire," the lieutenant colonel said. "Lucky hits. We're too far for them to be effective."

Arlan pulled his legs and arms close to his body, making as small a target as possible in case a shell made it into the interior. He noticed that the others were doing the same. Arlan looked toward St. George's and saw plumes of black smoke rising from three different places in the city, all targets of smaller helicopters that had flown below them from the west.

"Cobra helicopters from the USS *Independence*," the lieutenant colonel said. "The SEALs who are trying to rescue the governor-general are in a heavy firefight."

The Blackhawk descended into a clearing next to the beach at Grand Mal. Arlan could see a long dock a hundred yards north of the clearing and a few dozen homes and shacks near the dock. The clearing itself appeared to be a makeshift soccer field. Three similar helicopters were on the field, and a half dozen troops had formed a loose security perimeter around the landing area. As the group disembarked from the Blackhawk they were greeted by Charlie's friend, Colonel Faulkner, who stood with two other officers next to the helicopters.

"I heard you were mounting a beach landing here," Charlie said to his friend while they shook hands. "Where are your troops?"

"They'll be here shortly. We're checking out the beaches to see where it's best to land."

Lieutenant Colonel Hegel smiled and said, "I thought you marines would have already stormed the beach by now."

"We've been busy cleaning up the other airport," John said.

The lieutenant colonel laughed and said, "Jesus, you marines think you're so tough. We had a real army to contend with. You had to deal with some heavy surf and a few mangroves. I'm glad you could finally join the fight. But it looks so far like you're doing nothing but entertaining the locals." He laughed and nodded to the dock, where a couple of dozen locals stood, some cheering.

The lieutenant colonel said, "I need to get going. I'm here to do a little recon south of here before we move toward the campus tomorrow."

"Don't get shot," Colonel Faulkner said with a smile.

The lieutenant colonel shook hands with everybody, wished them luck and walked back to his helicopter.

John said to Charlie, "You can stay here on the beach and spend the night with the mosquitoes or you can come with me to the *Trenton*, which is about five miles offshore. I understand the man you've been looking for is in St. George's."

Charlie shrugged and looked at the others for some input.

John said, "We can try to get you closer to the city, but I can't guarantee your safety. We haven't taken out all of their guns yet."

"We could walk. St. George's is just a mile or so over that hill," Captain Jay said, pointing to a steep hill that separated them from the city. "From what we've seen so far, the locals seem to support the invasion. We'll be all right."

Charlie said, "Before we go on a wild goose chase I need to call Desmond to see if he's seen Boiled Bob or Lisa return to the boat."

Captain Jay said, "The son-of-bitch is in St. George's, being held by a Special Forces team. Haven't you been listenin'?"

"What if it's not him? It doesn't make sense that he was a patient in a mental hospital. He's only been on the island a couple of days," Charlie said and tried to reach Desmond on his radio. He couldn't get through. He turned to the colonel and said, "My radio isn't working. Can I use yours?"

The colonel handed his radio to Charlie and said, "We've been having problems with communications. They seem to be hit and miss."

Charlie missed—again. He handed the radio back to the colonel and said, "Where in St. George's does Delta have the man they think is Boiled Bob?"

"They're hunkered down somewhere near the harbor, where we're not bombing, and are going to stay there until we secure the city. I don't have an exact location. I know they've hooked up with a SEAL team that took out the transmitter for Radio Free Grenada. Both teams are waiting for extraction."

"I find it hard to believe the man the Delta guys have is our man," Charlie said.

"I passed the photo you gave me on, and we have positive ID. I think you need to check it out."

Charlie shrugged and looked toward the rest of the group and said, "I tend to agree. And I think Jay is right. We can find the harbor from here." He pointed to a small crowd of locals who'd gathered on the dock. "We'll be able to get a ride from a local who wants to make a few bucks."

Nobody protested. Arlan wanted to say that he didn't want to march into hostile territory but knew it would do nothing to change the inevitable.

* * *

Desmond drove back to the temporary command post at Point Salines to look for Charlie. When he arrived, he was told that Charlie and the rest of his group had gone with the lieutenant colonel to a beach north of St. George's and, from there, they would enter the city to collect the man they'd been looking for—the boat thief.

"But dat is not possible," Desmond told the officer. "We have him back on de boat."

"Are you positive?" the officer asked.

"Yes. Tis him. We have de girl too. She's safe."

The officer tried to reach his boss on the radio and failed. He tried every five minutes for the next thirty minutes, finally reaching him on the seventh try. He explained the situation to the lieutenant colonel, who immediately broke communications with the officer at Point Salines to call Colonel Faulkner, whom he'd left on the beach with the group of American civilians an hour earlier. It took him four attempts before he reached the colonel.

"What?" Colonel Faulkner said. "I'm on my way back to the ship. Charlie and his group have gone into St. George's on foot."

"Shit."

"Yes, Lieutenant Colonel Hagler—shit."

"John, my radio is off and on. Can you call the command center from the *Trenton*? See if they can get a message to the Delta team?"

"Already on it. Out."

The colonel's helicopter landed on the *Trenton* ten minutes later. He rushed to the bridge and called the command center on the USS *Independence* and told the officer in charge what was going on. The officer relayed the message to his commander who shouted loud enough for the colonel to hear… "Tell that son-of-bitch we have a battle to win. We're not in this to babysit some fool civilians looking for a fucking boat thief."

"Did you get that?" the officer asked the colonel.

"Yes. The civilians are on a mission to rendezvous with our Special Forces to pick up the wrong man—and they're on their own for a while."

Chapter 17

DAY 13: OCT 26 (Morning)

Arlan could no longer take the pain in his shoulder and rolled onto his back. He hadn't slept on a cot for many years and remembered in the middle of the night why. There was no way to be comfortable, unless you were unconscious.

"Jesus, Charlie. Was this the only place you could find where we could sleep for the night? If you call this sleep," Captain Jay said as he rose from his cot and stretched. "Why'd we listen to that taxi driver anyway? This place is a shit hole."

"His cousin owns this place and opened it up for us. Otherwise we'd have been on the streets. Everything else is closed," Charlie said and rubbed his back while sitting on the edge of his cot. "I've slept on worse. We could have stayed on the beach and be bitten by mosquitoes all night."

"Wh-what were those bugs b-biting me all n-night in here?" Tommy asked and nodded to the floor of the large room that was part of a youth hostel located in the center of St. George's.

Rat-tat-tat! Boom! Boom!

"I guess there's still a war going on," Arlan said. "I didn't hear much gunfire or shelling last night."

"It's a daytime war, Rookie. Made for TV. There'll be a movie about this island brawl one day. Wait and see," Captain Jay said with a snort.

"Grab your gear, and let's find the Delta team," Charlie said while tinkering with his radio, which still received nothing but hissing and crackling.

"Wh-what gear?"

Charlie ignored Tommy and said, "They're somewhere near the harbor, and my guess is they'll be as far away from the old forts as possible, which are getting hammered about now. I say we walk to the southernmost part of the harbor and move north until we find them, or they find us."

Everybody agreed, and a few minutes later they walked on the narrow streets of St. George's which was a typical Caribbean capital—wood and stone historic buildings, none more than three stories tall, many in disrepair, mixed with modern, but rundown, concrete structures, which were often government offices.

The air was humid, and the haze of exploded ordnance permeated the air. The sun shone through occasionally, but for the most part, the sky above the city was socked in by the repercussions of war. At least there were no military roadblocks and no fighting in the streets. US helicopter attacks and return gunfire was limited to Fort Rupert, at the harbor entrance, and Fort Fredrick and the prison, above the city on the steep hillsides.

Arlan would have thought that the city would be a ghost town. It wasn't. The streets weren't crowded, most residents choosing to stay inside while a war played on outside, but there were people milling around. They seemed concerned but kept their smiles and greeted each other warmly, while treating strangers with polite suspicion. The noises Arlan heard as they walked were as eclectic as the city—mufflers from passing vehicles, friendly shouts from the locals to each other, children playing soldier, the thumping sound of low-flying helicopters, shells exploding near the forts and return small arms fire, dogs barking and roosters crowing.

They'd walked a few blocks west to the harbor and then turned south and followed the warehouses, bars and funky West Indian shops that made up the harbor's edge, where tourists would normally be seen. But they were gone.

Several blocks later they heard a whistle from a warehouse opposite the harbor. A man with a black and green painted face that matched his fatigues and a floppy bush hat stepped from the warehouse. He had a short assault rifle slung loosely around his shoulder but didn't hold it in a threatening way.

"You guys lost?"

"N-no. We know exactly wh-where we are," Tommy answered with a grin.

The soldier stared at Tommy for a moment, probably wondering if he'd confronted a drunken tourist.

Charlie said, "SEAL team?"

The soldier nodded, still looking at Tommy. He then asked, "Who are you?"

"We're looking for someone. We've been told a Delta team has him," Charlie said.

The SEAL nodded with recognition and pointed up the block. He said, "They're up there holed up in a drugstore watching our asses, while we watch theirs from this end of the block." The SEAL looked at the group and said, "You the guys chasing the band of rapists and murderers around the islands?"

Tommy said, "W-we don't know about any r-rapists. There w-was a murderer, but he's d-dead now."

The SEAL frowned and looked to Charlie, who nodded. With a look of respect, the SEAL said, "We've heard of you."

Three other SEALs stepped out of the dark warehouse opening. All were wearing floppy hats and had automatic weapons slung around their shoulders.

Another round of shells exploded across the bay at Ft. Frederick.

Charlie asked, "Are you trapped here?"

"Yes and no. We could get out of here, but we have a problem. We need to take out an anti-aircraft placement that our attack choppers can't seem to locate."

Charlie said, "We choppered in to Gran Mal Bay late yesterday with the Rangers and met with Colonel Faulkner on the beach. He's on his way to get you and the Deltas out of here."

"We figured as much, but our radio communication is shit," the SEAL said and then shouted down the block. "Hey, ground pounders, we got a group coming your way for the crazy." He then nodded up the block and said, "Your man's up there. He's crazy, though. Hope it's him."

Captain Jay said, "What do you mean?"

The SEAL waited a moment and said, "Listen. If those Delta guys thought he was your rapist, they'd have offed him just to save you guys the trouble. We'd have done the same." He paused and said, "He's a dead ringer for the guy in the photo we were shown, but he's crazy—like he's been living in a nuthouse for a long time." The SEAL shrugged and said, "You'll see."

The group walked down the block and was met by two Delta Force team members. They looked a lot like the SEALs as far as the weapons they carried were concerned, but they were dressed in civilian clothing and wore camouflaged floppy hats.

"I'm Master Sergeant Cummins. Call me Mark. Come on in," the shorter of the two said, looking up at the rooftops and down the street in both directions and paying particular attention to a location two blocks farther down the road where two other Delta members were crouched behind an old truck, looking up and to their left. One had binoculars. The other turned and held up two fingers toward the Delta soldier who had invited Charlie's group into the drugstore.

Boom! Boom! Boom!

"That was close," Arlan said as they walked into the store. Captain Jay frowned and nodded for Arlan to follow the others.

"That's an anti-aircraft setup on a rooftop a few blocks from here. Must be well hidden up there. It's already taken down two of our gunships. We've been trying to call in a strike, but our damn radios won't work," Mark said, holding the handheld radio out. "Come on. He's back here. Won't shut up. Driving us crazy."

Arlan glanced around the store. A few items had fallen from shelves, but the store was intact. A pay phone hung on the wall near the cash register. As they walked toward the back of the store Arlan picked the phone up and heard a dial tone. He laughed and said to Captain Jay, who was just behind him, "It still works."

Captain Jay didn't laugh, or smile. He motioned for Arlan to follow the others.

They walked into a back room and saw two more Delta soldiers standing over a man sitting in a chair at a small table. The man wore a soiled, blue jumpsuit and had his head turned toward one of the soldiers. He was white, thin and had long, scraggly hair and a beard. He wore a camouflaged floppy hat, similar to those the soldiers wore.

"I'm a Delta man," he said with a laugh. "Delta mon, Delta mon, Delta mon, me son," he repeated, this time with a West Indian accent.

The two soldiers looked toward the door. One smiled at Mark and shook his head. The man in the chair followed the soldier's gaze and turned his head toward the door. Captain Jay stomped toward the chair and knocked the man in the jumpsuit to the floor. The two Delta soldiers grabbed Captain Jay. Tommy, Arlan and Charlie were on Captain Jay a second later.

"You prick. Where's Lisa?" a red-faced Captain Jay shouted and tried to break free of the soldiers.

The man on the ground showed no recognition of Captain Jay, or anybody else in the room, except his Delta babysitters. He smiled while on the floor, grabbed the floppy hat that had been knocked off his head and said, "Delta mon, Delta mon. I and I am Delta mon."

Arlan frowned and looked to Tommy, who looked just as confused. Even Captain Jay relaxed a little, the red leaving his face.

Charlie didn't know Boiled Bob as well as the others. He asked, "Is this Boiled Bob?"

Nobody responded.

The man in the jumpsuit stood, walked back to the chair and sat. "Boiled Bob, Boiled Bob, Boiled Bob. I'm Boiled Bob," he said with a broad grin.

Arlan said, "I don't think this is Boiled Bob. But damn, he's his twin."

The resemblance was remarkable—same size, same hair and the same wild eyes.

"S-something is not r-right with him," Tommy said.

"No shit, Sherlock," Captain Jay said.

"Who are you?" Arlan asked the man, who was rocking gently forward and backward with a smile.

The man cocked his head as if thinking about the question and said, "Who are you, who are you, who are you?"

"Jesus," Charlie said and looked to Mark for an explanation.

The man in the chair then said in a strong, coherent voice, "I'm Boiled Bob of the Delta Force team."

Boom! Boom! A slightly more muffled sound of ordnance being fired from the anti-aircraft weapon shook the drugstore walls.

Mark glanced at the man in the jumpsuit, then turned to Charlie and said, "We were part of a team sent in early yesterday to rescue some people at the prison. It was heavily fortified and got too hot to safely rescue the prisoners. We had to abandon the mission."

"We learned that from Colonel Faulkner. He's coming to get you guys out today sometime," Charlie said.

Mark pointed to his radio and said, "These are shit, and we haven't heard anything, but we figured as much."

Arlan absentmindedly put his hand into the front pocket of his shorts and felt his wallet—a rubber band stretched around a driver's license, a few bills and a plastic card. He then thought of the pay phone he'd seen near the cash register when they entered the store.

Charlie nodded to the man in the jumpsuit and asked, "How'd you end up with him?"

Mark said, "We knew some other Special Forces were in the area, so we decided to get close to the harbor after we abandoned the prison. A lady dressed like a nurse spotted us and led three people dressed in jumpsuits to us. She recognized us as US military, probably from our weapons and color, and told us that we were responsible for bombing her hospital and, therefore, responsible to take the two women and this man off her hands and to safety."

Charlie frowned.

"It's not like we had a choice. She told them to stay with us and left. The three people in jumpsuits followed us. We ran into the SEAL team just a little ways from here. We all agreed to take up positions close together and wait for reinforcements. We took this end of the block. They took the other. The three people the nurse left with us stayed close, probably scared shitless of the bombs and gunfire."

"Wh-what happened to the w-women?" Tommy asked.

"The owner of this drugstore saw us, recognized the jumpsuits as patients from the mental hospital and asked if he could help. We told him our situation, and he said we could hole up in his store. His wife came and took the women to their home. This guy…" Mark said and pointed to the man at the table who was now mumbling. "They said he had to stay with us. They didn't have room for all three."

Boom! Boom! Boom!

Arlan looked at Boiled Bob's look-alike and shook his head. Even Captain Jay had to admit that this wasn't him. Arlan pulled his rubber band wallet from his shorts and thought about the phone again. Then it clicked.

Arlan asked the Delta master sergeant, "Are you based at Fort Bragg?"

"Yes."

Arlan pulled an AT&T calling card out of the rubber band, handed it to the master sergeant and said, "Call them up from the pay phone near the cash register, and have them contact your ship offshore to call in the strike."

The three Delta soldiers, Tommy, Captain Jay and Charlie stared at Arlan for several seconds.

The man in the chair rocked back and forth and said, "Fort Bragg, Fort Bragg, Fort Bragg."

Mark took the card and walked into the main store and to the pay phone. In a few seconds Arlan heard him talking to an operator and reading the numbers off the front of the card. A minute later Arlan and the others could hear a series of "Yes, sirs" and "No, sirs," and then Mark gave a description of the building where the anti-aircraft weapons were located.

Charlie looked at Arlan and said, "What the hell?"

"It's from your friend who I let stay at my house when you were off island, the AT&T executive. He and his wife had a great time and sent the card as a thank you gift, I guess. I've never used it."

"Shit, Rookie," Captain Jay said, "You're smarter than you look."

Arlan smiled and said, "I'm just tired of hearing those guns go off. My ears hurt."

A few minutes later Mark came back into the room and said, "Heads down in five minutes. I'm going out to get my guys and warn the SEALs. Shit's going to go bang soon." He started to leave and then turned to give Arlan his card back and said, "Good job. Did you know there was a two hundred dollar-credit on this card?"

Arlan was surprised. He glanced at Charlie and then told Mark, "Keep it. You might need it to call in more strikes."

"I'll have the government send you a new one," Mark said and left.

Five minutes later the sound of helicopter blades chopping through the air grew as gunships flew close overhead. A series of deafening explosions shook the drugstore so hard bottles fell from shelves. Everybody instinctively ducked, except the man in the jumpsuit. He laughed, stood and jumped around the room. "Boom. Boom. Boom," he shouted and then said, "Let's go get 'em."

Tommy was closest and grabbed the man before he made it out of the room.

"Y-you need to be c-careful," Tommy said as he led the man back to the chair.

"I-I need t-to b-be careful," the man replied, stuttering with a smile.

Arlan looked at Tommy, expecting him to knock the man to the ground.

Tommy smiled at the man and said, "W-we need to give you a n-name."

Then, with lucidity and clear eyes, the man said, "I'm Ben Joseph. I moved here with my family from Canada when I was young. They are dead now."

"Why are you a patient in the hospital?" Arlan asked him.

The man's crazy eyes returned, and he jumped up again and shouted, "I'm Boiled Bob, Boiled Bob, Boiled Bob."

Arlan shrugged and said, "Okay. We'll call you Bob." He then added, "It's clear that you're boiled."

Mark returned and said, "That should allow the troops to get in here quicker. Thanks again for the card," he said to Arlan. "I learned on my call that the marines have landed just north of here at Grand Mal. They're heading here to rescue our guys and the governor-general, and then they'll move south to the other medical school campus at Grand Anse. The 82nd Airborne and some Rangers are moving north to the campus from Point Salines. There seems to be a lot of resistance near the campus. We're joining up with them a few hundred yards south of here in two hours." He looked toward the man in the jumpsuit who was saluting him and said to Charlie, "Can you take him with you?"

"Where?" Charlie asked.

"Can we take him back to the hospital?" Arlan asked.

"The hospital is destroyed. I learned on my call that a bunch of the patients were killed. This guy's lucky," the master sergeant said.

Charlie said, "What are we supposed to do with him?"

"I don't know, but we can't take him into a battle, and I don't want to leave him here by himself."

Charlie looked to the rest of the group and said, "I need to contact Desmond. It's clear that this guy isn't Boiled Bob."

"I'm Boiled Bob. Boiled Bob. Boiled Bob."

Charlie rolled his eyes and said, "The real Boiled Bob may have returned to the boat, if he's still alive."

Captain Jay put his hand on the shoulder of the man in the jumpsuit and said, "No. You're Bob. Just Bob."

"Just Bob. Just Bob. Just Bob," the man repeated with a grin.

Charlie turned to Mark and said, "Can you get us a ride back to Point Salines?"

"I would think so. Come with us to the rendezvous point. The marine colonel is a friend of yours, and I'm sure he can spare one of his choppers to ferry you guys and your new friend to Point Salines. We need to leave in an hour."

The bombing and return fire stopped less than an hour later. The drugstore owner returned and said he'd learned from the local grapevine that the US forces had control of the forts and the prison. As far as he was concerned, the fighting was finished, and he and other business owners were returning to their shops to clean up.

"Can you take this man from us?" Charlie asked the store owner and pointed to Bob.

"No. Der are too many people at my house. Some of de patients from de hospital are wander*in* around the streets. I heard dat some of de nurses and doctors from de hospital are look*in* fo a new building to house dem patients. You will have to keep him wit you, or let him go."

"We c-can always bring him back h-here later. Or m-maybe the military at P-Point Salines can t-take him," Tommy said. He looked over at the man in the jumpsuit and said, "Y-you okay, Bob?"

Bob saluted Tommy and said, "O-okay, s-sir."

Tommy smiled and shook his head. Everybody else laughed.

"Bring him," Charlie said. "Let's go."

Chapter 18

Day 13: Oct 26 (Afternoon)

The Delta and SEAL teams led Charlie and his group along the mile and a half road that ran south from St. George's to the north end of Grand Anse Bay. The hillside road had given them a view out to sea where they could see a dozen military landing craft filled with marines from the 22nd Amphibious Unit cruising from the north toward the beach at Grand Anse Bay. There they would land at the north end of the beach and rendezvous with the Delta and SEAL teams.

The medical school campus at Grand Anse was a thousand yards farther down the beach to the south. Arlan could see US gunships striking positions on the hill above the campus. Twenty minutes later the marines landed in the landing craft and started to disembark and form up. The same three helicopters they saw with Colonel Faulkner on the beach north of St. George's the day before landed on the beach just beyond the landing craft, and Colonel Faulkner disembarked with two aides.

"About time the cavalry showed up," Charlie shouted to his friend as the two groups met a hundred yards up the beach.

Boom! Boom! Rat-tat-tat!

Arlan ducked and looked a half mile down the beach at the attacking helicopters and return gunfire from somewhere up in the hills.

"Better late than never," John said and nodded to the Special Forces teams. "Good work back there. How'd you figure out to use the damn pay phone to call air strikes?"

Mark, the Delta leader, nodded toward Arlan and said, "He figured it out."

John looked approvingly at Arlan and said, "Good thing you were along. These muscle heads would never have figured that out." He turned to Mark with a smile and said, "That damn rooftop weapon did a lot of damage and held us up for half a day."

John then looked to the back of the group at the man in the jumpsuit wearing a floppy military hat and a goofy smile. "Who the hell is that?" he asked. "Looks like your man in the photo."

Charlie said, "It's not."

"Th-this is our n-new recruit," Tommy said. "H-his name is B-Bob."

"Boiled Bob, Boiled Bob, Boiled Bob," Bob repeated.

Tommy looked at him and said, "N-no. Not B-Boiled Bob, just B-Bob."

"Just B-Bob, just B-Bob, just B-Bob."

The colonel rolled his eyes and looked to Charlie for an explanation.

"A patient from the mental hospital that was bombed. Looks exactly like the man we're looking for," Charlie said.

"What's he doing with you?"

"We've sort of adopted him. He has no place to go until somebody finds a place to house him and the rest of the patients that survived."

Rat-tat-tat! Boom! Boom! Boom!

"Jesus, what a war," John said, to nobody in particular. He then looked down the beach at the helicopters flying low through the smoke.

"Well, we've got some students to rescue. What can we do for you?" he asked Charlie.

"It would be great if you could give us a lift over the hill, back to Point Salines. My radio still doesn't work, and we need to contact my man here on the island. He may have the real Boiled Bob."

"That's the least we can do for you," the colonel said and shouted to one of his aides to get one of the birds ready to take five civilians to the command post at Point Salines.

Charlie and his group thanked John as they climbed into the helicopter for the five-minute ride that would take them out over the ocean to avoid the gunfire on shore and then circle back to land at the Point Salines airstrip.

Desmond was waiting at the compound when the helicopter landed. He'd been told by the Ranger officer he'd talked to the day before to check back every couple of hours to see if he'd made contact with his friends. On his third visit to the command post since early morning he was told that a helicopter carrying his friends had just left Anse Bay and that they would be landing momentarily.

Arlan couldn't believe the activity he saw at Point Salines as the helicopter approached. There were many more troops, vehicles, planes, helicopters and pallets of equipment and provisions lining both sides of the runway than he'd seen the day before. The temporary concertina wire prison had doubled in size. Arlan strained to find Long Bill and the large Dread. He thought he saw them just as the aircraft touched down, but at ground level he couldn't see the prisoners through the sea of troops and hardware.

Desmond crouched and ran toward the helicopter, its rotors still spinning so it could return to the action at Anse Bay after dropping off its passengers. The group disembarked with Tommy bringing Bob out last. Desmond stopped in his tracks.

"Dis mon look just like Boiled Bob."

"Just Bob, just Bob, just Bob," Bob repeated. He then saluted Desmond, accidentally knocking the floppy hat off his head.

Tommy picked it up and placed it back on Bob's head. He said, "S-still okay, B-B-ob?"

"S-still okay, s-sir."

Desmond frowned. Charlie nodded and said, "What do you have?"

Desmond, not taking his eyes from Bob, said, "We've got Boiled Bob on de boat. Lisa is okay and staying on de sailboat."

Arlan, Charlie and Tommy let out sighs of relief.

Captain Jay fumed and said, "Let's go get the son-of-bitch."

Arlan looked at Captain Jay, smiled and said, "And Lisa."

"Yeah. That too."

Desmond led them to his van, looking back at Bob several times. He finally said, "He's from de mental hospital. I can tell by de clothes."

Charlie said, "In a moment of lucidness he said his name is Ben Joseph and that he grew up here."

Desmond turned and said, "Dat's him. I now know why dat photo of Boiled Bob looked so familiar when I first saw it. Dis mon and his family came to de island about twenty-five years ago. His fadder was a bad mon. Used to beat Benny." Desmond looked at Charlie and said, "Dat's what we called him. He had an older sister too. I tink de fadder raped her. De mudder sailed away wit anodder mon and about ten years ago de fadder was found dead. Burned up in his car. De police taut Benny did it and put him in de mental hospital. Nobody wanted him to hang. De sister went away. Benny has been in de hospital fo a long time."

"Was he always this crazy?" Charlie asked.

"Not so much before he went into de hospital. But he was beaten bad by his fadder many times. Years of living in dat hospital could have made him dis crazy. Dat's a bad place."

They stepped into the van, and Desmond drove past the troops and equipment to the road that would take them over the hill and to the dock where the boats were tied. Arlan spotted Long Bill and his Dread friend standing at the back of the coiled concertina wire fence that now contained hundreds of prisoners. Both were still handcuffed.

Ten minutes later Desmond pulled the van into the parking lot near the dock. Captain Jay couldn't get out fast enough. He stomped down the dock shouting for Boiled Bob. Two large West Indian men stepped from Charlie's boat onto the dock and blocked his access to the boat. Lisa appeared on the deck of the *Happy Hobo* and called for Jay, who stopped, climbed over the rail of the *Happy Hobo* and hugged her. Arlan could hear, "How you doin' sugar puddin'?"

Captain Jay then turned and stepped back onto the dock and shouted for Boiled Bob.

Charlie, Desmond and Arlan hurried down the dock. Lisa stepped off the sailboat and hugged Arlan and Charlie. Tommy lagged behind with Bob. Lisa's jaw dropped when she saw the man in a jumpsuit stop next to the boat and salute. Desmond's men looked confused. One of them glanced back into the cabin to make sure their prisoner was still there. Captain Jay continued to shout for Boiled Bob and tried to step onto Charlie's boat. Desmond shook his head at his men telling them to not let Jay pass. They moved close together, blocking the opening in the boat's rail, the only place where Captain Jay could board.

Lisa leaned, or fell, back against the rail of the *Happy Hobo* and continued to stare at Bob.

Tommy said, "I-it's okay, Lisa. He's n-not Boiled B-Bob. Just l-looks like him."

"Boiled Bob, Boiled Bob, Boiled Bob," Bob said.

Tommy shook his head, put his hand on Bob's shoulder and said, "His n-name is Bob, j-just Bob."

"J-just Bob, J-just Bob, J-just Bob," the man in the jumpsuit repeated with a big smile.

Desmond's men laughed.

Boiled Bob heard the commotion on the dock and recognized the voices of Captain Jay and Charlie and that stuttering prick, Tommy. This was his worst nightmare. He struggled against his restraints, but he was going nowhere.

Captain Jay continued to shout. His face was red, and he shoved one of Desmond's men, who shoved back. "Let me onboard, or I'll kick your black asses," Jay shouted.

Desmond moved toward Captain Jay. Charlie stepped close and said to Captain Jay, "You need to back off. We've got him. And we have your girlfriend and the boat. We're done here."

"Bullshit. I'm gettin' even with that asshole. He raped Lisa."

"He didn't rape me," Lisa said in a hushed voice.

All eyes turned toward Lisa, who had stepped away from the sailboat.

Her voice stronger, she said, "He tried to several times but couldn't get an erection."

Desmond's men fidgeted, fighting smiles.

Boiled Bob heard Lisa, and his face reddened. "Bitch," he mumbled.

"He might have raped me when I was passed out after he pulled me from the water. But how would I have known." With an even stronger voice she looked toward the cabin of Charlie's boat and shouted, "How would I know if Boiled Bob stuck his dick into me? It's so small I would never have felt it!"

Desmond's men laughed.

Boiled Bob fumed inside the cabin. "I'll kill that bitch once I'm loose," he said to himself.

The man in the jumpsuit laughed and said, "Little weenie, little weenie, little weenie."

Lisa smiled, and Captain Jay seemed to have settled down.

Who the hell said that? Boiled Bob wondered.

Charlie said, "Bring Boiled Bob out here. We need to make a decision."

Desmond nodded, and one of his men walked into the boat's cabin and returned with Boiled Bob uselessly struggling in his captor's tree trunk arms. He saw Lisa and sneered. Captain Jay was a few feet away, being restrained by Charlie. Arlan and Tommy stood back with a man in a jumpsuit wearing a floppy camouflaged hat. Boiled Bob stared at the man for a full minute. The man saluted him.

"Who the fuck is that?" Boiled Bob asked, standing motionless.

"Th-that's you," Tommy said with a laugh, which brought smiles to everybody except Boiled Bob.

Arlan laughed but stopped when an idea began to nag at him. Something Tommy had just said.

Charlie pointed to Boiled Bob and said, "I'm not hauling his sorry ass back to St. John. He either goes to prison here or dies here."

"There's no proof he did anythin' here to send him to prison," Captain Jay said and licked his lips. "I can gut the son-of-bitch right here, and we can dump his body in the bay. I'm sure there are plenty of war casualties floatin' around this island."

"There's proof back on St. Marten," Arlan said.

Boiled Bob shouted, "I didn't do that!"

"That was Maynard. And he's dead," Jay said and nodded to Tommy.

Boiled Bob recoiled and wondered how Maynard had died.

Charlie looked over to Lisa and said, "What do you want to do with him? You suffered more than anybody else."

Lisa stared into the bay and shook her head. She didn't want to decide.

Desmond nodded toward Boiled Bob and said, "We can take dis Boil Bob and find a hole to put him in."

The man in the jumpsuit coughed and looked down at his clothing. In one of his rare lucid moments he said, "The hospital is a hole."

"Tis fo tru," Desmond said with a tinge of embarrassment.

The idea brewing in Arlan's mind had come to fruition. He said, "I have an idea."

Everybody waited for Arlan to tell them his idea.

"Let's take him back."

"B-back where?"

"To the mental hospital."

"I, f-for one, don't want to see h-him go back th-there," Tommy said and placed his hand on Bob's shoulder. "B-besides, it's blown up."

Arlan said, "I'm not talking about him," pointing to Bob in the jumpsuit. "I'm talking about him," Arlan said as he turned and pointed to Boiled Bob.

Charlie smiled. After a moment Captain Jay laughed, as did Desmond and his men. Lisa even grinned.

Boiled Bob, realizing what Arlan meant, tried to run and was grabbed immediately by Desmond's men. "What the fuck are you talking about? I'm not going to any mental hospital."

"Would you rather be dead?" Charlie asked and shrugged. "Because none of us gives a damn either way."

Arlan said, "The owner of the drugstore told us a group of nurses and doctors were scrambling to find a temporary home for the patients that survived the bombing. I'm sure the US military will help with that effort once we explain the situation to Charlie's friends."

Nobody spoke. Arlan looked around and saw that everybody was deep in thought, except the two Bobs. Boiled Bob was straining against the two large men who held him, mumbling, "Fucking idiots. Mother fuckers…"

Bob in the jump suit looked at the struggling Boiled Bob and, with clear eyes and a cold stare, said, "Your name is Ben Joseph." He then saluted him and said, "Goodbye, Ben Joseph." He laughed, turned toward Tommy and said, "Just Bob, just Bob, just Bob."

"Y-you finally g-got it right, B-bob."

Arlan said, "We need to exchange their clothes."

Desmond nodded toward his men, who held Boiled Bob down and stripped him of his shorts and T-shirt, Boiled Bob screaming and kicking the whole time. With his clothes off they stood him upright, naked.

Arlan looked to Bob with the jumpsuit and said, "Bob, we need your clothes. We'll give you some new clothes in return."

Bob smiled, took off his jump suit and stood naked on the dock next to Tommy.

Lisa couldn't take her eyes from Bob's genitals. All the men were taken aback too. Lisa smiled and said, "Well, at least we know they're not identical twins."

Captain Jay said, "Jesus, Bob, what do you do with that? Hit baseballs?"

Bob seemed not to be embarrassed. He liked the attention. He looked over at the still struggling Boiled Bob and said, "Little weenie, little weenie, little weenie."

Boiled Bob was humiliated. He tried to cover his small penis with his thighs. Desmond grabbed the jumpsuit and told his men to put it on Boiled Bob. Arlan then went into the cabin of Charlie's boat and took a spare clean T-shirt and shorts from his overnight bag. He stepped back onto the deck and handed them to Bob, who saluted him and said, "Thank you, sir, thank you, sir, thank you, sir."

"You're welcome, Bob," Arlan said and patted his arm.

Boiled Bob struggled while the men put the filthy jumpsuit on him. Then he started to think that maybe this wasn't a bad deal. Once in a mental hospital and with these gorillas nowhere around, he could easily escape. And these idiots would probably never know it. He smiled inwardly and resigned himself to be led away to wherever the hospital was.

Desmond and Charlie left to talk to the commander at Point Salines. Desmond's men returned Boiled Bob to the cabin and restrained him. He seemed much calmer. Lisa and Captain Jay relaxed on the *Happy Hobo*. Tommy, Arlan and Bob had joined them, but Lisa was uncomfortable with the Boiled Bob lookalike on the deck with her, so Tommy suggested they move to the cabin of Charlie's boat to antagonize Boiled Bob.

They could hear large aircraft taking off and landing at the Point Salines runway. An occasional helicopter flew by, and a spattering of gunfire could be heard in the distant hills.

Charlie and Desmond returned just before sundown.

"Okay. Here's what we know." Charlie then explained. "This invasion is about over. There are a few pockets of resistance around St. George's. The campus at Anse Bay has been taken, and the students are being flown home. However, it turns out that there's a third campus on that ridge over there," Charlie said, pointing to the hill on the east side of Prickly Bay. "We're going to hunker down here for the night and part of tomorrow while the military cleans things up. The Rangers will move in early tomorrow to rescue the students on that ridge. The commander tells me that the only thing left to do after that is to take the Cuban construction camp that's located a few bays farther to the east. If all goes well, we'll be getting a military escort into St. George's about mid-morning, where we can deliver Boiled Bob and be done with this nonsense."

"What are we going to do with the new Bob?" Arlan asked.

"That's a good question," Charlie said.

Chapter 19

Day 14: Oct 27

Around eleven in the morning the distant gunfire slackened considerably, and Charlie announced that it was time to leave for St. George's with Boiled Bob. Desmond and his men stayed back to watch the boats and the new Bob. Lisa chose to stay behind, not wanting anything to do with the real Boiled Bob. She wanted Captain Jay to stay with her, but he protested, not wanting to miss the chance to pummel Boiled Bob if he tried to escape.

Charlie drove, Arlan rode shotgun and Tommy sat in the back near the handcuffed Boiled Bob to make sure Captain Jay, who sat on the other side of Boiled Bob, didn't skewer him in route. Along the way the van was forced to take several sharp turns. Each turn where Boiled Bob leaned into Captain Jay was rewarded with Jay elbowing him in the ribs. Arlan glanced back at each left turn and saw the intensity of the jabs increase as the trip progressed. He was sure Boiled Bob had suffered several bruised, if not cracked, ribs.

On the road that led north from Point Salines they met up with a military truck with two soldiers in the front and two more in the back, one manning a .50-caliber machine gun. The military vehicle led the van three miles north, past Anse Bay, and into St. George's. They heard sporadic small arms fire from the hills but saw no violence along the way. In some places, locals celebrated the successful invasion, many holding hand-written signs thanking the US for saving them from communism.

As planned, the escort truck drove to the harbor and to the street where the drugstore was located. About half the shops along the street were open. *They'll have a hard year ahead of them*, Arlan thought. Tourists would probably stay away from the island for a while.

Charlie parked the van on the street outside the drugstore and Boiled Bob, wearing the mental hospital jumpsuit, was led into the store. The owner, who was restocking shelves, recognized them and greeted them warmly.

"Tanks fo watch*in* Ben," he said and looked toward Boiled Bob.

"We didn't know you knew him," Charlie said.

"We all know Benny. He was dealt a bad hand. I've not seen him since he was sent to de hospital, but when he was younger he and his sister would come in here to get away from der fadder."

Boiled Bob remained quiet, but his head was screaming, *I'm not Benny you stupid fuck.*

The store owner looked at Boiled Bob's menacing expression and said, "I tink he has become more angry since I knew him."

"He's violent too," Captain Jay said. "He's gonna need restraints and guards."

"Have you found a place for the patients from the hospital?" Charlie asked.

"Yes. De two girls we kept wit us were taken to de new facility dis morning. I'll call a nurse who is working der. It's a short way from here. She can be here in five minutes."

The store owner walked to the pay phone near the front of the store and made the call. Boiled Bob didn't like what he'd just heard. He looked around the store for an exit.

"It l-looks like your g-going home, B-Benny," Tommy said with a smile.

"Fuck you T-Tommy," Boiled Bob said, spittle flying from his mouth.

Tommy stepped close to Boiled Bob and said without stuttering, "If you think you're in the clear you're as crazy as the people you'll be living with the rest of your life."

Boiled Bob felt Tommy's hand cup his balls and squeeze. He screamed, bringing the store owner scrambling over.

"What tis de problem?"

"H-he's been this way since w-we took him," Tommy said.

"I think he's shell-shocked," Charlie added.

"I told you he's gonna need restraints," Captain Jay said.

As soon as Tommy let go, Boiled Bob bolted toward the back of the store, hoping to find an exit. The pain from his ribs was debilitating. He somehow found a door, but it was blocked with boxes and office furniture. Breathing heavily and doubling over from pain, he ran back toward the front of the store, chased by Tommy, Arlan and Captain Jay. He exploded out of the entrance door at the same time the nurse was entering. He bowled her over and kept going. What he didn't expect was to run into the US military. The four troopers from the escort vehicles were on him in seconds. They took him to the ground and held him there.

Boiled Bob lay on the ground, in pain and defeated. The simple task of taking a breath was agonizing. He stared up at his captors and wanted to kill all of them. *Where was Maynard when he needed him,* he thought.

"We heard a scream from the store and decided we should check it out," one of the soldiers said. "Looks like your patient is a flight risk," he added.

Tommy stopped and helped the nurse to her feet.

The nurse stepped toward Boiled Bob with Tommy's assistance and said, "Benny, what's gotten into you?"

"I'm not Benny, bitch. I'm Bob, Bob Blight, from Miami!" Boiled Bob shouted.

"Oh, Benny, poor Benny," the nurse said and shook her head.

"I'm Bob, damn it! Bob. Bob. BOB!" Boiled Bob shouted.

Perfect, thought Arlan and smiled.

Boiled Bob looked toward Arlan and realized his mistake.

"You don't understand," he pleaded. "These men have kidnapped me and have replaced me with the real nut job... whatever his name is." Boiled Bob grimaced in pain and said, "I'm Bob. Boiled Bob. How can you not see the fucking truth?"

The nurse shook her head and looked to the men around her. She said, "Benny is a mimic of sorts. He always claims to be somebody else… anybody he's met or has been told about. And he changes his personality to fit his new name. Sometimes it lasts for a few hours. Sometimes it lasts for months." She paused and said, "I've never seen him so angry. The bombing must have had a very bad effect on him."

The soldiers stood Boiled Bob up.

"What do you want us to do with him, ma'am?" One of the soldiers asked.

The nurse frowned at Boiled Bob and said, "Oh, Benny. What has happened to you?" She then looked at the soldier and said, "We have been given part of the prison that you liberated yesterday to use for our patients. We have plenty of security, and I've been told that there will be significant financial aid from the US to help us build a new hospital with modern upgrades and security. He won't be a bother to anybody."

Boiled Bob shouted, "You stupid bitch! I'm not Benny. I'm Bob!"

The nurse shook her head and said, "Of course, Be… Bob. Don't worry. Everything will be fine. You'll be home in no time."

Captain Jay snorted and let out a laugh.

The nurse turned to him and said, "This is not funny."

"Of course not, ma'am," he said and turned away with a smile on his face.

"Can I depend on you soldiers to escort Ben… Bob to our new facility? There are already other US soldiers and doctors there."

The soldier looked toward Charlie. Charlie nodded and said, "We can find our way back. I think you should do as the nurse asks. I'll let your commander know where you are."

"Thank you, sir," he said and then nodded to the other soldiers, who put Boiled Bob in the back of the truck and hopped in with him.

"You can ride in front, ma'am."

"Thank you," she said and turned to Charlie and the others. "Thank you so much for taking care of our Benny. He'll be in good hands." With a sad look she walked to the truck and got in the passenger side.

Boiled Bob glared at the group as the truck slowly drove away. All were grinning. As the truck turned the corner Captain Jay smiled, raised his arm and waved at Boiled Bob with his fingers, like a child.

* * *

Charlie drove the van to the dock and let everybody off, motioned for Desmond to hop in, and they drove away. On their way out of the parking lot Tommy shouted, "Wh-where are you g-going?"

"I need to make a couple more phone calls. Then we're out of here," Charlie shouted with his gruff voice.

Tommy and Arlan entertained Bob, who'd made himself at home with Desmond's men. They played dominoes for a couple of hours, after which Desmond's men claimed that Bob was a shark. Charlie and Desmond returned, both carrying two large duffle bags from the van onto the dock.

"Provisions," Charlie said to Arlan and Tommy as he set his bags down. Charlie looked around and asked, "Where's Captain Jay and Lisa?"

Captain Jay and Lisa had gone for a walk earlier. Tommy had suggested that they would be screwing on the beach someplace because it was too crowded around the dock. Arlan laughed, causing Tommy to say that when Jay and Lisa returned scratching the mosquito bites on their asses then he would be proven right.

"They've gone for a walk," Arlan said and glanced at Tommy, who had a big grin.

"Put these three bags on the sailboat," Charlie told Desmond and then carried one bag onto his boat.

Ten minutes later Captain Jay and Lisa returned.

Captain Jay scratched his ass and asked, "What's the plan?"

Tommy and Arlan exchanged glances and laughed.

"What's so funny, Rookie?"

"Nothing," Arlan said and noticed the bracelet he'd found where Lisa went into the water was back on her wrist. "That's a nice gesture," he said, nodding toward Lisa's wrist. "More sentiment than I'd have ever expected from you."

Tommy laughed.

Captain Jay frowned.

"How was your walk?" Arlan asked.

Captain Jay scratched his ass again and said, "None of your business."

Charlie, who'd been on his radio, stepped onto the dock and said, "Forrest is flying in and bringing a crew to sail the *Happy Hobo* to Tortola where it will be in dry-dock for a while to fix the damage Boiled Bob inflicted on it. He'll be landing in an hour or so. You can fly back with him or come with me to Dominica. I'll need some help with Bob." He then turned to Desmond and said, "I'll see you in a couple of weeks."

The two men shook hands. Desmond nodded to Tommy and Arlan and left with his men.

Charlie looked to the rest of the group and said, "Who's coming with me and Bob?"

"What's that mean?" Arlan said.

Charlie smiled and said, "I called Winston up on Dominica. It turns out the government owes me a favor for helping to stop a coup by a bunch of racists from Canada and the US who tried to take over the country a couple of years ago. Winston called in the favor and was told there is a nice foster home that will take Bob. No questions asked."

"When are we leavin'?" Captain Jay asked. "You'll need help with the boat. You'll get lost without my navigation skills."

Charlie smiled and said, "We're leaving as soon as you get us untied."

Arlan watched Desmond and his men drive off. He then looked out into the bay and thought about St. John for the first time in a fortnight. He doubted anybody missed him, or Tommy or Captain Jay, or cared where they were. News that Lisa had been abducted had already been recycled and likely forgotten or dismissed as rumor. *That's the way islands are*, he thought. People come and go, and those who live there give everybody the same privacy they take. With no TV and little daily news service, most island residents would know little of what happened on Grenada. Arlan looked back to the mountains, where a few smoke plumes drifted, and smiled, not at the insanity of war, but at the thought of returning to the peaceful insanity of his island, where he had a project to run and a house to take care of. He looked to Charlie's boat and Captain Jay readying the bow line. St. John would have to wait a few more days. He wanted to see this thing through to the end. Tommy could handle the project for a few days.

Arlan looked to Tommy and said, "I think you need to get back with Forrest to check on the project and Frank." Arlan thought about inspector Blake and said, "I wonder who won the beauty contest."

Tommy laughed and said, "I'm s-sure his daughter looked good in the d-dress."

They both laughed at the thought of seeing Blake's daughter, the size of an NFL lineman and always smiling, popping out of the dress Arlan had bought for her.

Arlan shook Tommy's hand and said to Charlie, "I'll come along to watch Bob. Tommy needs to get back to make sure our contractor hasn't gone broke and sent everybody home. He'll fly out with Forrest."

Charlie and Tommy shook hands, and Charlie said, "Desmond will be back with Case and Henry a little later. You can get a ride to the airstrip with him. Forrest is expecting a passenger or two for the ride back."

"N-no problem. I'm g-getting tired of boats anyway."

Charlie smiled, then looked to the others and said, "Once we're on Dominica you guys can take your boat back to St. John. I need to stay on the island for a while to round up all of the weapons the Dreads have collected from the Cubans."

Lisa hugged Tommy, then stepped onto the trawler behind Charlie. Arlan and Captain Jay untied the bow and stern lines and prepared to push off.

Tommy stepped close to Bob and said, "Y-ou take c-care of yourself. And k-keep your r-rudder dry." He then hugged Bob, who kept his arms rigid at his side, completely lost on the dynamics of a hug.

Instead, Bob whispered into Tommy's ear, "Thank you." He then backed away with a grin and said, "K-keep my r-rudder dry, k-keep my…"

Before Bob could repeat it a third time Tommy took his arm and led him onto the boat. He stepped back onto the dock as Arlan and Captain Jay shoved off and stepped onto the boat.

A Fortnight of Fury

Bob saluted Tommy as the boat rumbled away from the dock and into the bay.

Epilogue

The boat ride to Dominica had been uneventful. Forrest and Tommy had buzzed them with the Aero Commander on their way north. Lisa could not warm up to Bob, not because he wasn't charming, in his own way, but because she couldn't get past his uncanny resemblance to Boiled Bob. She and Captain Jay had stayed behind at Charlie's home in Portsmouth when Winston had come to take Bob to his new home.

Charlie and Arlan went along and had been impressed with Bob's new surroundings. A wealthy Brit, whose family had owned his estate on Dominica for five generations, and his wife had recently lost a mentally challenged son in a boating accident. The son would have been about Bob's age, and the estate was set up with a live-in nurse, security and a plethora of activities that would keep Bob happy for a lifetime. The couple and Bob had hit it off immediately.

It was time for Arlan and Charlie to leave, and Bob, still wearing his floppy bush hat, saluted each one after an awkward hug. As Charlie and Arlan walked back to Winston's car, Bob followed them and said, "You are both my big brothers." They turned to see him salute and then skip back toward his new home and foster parents.

Arlan took a flight to St. Thomas the next day, leaving Captain Jay and Lisa to return to St. John on the dive boat. He hoped they would take their time and turn it into a romantic trip. Upon landing, Arlan called Tommy from the airport and asked him to pick him up at the dock on St. John. He'd be taking the noon ferry from St. Thomas.

Arlan had a good idea what to expect when he arrived, and the island didn't disappoint him. The tranquil island's village of Cruz Bay came alive twice each hour—ten minutes before the hour, when the ferry was loading up to go to St. Thomas and twenty minutes after the hour, when the ferry crossing Pillsbury Sound from St. Thomas arrived at Cruz Bay.

The ferry that left St. Thomas at noon bumped the Cruz Bay dock twenty minutes later, and the passengers disembarked. The few tourists that were on the ferry stood on the dock looking confused. Locals greeted friends with big smiles and fist bumps and waited for the boat's crew to offload boxes of provisions they'd purchased on St. Thomas.

Arlan walked down the dock and took in the familiar smells and sights of home. He looked across the bay to Gallows Point. The construction was taking shape, and he hoped that he'd done the right thing by tearing down the old cottages and building a new project. Time would tell.

"Okay, Arlan, me son?" Beaver, one of the taxi drivers who'd walked onto the dock to solicit fares from the tourists, asked when he passed Arlan.

"Okay, Beaver," Arlan answered.

Tommy had parked the Jeep near the ticket booth and was holding court with a couple of local carpenters in the small, open-air bar a few feet away at the end of the dock.

Arlan stepped up to where Tommy leaned on a recently varnished wood bar, and Tommy handed him a cold Heineken, still talking to the carpenters. One of them nodded to Arlan and said, "Hey Arlan. What's up? You been off island or something? I haven't seen you for a few days."

"Just a short trip. No big deal," Arlan said and took a drink of beer.

"You missed the news of the invasion then."

Arlan raised his eyebrows and smiled.

"Yeah, Reagan went into Grenada and squashed it. Something about Bishop being executed."

The other carpenter broke in and said, "No. I think it was to rescue some American students."

Arlan and Tommy looked at each other and smiled.

213

"I guess I missed it," Arlan said.

"Hey, did you hear some rumor about Lisa being kidnapped?"

"Yeah. I heard about that," Arlan said. He then added, "She and Captain Jay took his boat down island for a few days. That's all."

One of the carpenters laughed and said, "I figured so. This place is one rumor after another. Glad nobody really gives a damn. That's what makes it such a great place to live."

A couple of locals walked by and said, in unison, "Okay?"

All four said, "Okay."

The short, homeless Willie, wearing a dirty T-shirt and baggy shorts with holes where the pockets should have been, stumbled up to the bar and sat on one of the few brightly painted stools on the other side of the carpenters. The bartender rolled his eyes and asked, "Willie, do you have any money?"

"No."

The bartender looked toward Tommy and Arlan, who both nodded. The bartender shook his head, reached into a cooler and pulled out a can of Old Milwaukee beer. He placed it on the bar in front of Willie and said, "You only get one, and then you'll need to move on."

Willie smiled and took a long drink and then mumbled to himself, something locals were used to.

A tourist couple, fresh off the ferry, sat at a small table near the road, their bags resting on the ground near their feet. Arlan had seen them recoil a bit when Willie stepped up to the bar. They nervously looked at the other customers and, when they saw that nobody else in the bar paid Willie any attention, they relaxed, each taking a drink of peach-colored slush from plastic cups. They quickly resumed watching their surroundings through tourist masks—the uneasy smile at everything and everybody, hiding their giddy nervousness of being on the friendly but unfamiliar funky island for the first time. Arlan had seen the look hundreds of times. He smiled and wondered if he'd had the same look the first time he stepped foot on the island.

One of the carpenters turned back to Tommy and Arlan and said, "There's a Halloween party at the Backyard tomorrow. You shouldn't miss it. Those parties are always great."

Arlan smiled and remembered last year's party when a local artist, originally from Connecticut, walked into the popular bar and forgot it was Halloween. He walked to a storage closet, returned a few minutes later with a wet mop on his head and declared he was a white Rasta.

Tommy said, "Maybe we'll s-see you th-there."

"Sounds good to me," Arlan said.

"Okay. Okay," the carpenters said and walked across the street to the park.

The activity that accompanied the arrival of the ferry had dwindled. Most of the taxis had gone, and a handful of vehicles belonging to locals who were loading boxes of provisions were pulling away from the dock and starting their trek through the village, dodging chickens and dumpster dogs, and up the steep mountainous roads to their homes. The vehicles' occupants smiled and shouted "Okays" to pedestrians they passed whom they knew, which was just about everybody.

Willie continued to mumble and looked around the bar. Locals knew that if they made eye contact with Willie during one of his mumbling sessions, he'd launch into a diatribe about whatever was on his mind. The tourist couple made the mistake of looking at Willie, who then decided to raise his voice and ramble on about Maynard and his big knife and that he was going to kill that bad mon the next time he saw him.

The bartender and a handful of locals shrugged and went about their business. The tourist couple dropped their smiles, grabbed their bags and walked to the park across the street, leaving half-full drinks on the table.

Arlan and Tommy watched and smiled. They finished their beers and walked toward the Jeep. Tommy stopped and said, "W-wait a minute."

He turned back and patted Willie's shoulder. Willie smiled and shut up. Tommy leaned in and said, "You d-don't need to worry a-about Maynard ever again."

Willie looked at Tommy with bloodshot eyes and chugged his beer.

Tommy turned and walked with Arlan to the Jeep.

Arlan looked back at Willie and asked, "Do you think he understands?"

"D-does it matter?"

Arlan sighed and looked out into the bay.

After a moment he asked Tommy, "Is Frank still on the job?"

"B-believe it or not, he is. And h-his full crew is there t-too."

"Damn. That's surprising."

Tommy grinned and asked, "Y-you know what's m-more surprising?"

Arlan shrugged and said, "What?"

"Blake's d-daughter won the b-beauty contest."

They both laughed as Tommy backed the Jeep into the road and drove up the hill toward Gallows Point.

THE END

About the Author

David Culberson grew up in a small town in Middle America. After a higher education in a warmer climate, he spent the next four decades living and mixing with the cultures of the Caribbean, Mexico and the Great Lakes, where he pioneered and built several low-impact, sustainable resort properties.

He currently lives with his wife and Border Collies on Lakes Michigan and Superior and keeps a home on the Caribbean Coast of Mexico.

www.ingramcontent.com/pod-product-compliance
Lightning Source LLC
Chambersburg PA
CBHW031100020726
47495CB00007B/1981